Ripping the Veil

RIPPING THE VEIL

JAN SMOLDERS

iUniverse, Inc.
Bloomington

RIPPING THE VEIL

This is a work of fiction. All of the characters, names, incidents, organizations, and dialogue in this novel are either the products of the author's imagination or are used fictitiously.

iUniverse books may be ordered through booksellers or by contacting:

iUniverse
1663 Liberty Drive
Bloomington, IN 47403
www.iuniverse.com
1-800-Authors (1-800-288-4677)

ISBN: 978-1-4759-8525-2 (sc)
ISBN: 978-1-4759-8524-5 (hc)
ISBN: 978-1-4759-8523-8 (e)

Library of Congress Control Number: 2013906397

Printed in the United States of America.

iUniverse rev. date: 5/9/2013

ortioned and cleverly handled its seven or eight extra
ce. *And sometimes to good effect.* When she stood next
n, she looked just the right partner; her nose could
One of my tests. I want them tall and strong. The wits test

re on a long break from the three-person business she
Its specialty was tracking wayward husbands and wives.
s in high demand and paid well. And she was good at
it could get her in trouble. For those cases, she had a
so far she had always managed to get her work done
er weapon. She had another two weeks to look forward
paradise. Business would go on at home.
r hair in a knot and swung her delicate batik sarong
d body to walk to the sliding glass door and the balcony
kin anticipated the heavy Caribbean air, still cool this
d welcome her.
nced sideways, she noticed a message slipped under
Management must be announcing its umpteenth water
aintenance. They've been saving up the work for my stay,
ardly.
stiff early in the morning, she bent down and picked
wrinkled envelope. *Thick.* She opened it with dismissive
pping it with her index finger, slightly irritated. *Always*
I travel to these kinds of places. No water for hours. I'll
unt.
alance made way for inquisitiveness when she noticed
ond envelope inside. It read: Only for room 302.
a love note from Humberto. This would be the first one
e almost four weeks she now had known the young man.
n him in five days. He wasn't answering her calls. She
to have found better company, although he always said
time with her. *And I paid him enough.*
d the second envelope, anxious to read Humberto's
she noticed the words written on a third envelope

ACKNOWLEDGMENTS

For their contributions to this manuscript, I express my sincere thanks to my spouse, Lut; to my daughter, Helena, and her husband, Peter Fellows; and to Michael Hennelly and Jeff Stewart.

PROLOGUE

6:30 a.m.
Friday, April 3, 2009
Punta Cana Paraíso Resort, on
Republic

All was peaceful. Silky, foamless, a
the east, their cadence regular a
Most of the three hundred guests
exceptions being European jetlag
with poor bladder control.

The guest in room 302 rubb
low sun as she woke up. She had
she went to bed last night after h
to its rhythm in solitude from h
the fullest the Barceló rum she h

She now rubbed and stret
perfection. She fantasized about
last night at the hotel bar. He h
room door, kissed her hand, wis

Relaxed, she yawned as sh
pictured the gray skies that woul
She smiled as she looked appro
She saw a woman in her early si

It was well p
pounds with
to a six-foot
touch his chi
comes next.

She was
owned and ra
This activity
it. On and o
gun permit,
without usin
to in this litt

She tied
around her n
behind it. H
early, that we

As she g
the room do
shutdown for
she fretted in

Still a li
up the slightl
nonchalance.
the same whe
demand a dis

Her non
there was a se
It must b
from him in
She hadn't se
figured he ha
he had a grea

She ope
message. The

that sat in the second one: Strictly personal and confidential. For the occupant of room 302 only.

Why such cold, official words, Humberto?

She saw her hands tremble as they held the sheet that was inside the third envelope. She read it aloud to herself.

"Dear occupant, we have noticed many visits to your room by a man we know well. We think it is very probable that he has infected you with the HIV virus. Do not panic. We can help you, discreetly and with a caring attitude. We have a good local doctor who will test and treat you strictly confidentially. Do not contact hotel staff. They cannot be trusted. Call us at 3346977. We want to help."

She paled. She saw goose bumps over her entire body as she dropped her pink sarong and threw herself on the bed. She cried helplessly, impotent, without recourse. She reached for the phone. She would call her daughter, her only confidante. Or Solange, her best employee.

Then she reconsidered.

She stood up and looked at herself frontally; she saw a cold body, beautifully tanned but shivering. She picked up her sarong, threw it around her waist, and walked out on the balcony.

The waves still looked unperturbed by her tragedy. Their song had not changed. Her mirror had just told her she had aged ten years, but she felt helpless like a child.

The breeze blew softly under her sarong, caressing her legs, telling her she was still part of the world. But she cried again.

Did Humberto give me the virus?

CHAPTER

Monday, January 12, 2009
Valencia, about fifteen miles west of Santo Domingo

Luis, a go-getter bachelor businessman in his early forties, entered the office of Dr. Barone around noon. It was located on the first floor of the doctor's two-story stucco building.

This was Luis's second visit. He had been very successful in his commercial ventures. In his exuberance, he saw no limits to the piles of money he would amass in the future—"the near future," he liked to say. He probably wasn't that far off in his assessment; he worked long, irregular hours. But he also partied hard and lived the good life. He spread the money around and unfortunately collected around him a crowd of fair-weather friends of both genders. Today, as he entered Dr. Barone's office, he just knew one of his female companions had gotten him in trouble. Hard to say exactly which one, but he had to see Dr. Barone again.

"After the two positive Rapid tests of last week," the doctor explained, "I now have the result of the Elisa test. It's more thorough and reliable and … it confirms that you carry the HIV virus."

Luis was speechless.

"It's not a death sentence; it can be controlled," the good doctor assured him, grabbing and shaking his right shoulder to encourage him. "A strong, young man like you can fight this virus for many decades, very successfully. I always say it's a bit like living with diabetes."

The diagnosis was a blow to Luis, who sighed, desperate. "So it's true … HIV … Maybe I can beat it, as you say, but the damn virus will ruin my checkbook and my reputation. There goes my whole business." He saw the doctor smile. *He wants to encourage me.*

"Wrong, my friend. We can control the virus and help you keep your reputation intact. Your finances may suffer a bit, but I understand you have a good money cushion. Nobody has to know about your HIV. The assistance we can provide is complicated, hard work that never ends or slows down. It won't come cheap, but it can safeguard both your health and your reputation."

"That sounds almost too good to be true, Doctor." Luis sighed, unconvinced.

Dr. Barone smiled again. He looked impressive and confident, also compassionate—the lanky, graying doctor, athletic, in his fifties, a picture of controlled serenity. "My friend, relax. And believe me. I know what I'm talking about. Let me explain. A man of your means can pay for the best medicine. You don't have to take the cheap antiretrovirals, the crummy ARVs you can get free from the government. For those, I'd have to put you on their dreaded list where they give you a code number. It's a 'secret' list but not much more so than the number of mistresses the president of the country has at his disposal. Crooks will sell you the codes on that list. On the web. I'll keep you out of that kind of trouble and in good physical shape if you want me to."

"I want you to," Luis hurried to answer.

"Of course you do. That's always the immediate answer. But you must understand a couple of things before you say yes." The doctor sat down.

"Go ahead, tell me. I'll beat this damn beast. It's *my* frigging body."

"It sure is. Good attitude. Now these are the damages: a good deal of money, and you'll have to follow strict rules, always, no exceptions, for the rest of your life. A long life. I bet we can make it that."

"Rules?"

"I'll explain. Let's talk about the money first." The doctor shifted his body a couple of times in his armchair before he continued. "I know you've got the resources, so I can speak frankly and concretely off the bat. Medicines will be expensive. Figure 10,000 dollars a year. Most of it will have to be cash. First-class material they are, these pills, and nobody will ever know you're on them; I take care of that. Next comes testing, finding out how your viral load is evolving. If it goes up, you get sicker. If down, better. Got it? We want to get it so far down that our tests don't find the virus anymore. Just like Magic Johnson. We test you every three months, not the ordinary six-month routine. Five hundred dollars each time, plus some extra because I'll get you in there for testing at late hours, when nobody else is around, through our secret side entrance. Well hidden. Overtime and hush money. All secret. People must be paid."

"My health is worth it, Doctor, and the discretion is of paramount importance to me. In my line of work …"

"The discretion doesn't come free either, Mr. Flores, Luis. I've just put in a call for Carla to come over. Carla Fuentes. She should be here within fifteen minutes. Who's Carla? Smile, man. A gorgeous woman, if you ask me, a good soul, and a perfect coach for you to keep that discretion assured. She'll encourage you and tell you how to adhere very well to your treatment schedule. She'll also be accessible 24/7 to handle your questions about what to do and what not, in order to protect your secret. At some point, you may feel threatened by inappropriate questions or insinuations, or by unexpected comments on your behavior or appearance, or on your working and drinking habits. You may even let something slip. That's where she comes in, and—"

"I understand," Luis interrupted, getting impatient. "Hand-holding."

"Call it what you want. A soft hand, I'd say, belonging to an angel; you'll see. But angels don't come cheap. Carla's first class. She works with our community support organization. It guides its members, such as Carla; it controls their work, updates their skills, keeps them motivated and, ultimately, protects you. I'd like you to see our group's mission as comprehensive, private care of the highest standard, driven to perfection. When I say comprehensive, I'm talking about: the meds

I mentioned, of the highest quality; tests perfectly done with high frequency, discretion, and flexibility; personal coaching and counseling; legal advice; message and response formulation, etc. Our 'protective veil' provides complete peace of mind. We're proud of our capabilities and performance. The organization will of course charge you a fee, of which Carla will get a part."

And he too. Great sales pitch, well-rehearsed and delivered. But I must ... "Okay ... How much?"

"For each case we agree to take on, the fee is set by a coordinator for the Santo Domingo region. He takes into account such factors as the financials of the patient, the importance and vulnerability of his social status, the daily business activities of the patient and the level of complications these activities can lead to, and the extent to which we expect the particular patient himself to proactively cooperate in his own protection scheme. The latter is a judgment call. Then we have—"

"So when will I know how much?"

"Let's have you see Carla first," the doctor suggested with another encouraging smile and a wink. "Meanwhile, I'll talk to the coordinator. Come with me, in this small room. Operation Discretion starts now."

Luis had been sitting in the special room for about ten minutes when Carla breezed in through a door he hadn't even noticed, his mind far away from there. She looked radiant, a picture of health, early forties, smooth olive skin, confident and reassuring, her sleek, raven, shoulder-length hair flying freely around her cheeks. She greeted Luis with a long embrace. That was a surprise but also a welcome consolation to Luis.

"Mr. Flores, Luis, I'm here to protect you," she said as she sat down, sounding and looking confident. "And I know how to. Discretion and caring, that's us; that's me. I'm your friend; you can lean on me. I help people, day in, day out. Very rewarding work."

Luis was overwhelmed by the whirlwind of positive words emanating from between Carla's full lips and circulating through the small room for the next ten minutes. Her phrases filled the small space with hope, although he also discovered new grounds for fear and apprehension as he listened to her. Above all, he welcomed Carla's encouraging suggestions as they rained down on him. A soft, soothing drizzle. He decided to put his lot in her hands. *These hands look soft indeed. The doctor seemed to know how soft.*

"Carla," Luis volunteered, "you're a godsend. My life collapsed twenty minutes ago. But I'll rebuild it, with your help."

She didn't answer but stood up slowly, flaunting her tall body, right curves in right places, and smiled confidently, her eyes trained on Luis. "I'll help you," she said as she walked up to him. She bent down, so her lips touched his sideburns and almost his left ear, and whispered, "I'll care for you."

Even under all this stress, Luis couldn't help noticing her impressive cleavage.

At that moment, he heard a cough. Dr. Barone had entered the room. He carried a sheet of paper. His glasses sat low on his nose.

"Hi, Carla. Good you made it here so soon. I see you met Mr. Flores."

"We met, Doctor. Indeed. I'll take good care of him. I think he fits wonderfully in my group of patients."

Dr. Barone looked at Carla and said, "Could you leave me with Mr. Flores for a minute?"

"Of course, Doctor. I'll be at the reception," she answered and left the room, throwing a little smile at Luis.

"Well," the doctor continued, "I have some good news. I got our coordinator down to three thousand dollars a month. Cash." He glanced quickly at Luis and hurried to go on. "That includes additional charges for late visits here and in testing rooms. You're lucky that Carla likes you in her group. She can be picky. I'm sure you'll rank high on her list of favorite patients."

"Three thousand?" Luis groaned, incredulous.

The doctor frowned, looked over his glasses, leaned his head forward, and lowered his voice to add, "I stuck my neck out for you. I told the coordinator you would be a case without much social complication. Straight case. Favorite case. That's how I got him down so much."

Luis took a deep breath and exhaled. He whispered, "I must do *something.* I don't want to end up on the damn government list or in graffiti on neighborhood walls … Okay … Worst deal I ever made. But what's my choice?" He put his head in his hands, his elbows weighing down on the table, and he felt the doctor's hand on his back.

"Other services charge more. Believe me, my friend. And we're first class."

Dr. Barone called Carla back in and said, "He's in your capable hands, Carla. This man counts on us. On you."

Carla looked at Luis and then answered, "Mr. Flores will be a good patient. I already know. He's going to be just fine."

After the meeting, Carla walked Luis out of the room through the back door and then across the parking lot to his car, her right arm low around him, comforting him.

Luis felt her hand on his waist, a balm on his wounds.

Standing behind his car, out of sight from the front door, Carla kissed Luis good-bye on the cheek and said, "I'll call you tonight. Let's shoot for six o'clock. We must get going right away. Your first days are the most critical and dangerous ones. No experience yet." She touched his chin briefly with her index finger.

Luis was half-dazed and said a quick thank-you before he opened his car door.

As Carla walked away, her gait elegant and confident, he kept gazing at her, the person who would have to be his guardian angel for many years. *She doesn't look back. Maybe she's already thinking about the next patient.*

CHAPTER

Carla called Dr. Barone from her car. *I like this Luis. What a chest. And eyes.* "I really think he fits in my group, Doctor."

"No doubt," he said. "I noticed when I walked in."

"Oh, please …"

"No, I know that keeping those patients under control can be like making cats march in a line, but you can do it. This one will last; he has good money."

"I'm glad you fixed these administrative matters with the coordinator, Doctor. I don't want to hear about the money. I have enough on my plate."

Dr. Barone disregarded Carla's reaction and enthusiastically went on, "We've got him on a starter fee, our normal practice. Once we know more detail about him, his business contacts and his finances, we may raise his contribution. 'Special, unexpected challenges we encounter with you, Luis. Sorry.' He'd have a hard time dropping out. He'll be smart enough to realize that in that case we could make life really miserable for him. And he'll understand that in order to do that we wouldn't have to violate any professional rule or run into trouble with any government agency."

As if I don't know, Carla thought as she pictured the doctor's grin. She said, irritated, "Doctor, I just told you I don't want to get involved in money matters." Then, recovering, she joked, "As long as I get my outrageously high salary and raises. Talk to you soon. Bye."

I'll kick off the program tonight. Not a day to waste. The sooner I start, the less trouble down the road. She would have to start telling Luis the tricks of not infecting any other person and of the best approaches to keeping HIV secrets away from nosy neighbors, relatives, colleagues, friends, officials, loan officers, employment agencies, architects, contract administrators, and many more. As an accomplished psychologist, she felt she deserved every penny of the good sum she earned each month, and her premium for keeping patients enrolled. She was providing a useful and caring service. "It isn't my fault that antidiscrimination laws aren't enforced," she would often say. "I help the victims of that situation avoid and deal with most of the disastrous consequences of those shameful practices."

From her little office, Silvia had heard slivers of the initial conversation between Dr. Barone and Luis. She was a physician, an assistant to the doctor. She was also his sometime replacement. Dr. Barone hadn't shared Luis's test results with her. That wasn't a total surprise, but a bit unusual. So was the fact that she had seen Luis disappear in the small, private room. *A patient with money.* Half an hour later, as she looked out over the parking lot, she observed Luis and Carla walking together. She saw, from her corner window on the side of the small building, that Carla kissed Luis good-bye. She noticed the Audi 8 he drove away in. She was sure Dr. Barone had made a diagnosis of HIV infection. The ritual had told her.

And she's driving this fancy BMW. On a counselor's salary?

Silvia had to admit she felt jealous for a moment. She barely scraped by on the alms she was earning there. But she also knew that Carla did a good job of coaching and that this was tough work most of the time.

CHAPTER

Friday night, March 20, 2009
The Malecón in Santo Domingo

Luis stepped out of his flashy white Audi, stood up straight, adjusted his belt, ran his fingers through his long, dark mane, and dangled his car keys in front of the valet parking assistant at the Vesuvio restaurant. He felt the warm, humid sea breeze hitting his face. He patted the doorman on the shoulder as he walked in and winked at him as he asked whether his friend Carla had arrived yet.

In fact, Luis knew Carla was waiting inside for him and that, when he would get to her table, she would demonstratively look at her watch. Then she would look at him, and her lovely eyes would say, "Again." But she would give the impression she understood when his muffled voice would tell her in the packed restaurant that he couldn't just walk away from a meeting where unscrupulous merchants were trying to cheat him out of four million pesos. He had hit on tough times; his profits had tumbled lately. He would hold her gaze as he would speak, and she would look for his hand to squeeze it. She would tell him he would survive, as he always had. She'd told him many times she admired his smarts.

Carla spotted him first.

"Hello, darling. Sorry," Luis said almost perfunctorily, half-absent, still absorbed in the misery of his meeting half an hour ago. He looked around for any friends or acquaintances amongst the restaurant patrons tonight. Once he had surveyed the field, he sat down.

"*Mi caballero,*" she teased, "I thought you'd forgotten me, distracted by one of the gorgeous women in your meeting."

"Good thinking. Two of them. Barely made it here." He laughed.

"How are you feeling? Any nausea? Still eating well?"

"So well I'm thinking of flushing the bloody ARVs down the damn toilet. I don't need them anymore." He saw a frown. He looked around to see whether anybody had overheard him. "Just kidding, of course. Thanks for asking. I know the rules. And you can check my appetite in a minute. Most important, I stocked up on condoms." He winked but immediately regretted his last sentence when he saw another frown on her face as she looked around.

"Quiet," Carla warned him. "You're paying for silence, for the organization to keep you out of trouble."

Luis felt like a schoolboy. Then he looked at Carla and figured he was sitting here with a stunning teacher. She reminded him of how he always dreamed of kissing his tall and beautiful second-grade teacher but never had the guts, or the reach.

Carla brought him back from that excursion, back to Vesuvio, suggesting they order.

Dinner was exquisite. Both knew the place well and were treated like king and queen. Luis's great-tipper reputation worked wonders.

When tiramisu time came, Luis proposed they take the dessert to his place and finish it there. "You know I play by the rules, and my viral load is low. Barone told me so earlier this week, and you know that, of course," he whispered.

Carla agreed with all of that, but Luis saw some hesitation on her face. *She's scared again. But I want her.*

She said, "I'll follow you in my car. When we arrive at your place, we'll have to talk, Luis."

I don't blame her. Don't know what I'd do if the roles were reversed.

When they reached his apartment on Avenida Independencia, he parked his car and then expertly parked hers millimeters behind his in the crammed private parking garage. He looked her in the eyes, took her hand, and they went into the elevator.

"Look. The ocean at night," Luis marveled as they walked up to the front window of his apartment, holding hands. "And the Malecón, it's beautiful but very scary. I'd need five bodyguards there for a stroll this time of day." He put his arm around her shoulder and pulled her head closer. He said softly, "You wanted to talk. Go ahead. You lay down the rules. I'm your pupil. What course will you teach your man tonight? Condom Techniques 101?" He laughed and took his shirt off.

"Maybe a new variation on the theme?" she teased.

Her frown has disappeared. "Hold on," Luis said as he heard an e-mail coming in and reached for his BlackBerry, his shirt in his left hand. "Somebody's still working tonight. The coordinator. And Barone gets a copy. What's the matter?"

He had barely read half the message when he started swearing and screaming. He flung his shirt to the floor in anger and brusquely pushed the BlackBerry under Carla's nose. "Here!" he shouted.

Carla read the message.

> *To the attention of Mr. Luis Flores:*
>
> *Dear Mr. Flores, Luis,*
>
> *Congratulations on your exemplary behavior as a patient we deeply care about. We trust the medical assistance, protection, and guidance we provide are of as much value as you expected.*
>
> *We recently have made a detailed review of your file.*
>
> *We found that in Santo Domingo, and all the way north to Puerto Plata, your stature and reputation are high and of considerable importance to your successes. They are, however, at significant risk because of your condition and the authorities' unfortunate lack of seriousness in the enforcement of the antidiscrimination laws.*

> *Consequently, your case requires even more attention and*
> *care than our initial assessment indicated.*
>
> *We have also gathered additional details on your financial*
> *situation and feel compelled, by our strict set of criteria*
> *ensuring fairness for all patients, to raise your monthly*
> *contribution to 5,000 dollars.*
>
> *We assure you …*

Carla stared at Luis, and he yelled, "Five thousand! You read it! Shit! No, and hell no! Over my dead body! I'll strangle the creep!"

She looks worried but not terribly surprised. Wait. Damn! Could this be Barone's normal game?

"It's a lot," Carla responded, "but is it much more than now? Does your fee include your ARVs?"

"Scandalous. We made a deal. I'll get to him—give him a piece of my mind. Shit," he thundered furiously.

"The coordinator must think you won't have much of a problem with this kind of amount … I don't know. You could discuss. He may not realize you have a bad slump in your business," she cautiously suggested.

"My money's none of his business. A deal's a deal. Where do I find the scumbag?"

"I don't have his number. The coordinator is off-limits for me."

He screamed, "I have Barone's number! He must be in on it." Now Luis saw fear in her face.

"But it's the coordinator, Luis. He decides."

"To hell with the frigging coordinator. I call Barone—"

She begged, "Please don't, Luis. Think it over. You're in good shape now, in every respect. Don't get yourself in all kinds of trouble. Please. Discuss. You can get that sum down." She put her head on his shoulders and ran her fingernails over his back.

"Who are you to tell me? Get out of here. Get out. I'm done with Barone and you, the whole frigging deal. Next week it'll be ten thousand! They got me cornered; they have all my personal information. They think they can charge whatever they want. Blackmail me."

She took her purse and walked away without saying one more word.

He remained silent as he heard her cautiously close the door behind her; he was dialing the number of Barone, who didn't answer. *Yeah, the chicken sees my name on his screen.* Luis left him a threatening voicemail. "Barone, you don't pick up, you gutless ass. I'll frigging kill you. You and your stinking coordinator are thieves, sharks preying on the sick, out for blood in the water. I'll go to the Ministry of Justice and file a damn complaint against you and your frigging boss, and against your entire network of crooks. You don't even have the guts to tell me things to my face. Tomorrow you'll be in the papers and on TV: extortion, racketeering, abuse of confidential information, overcharging for medicines, tax avoidance! I'll spend my last peso to expose you, scoundrel. Go to hell. Right now!"

Seconds after the voicemail arrived on his BlackBerry, Barone called Carla, who was on her way home. *Something must have gone awfully wrong with that fee raise, that unnoticeable dent in the guy's fat wallet.* "What the hell's going on?" he boomed. He was furious and indignant.

"I hadn't mentioned anything yet about a possible raise when he received the message from the coordinator, Doctor," Carla explained, her voice trembling. "I knew of course that he was on a starter rate, but I had no idea what the increase would be. He …" Carla started panting and blurted, "He just went off the cliff."

"I don't understand why he blows up over peanuts; the dude's rich."

"He is, I think, and you know. But I'm sure it's not just the money. Of course, his business goes up and down like everyone else's, and it's in a bad slump right now, he says. But what really set him off was the surprise. He was terribly angered that 'promises were broken.' His words, not mine," she hastened to add.

The doctor heard sobbing and asked, "Alcohol?"

"Barely any." Carla now sounded defensive. "He felt deceived, probably helpless and abandoned. I suggested he talk it over with you, but to no avail. He went berserk."

"Hmm. You should calm down, girl. Go to bed and forget about him. Take a Valium."

As he spoke these last words, Barone had switched to a controlled tone, and he managed to restrain himself as he put the residence phone down with less of a smack than he actually wanted.

He now called the coordinator and whispered, "Sorry to bother. Big promising newcomer, you know who. Nothing but trouble. Rich but dangerous rookie mouthing big words."

"I see. Not sure about phones. Careful," the coordinator grumbled.

"Understood. Threat imminent. Immediate action necessary."

"Address?"

"Have details. Close to favorite snack bar."

"Meet in parking lot, east side of hotel. Twenty minutes. Explain there. May have to 'talk' to him tomorrow."

"Today, immediately. I'll explain," Barone said, shaking, his voice breaking.

"Twenty minutes. Parking lot."

On Saturday morning, March 21, Santo Domingo radio and TV stations reported the breaking news at eight o'clock: a dead, male body had been found in the San Gerónimo area between Avenida Independencia and the Malecón. Around 7:00 a.m., details had emerged from the police department: The murder had all the marks of a robbery that led to a senseless killing; the person had no wallet or watch or ring. No cash was found on him, but he had an American Express receipt in his pocket.

That led to the identity of the victim, Luis Flores. He had been shot in the chest from close range. There were no visible indications on the body of any struggle.

CHAPTER

Silvia Herrera woke up this Saturday morning an hour later than on weekdays, when she would be on her way at seven.

She felt great as she stretched her limbs but also slightly concerned. *Getting a little stiff already?* At age thirty-eight, she was a picture of health. She had her svelte body under control, all of its five feet and eight inches. Her fair skin was smooth and tight. In meetings, she confidently swung her brown-black, time-saving ponytail. Her mirror didn't deceive; her measurements were good and kept that way by a rigorous combination of the right food and exercise. She walked confidently, healthy hips rocking, but with an appropriate modesty that came to her naturally because she was conscious of her professionalism and education.

She wasn't a stunner who would stop traffic, but she had a quiet glow. She knew. She felt that people who got to know her saw more beauty in her each time they came close to her, and it became more striking as she aged. She had no husband or steady boyfriend; she focused most of her energy on work and suffered fools badly. "If I never hit upon the right guy, it'll be their loss," she joked with friends, sometimes doubting herself a little.

When she stepped off her scale this morning and sat down with her two slices of whole grain toast, *pan integral*, and two chunks of papaya for breakfast, she was ready to enjoy a quiet weekend, to just let it all go. Maybe a little trip, by herself, to the Juan Dolio Beach if the sun wasn't too harsh.

Her bare feet lay on a little stool in front of her chair. She slowly curled her toes—it felt good—and she admired the purple polish. *My color.* She finished her *mora* juice, the delicious blackberry drink, and noticed the first whiffs of coffee aroma emanating from her brewer.

Then she switched on her little kitchen TV and heard, horrified, the astonishing news that a Luis Flores had been found dead, murdered. *Is this* our *Luis Flores?* In an instantaneous flashback, she saw him walking, maybe three months ago, in the parking lot of Dr. Barone's office, to his car with Carla, who had kissed him a lot longer than the customary split-second.

In an instant reflex, she called Dr. Barone to bring him the terrible news. He didn't pick up. She called Carla. No answer. She needed to talk to somebody. She called Jorge on his cell, Dr. Jorge Riquelme. He headed the Alliance in Santo Domingo. That NGO and Jorge had been instrumental in setting up AIDS treatment services in Valencia at Dr. Barone's facility and had close contacts with the Ministry of Health.

Jorge had already heard the news and was going to call her, he said. "Maybe the press will provide more information soon, Silvia. Relax. Nothing we can do to help your poor Luis, if it's him. A good patient, I understand."

"Could I come over?" *Oops. I'm inviting myself to a bachelor's place on Saturday morning. He's not going to be jumping for joy to show a messy place. Who knows who's still under the sheets there or sipping coffee with him?*

"I'm headed for Avenida Lincoln, Café Barahona, 9:30. Unbelievable portions, Silvia. Close to Independencia."

"Sounds good." Silvia wasn't being honest. She hated those places, and Jorge, a.k.a. the "refrigerator," didn't need this kind of breakfast. But she wanted to be with somebody who knew about Luis. To talk. "Can I join?" She almost begged. She didn't want to be alone. "I may just have coffee, Jorge," she quickly added, a bit afraid she might look asocial at the café.

17

Jorge laughed and then stopped and said, sounding more serious, "No worries, Silvia. Order something small. Tim is also joining us. The two of us can always help you out with the extra you leave on your plate."

"Tim? Oh, good. Does he know Luis?"

"I don't think so. We'll ask him. He's here on his way to Colombia. Always finds ways to arrange 'logical' Santo Domingo stopovers. He's going to make our city into a hub."

Silvia didn't feel like reacting to Jorge's joking. She knew Tim, or, more exactly, about Tim. He was actually Mathieu Timonier, a Frenchman, journalist for an economics magazine from Paris, *En Avant*. She was well aware that he had taken quite an interest in corruption cases in AIDS treatment and had struck up a real friendship with Jorge after the violent death of their good friend Julio Diaz. Julio was at that time the boss of Jorge at the Alliance. Tim had exposed the worst of that murder case, about half a year ago. He was now on a sabbatical from the magazine, she had heard.

"I'll be there. Thanks, Jorge."

"Good. As long as you don't pick food off my plate. I know these people who don't order food and then steal from their friends' plates," he said jovially.

"I'll be on my perfect behavior; don't worry," Silvia said quietly, sounding sad. *Of course, Jorge wasn't close to Luis.*

CHAPTER

Silvia dropped everything and ran to the shower. She barely had grabbed the soap when her phone rang. She didn't swear but wasn't pleased. Dripping water all over, stepping gingerly lest her wet feet slip on the tile floor, she got to her purse on the kitchen table to take her cell.

"Yes," she said impatiently.

"Silvia?"

"Hold on." Silvia had to do a minimal amount of toweling off. "Yes. Who is it?"

"Carla."

Words from a grave, that sound. "Carla! Is it Luis on TV? You know?" she screamed.

"I'm sure," Carla whispered and then sighed.

"Oh my God, Carla."

Silvia heard sobbing.

"How about Dr. Barone? Did he confirm?"

"He doesn't answer, on any of his phones. But I know, Silvia, that Luis is dead. And I'm scared. I loved him. They know that—they, Barone and his men. I lost my lover, and I may be next on the list."

"What? On TV they say it was a robbery, but you're saying you think *they* would murder, Barone and his … people? How can you say that?"

"They wouldn't murder. But they have lots of money ... I must flee. I'm afraid Luis made cruel accusations about fees, and threats maybe. He could be brutally honest and very angry when somebody tried to railroad him. Maybe he blew up. I know I'm in danger. I must get away. I don't want to be questioned by police. I could say the wrong things, get myself in more danger."

"Railroading, you said? Luis? Dr. Barone?"

"I'm scared."

"Poor girl." Silvia had trouble letting it all sink in. *So much.*

"I must flee. Maybe for a year. Longer. I can't hide in this country. I must disappear from the world," Carla cried.

"Carlita, relax. I'll help you." For a moment, Silvia hesitated. She was thinking. Then she said, feeling unsure, "How about hiding in a convent far away?"

"Anywhere, if it's safe."

She answered reflexively. "A place without the modern amenities you're used to?"

"Sure. If it's your suggestion, I know it'll be okay."

Silvia decided to go ahead. "In a remote area of Venezuela, my uncle runs a mission, a convent, where I bet you could be entirely safe as long as you're prepared to stay within the walls and not disturb the peace."

"I'll go."

"Without TV, electricity only now and then, silence, bedtime at 7:00 p.m. Healthy air, poor food, sew your own clothes, obligatory prayers—"

"Okay. Okay."

"Not so fast, Carlita. Think it over for fifteen minutes."

"I don't have to. Can you call there? I must get out. Immediately."

Now Silvia was silent. *Maybe I shouldn't have brought this up. But she's scared to death. She'll take anything. Why? Panicking. Does she know more than she's saying?*

"Okay. I'll call my uncle. I'll get back to you by noon," Silvia said.

"Let *me* call *you* then, from a phone booth, Silvia."

My God. That bad. "Okay, Carla."

"One more thing, Silvia. Please don't tell anybody I'm fleeing. Anybody. It could mean my life."

"I promise, *amiga*. Rest assured."

After the harrowing call, Silvia stood still for a while in her kitchen, reflecting. She dialed her uncle's number but couldn't get a connection. *This wet towel bothers the hell out of me.* She flung it to the floor and returned to the shower.

Twenty minutes later, she proceeded to Café Barahona, her uncle's Misión de Santa Teresita de Kavanayén in Venezuela on her mind. *I still have three hours.*

CHAPTER

Silvia made it on time for breakfast with Jorge and Tim.

As she arrived, both gentlemen stood up, ready to embrace her warmly. For a moment she disappeared in the long arms and against the thin, bony chest of the light-haired Tim, a full head taller than she. She wondered about the flavor of his chewing gum. She liked it. *French?* Next she was swallowed up in an embrace against the ballooning belly of "refrigerator" Jorge, shorter but much heavier than Tim. His black mane was greasier, and her hand on his back felt like patting a warm, giant marshmallow.

"Ready for a good bite," Jorge proclaimed after the greetings, and he put his right palm on his belly.

At the table, the discussion immediately turned to Luis.

"I know Carla, not Luis, of course," Tim said, "but you know both of them very well, Silvia. 'Knew,' we must say now for Luis. Unfortunately. What happened? Any idea?" His tone was considerate, and he looked at her with caring eyes as he spoke.

Silvia felt consolation and answered, "Tim, I really don't know. But," she continued after having glanced at Jorge, "what I do know is that Luis Flores was treated with more deference and with another type of caring than less well-off patients of Dr. Barone. Luis was catalogued as rich, meaning 'able to pay.' What I'm telling you, I've seen it with my own eyes. Carla had to play her psychologist's role in this, as a counselor employed by Dr. Barone."

"Hmm. But how did this lead to Luis's ending up shot to death?" Tim asked, looking puzzled.

Silvia threw a glance at him and refrained from shaking her head. She didn't answer.

"Why did Carla call you?" Jorge asked. "Why would Luis be robbed? Just the luck of the draw? Wrong place, wrong time? Did he flaunt wads of cash? What does she say?"

Now Silvia shook her head and said, "Carla's a dear friend. All I know is that she's devastated. She cared for her patient."

"And lover? I heard … Well, what do I know? But if it's not robbery, does she say who she thinks is behind this?" Jorge dug in.

"I didn't really ask. Actually, I kind of did, but she was in no condition to give an answer that made sense. She wasn't coherent, all over the map. She suffered a great loss and was scared to death. She did say that Luis could react violently when he felt he was being cheated. Luis had many business contacts. Something went wrong. He must have had a bitter argument … with … somebody."

"I'm the ignorant foreigner here, so I can ask stupid questions," Tim intervened. "In fact, I have two: Could she have sounded devastated because she feared she could be arrested, implicated? Or did she feel somebody she knows had something to do with this? Sorry, it's just my gut asking."

"Tim, for us locals who have to keep making a living here," Jorge quickly answered for Silvia, "those are things we can think about. That's all we can do for now, nothing more."

Silvia took over again. "I work closely with Carla, and all I really know is that she sounds scared and destroyed by Luis's death." *She feels she's got to run for her life, but I can't tell.* "Frankly, I came here because I felt so sad myself."

"Did you call Barone?" Tim asked.

"I did. No answer. Carla said that forty minutes ago his phones were still off. He probably wants to avoid calls; he's bound by professional confidentiality, of course. Maybe he'll just speak to the police once they find out Luis was his patient. Or he could volunteer to talk to them."

"The police may talk to you, Silvia." Jorge sounded concerned.

"No problem, Jorge. I'd tell them what I just told you and Tim. The plain facts. Luis wasn't my patient. I have no file on him."

Breakfast took over now. Eggs, bacon, plantains, more than even Jorge could wish for, all swept into two stomachs by rivers of sugar-laden coffee. Small talk came with it. Silvia sipped tea and felt guilty for not mentioning Carla's plan to flee, with her help. *She's a good person. She really loved Luis. Just for his money and the rich future he could promise her? He looked great. A real hunk but not my type. And he carried the HIV virus. Does she too?* Silvia had never seen a trace of a document on Carla. She wondered why Carla sounded so terribly scared this morning, whom she feared. The police? Dr. Barone? Somebody higher up? Why? Did Carla really fear violence against her? Or … exposure? *She needs protection—from whomever, in whatever form. I promised. I must call my uncle as soon as I get home. I'll always know where she'll be.*

"You're dreaming, Silvia? Your boyfriend coming over today?" Tim asked, sounding friendly.

He's trying to break my spell, changing the subject. Silvia managed a weak smile. "There isn't any boyfriend, Tim. Still waiting for that guy on the white horse to take me away. I really don't expect him today."

"White horse. That's a high bar. But you're playing it right. High, high bar."

"You think so, Tim? You mean it?" She looked at him. *He's taking his time to think up a riposte to match my little provocation.*

After a couple of seconds, he said, "Yes, but does it matter?"

Touché. Careful now. "Tim, I've always respected your opinions. Shouldn't I?"

"Okay, you win, Silvia. I must now concentrate on my bacon," Tim concluded with a little smile as he threw her a quick glance that was admiring and questioning at the same time.

"You're right; cold bacon isn't good for you, Tim," she agreed, to let him off the hook.

After breakfast, Silvia drove home. She would call her uncle in

Kavanayén. She knew that there, at the mission, they always had a room for unusual arrivals, even if they had to pack guests six to a room with one lonely forty-watt lightbulb and only four narrow, squeaking beds.

After a few minutes, she banned any Kavanayén thought from her mind so she could come back to her own life and enjoy reliving her verbal joust with Tim about the boyfriends. As she arrived home and stepped out of her car, she felt guilty about having inner pleasure on such a sad day. *Poor Carla. And I can't even call her.*

CHAPTER

In her kitchen, Silvia impatiently tapped her feet on the floor as she counted the rings of the phone in Kavanayén. *They don't pick up. Always like that. Uncle Armando probably has hidden his satellite phone in a drawer. It's an expensive toy. Ten rings, and I hang up. No. Patience. I need an answer for Carla right now.* She felt her nerves.

The ringing stopped.

She heard a young-sounding male voice. "*Buenos días,* you've reached Santa Teresita in Kavanayén. How can I help you?"

"I'm a niece of Father Francesco, calling from Santo Domingo. Is he available?"

"Oh, an international call. I know where the father is, in the kitchen. Give me thirty seconds. I'll run."

She heard the youngster's clattering steps as she visualized him storming away. *A novice, probably. I hope he doesn't drop the phone. It wouldn't be his best day.*

The sandal clatter stopped, and the young voice said, panting, "Father, your niece."

"Uh? Which one?"

There was a brief silence.

I bet he's cleaning his hands before he touches his favorite toy.

"Hello?" The father sounded apprehensive.

He fears we have a death in the family. I have to speak upbeat. "Uncle Armando, Silvia here. How are you?"

He sounded relieved as he said, "Oh, Silvia! Bless the Lord, you sound happy. What good news do you have for me?"

"We're all okay here, Uncle. How are you and your good people there?"

"The mission is doing well, thank God, and so are our villagers. Our *Pemones* are good people. God bless them. We help and guide them along the paths of the Lord's eternal laws and designs."

Of course. That last sentence shows up in all of his letters.

Father Francesco, Capuchin, born Armando Herrera, was in his early sixties, of average size, and soft-spoken. His appearance was that of an ascetic person, slight, exuding dignified modesty. He had a little gray hair left and wore old, heavy, dark-rimmed glasses.

The small, extremely remote community of Kavanayén, where he lived, was populated by Pemón Indians. Capuchin Fathers had established the Misión de Santa Teresita de Kavanayén in 1943. Silvia's uncle ran it with an iron fist and praiseworthy intentions. It was the heart and soul of the community.

Silvia felt she had to chat a little with her uncle before dropping her request on him. She asked, "So, how have you been, Uncle? What are you doing?"

"Me? You want to know? I'm arguing with a sister about the big inventory of perishable supplies. It's too big. As head of the mission, this old nag has to remain alert, you know. I must safeguard the material as well as the spiritual well-being of his community." He chuckled.

"So you're making the rounds of your immaculately clean kitchen?" She had to be careful not to make it sound like flattery.

"Clean? Yes. But you forgot to add 'outdated,' little niece."

"*Very well maintained* is the more correct phrase, Uncle. I know," she joked.

"Thank you. And … why are you calling?"

"Well, I have a request. I have a friend, Carla, who's in dire need of protection against violence. She's a good, well-educated woman. She cares for the sick. She's an easygoing person who wouldn't make trouble in your holy place if you would be so generous as to allow her to stay at the mission for a while. Carla could pay her way." *Whew. I said it.*

Father Francesco answered after a few seconds of silence. "I wouldn't be any good at protecting people from violent criminals, Carla." He laughed softly, sounding embarrassed. He explained, "I've never touched a gun."

"But, Uncle, she doesn't need such a kind of protection. All she wants is a hiding place, far away. You can offer that and a peaceful, rustic atmosphere—a calming environment," Silvia argued. Then she quickly added, "And above all, one that's good for her spiritual condition."

"Good girl. I mean you. She too, I'm sure. As you know, we rent rooms here in our guest building. Very economical. And food is limited in Kavanayén but cheap."

Silvia was concerned. "Uncle, she's in grave danger, she tells me, but I don't know exactly what it is. It would be better if you could give her a monk's cell, really inside of the mission. That's so much safer than a room in your guest building outside the mission proper."

"I see. You're right, although also that building is quite safe. You know it's only twenty or thirty meters away from the mission. So you must mean a sister's cell. Don't forget rules are different in that case. Our sisters don't run a hotel. You understand?" *He has a good point. But Carla must be protected.* "I do. So will Carla," she assured him. "Can she come immediately? She's in a huge hurry."

"She can ring the bell here as soon as the Lord delivers her here. But you know very well that Kavanayén means quite a trip." He laughed. "I still remember your litany of back and joint complaints when you visited here once with your father."

"You don't have to remind me. It still hurts when I think about it. Thank you so much, Uncle. Your many good deeds should shorten and smooth your own path on *your* big trip, the one you always talk about … the one to heaven … of course many years from now," Silvia joked.

"I don't know how soon or short or hard it'll be, but when the Lord calls me, I'll be ready for the voyage, and I trust he'll guide me, Silvita.

28

And as I hear you talking, I know that you, my little niece, have your compass right. You'll make it to heaven too."

"Trying, Uncle. Trying."

Happy about the good news from Uncle Francesco, Silvia waited for the call from Carla. She knew the poor girl would be safe in Kavanayén.

The village was situated in southern Venezuela, close to the borders of Guyana to the east and Brazil to the south, in the Canaima National Park. It had a seldom-used landing strip, 700 meters long, just a wide, rough dirt path. It was partly overgrown and often flooded, and not suitable for the faint of heart or spine. The normal overland voyage to Kavanayén meant a seven- or eight-hour drive south from Ciudad Guayana, including a long way through the Gran Sabana, and then from Luepá on, an excruciatingly difficult final forty or fifty kilometers west. The dirt road had no markings or signs. It was not only rough, but also prone to confusing and aggravating drivers; they would see the road splitting here and there in two or three paths created in the mud by travelers who days or weeks before had tried to find the least muddy, most manageable passage during heavy rains and floods. The different paths would lead the traveler into woods and over little creeks. They offered no guarantee that they would lead him to Kavanayén, but they might deliver him there.

Seated at her kitchen table, Silvia prepared a note with the exact details of the location of the mission so she would be able to dictate them correctly to Carla over the phone. She wondered how she could help her further. She wasn't allowed to divulge her uncle's phone number. He always worried about the excessive cost of calls, outgoing and incoming, on his cherished satellite phone.

When she was done writing, Silvia stood up and went to her tiny balcony overlooking the Jardín Botánico. Noisy cars were racing by under her, but her mind wandered far away from Santo Domingo.

She saw Carla walking solemnly in the narrow halls of dark and cool buildings, careful not to make noise, smiling at sisters, chatting at mealtime. *She'll have to get up before the roosters. She'll have to get a uniform, a habit.* Silvia tried to picture Carla, who would now, within minutes, enter a phone booth to call her. *Phone booths can be disgustingly dirty, full of chewing gum and cigarette butts. Only poor people without cell phones use them, or cats who manage to slip in, or regular folks who are in trouble or hiding something.*

Carla called at noon.

As Silvia picked up, she heard a door being slammed several times and then a muffled voice saying, "I made it, Silvia. I have trouble keeping this thing shut. Did you call Venezuela?"

The booth's acoustics are terrible. And she sounds a bit rude. It must be stress. "You're all set, Carla, your lodging."

"Really? Good. Thank you, Silvia. You're a dear friend," Carla responded without much emotion.

She's low on energy, Silvia figured as she hurried to give Carla the details and explained that if she wanted to call Kavanayén, she should go through her, Silvia.

Carla sounded nervous when she abruptly ended the conversation, just saying, "Okay. Thank you, *amiga.* I have it all written down. You're saving me. I'll manage from here on."

"When do you think you can leave, or, better, get there? I should give my uncle some idea when to expect you."

"I'll leave as soon as I can. I'll get there. I must hurry and get out of this booth. Thanks again."

Silvia felt strange. *Of course, she's tremendously stressed. And how many problems does she have I don't even know of? Was anybody watching her? Was she afraid somebody would be?* Silvia was convinced Carla would have to call her again. *She didn't seem to worry about travel arrangements. It's not simple, traveling to Kavanayén. She'll find out.*

After the call, Silvia was tempted to phone Tim. Just for a little chat. She didn't.

She decided to have a quiet afternoon, check her snorkeling equipment, and make a little bag for an early drive to Juan Dolio Beach tomorrow morning. Even there she would be checking her cell often for Carla, except during those precious short periods she would spend underwater, a few of them maybe even in the company of curious little fish who might want to swim along with her for a while.

CHAPTER

Nine-year-old Marcelo Lima was taking a breather. It was morning recess on Monday, March 23, on the playground of the San Pedro elementary school in the prosperous Jardines del Sur section of Santo Domingo. He'd been playing soccer with a large group of boys. A supervisor was walking the grounds in circles, the radius of which kept getting shorter as he kept checking his text messages. He seemed blissfully detached from the dynamics within the noisy young crowd around him.

Marcelo was a good player, proud of his goal-scoring record, which was known to all his teammates and opponents. He also had to suffer the not so occasional foul kick in the shins, or the elbow in the stomach from a jealous opponent. He always figured it came with the territory of being a good, and therefore sometimes envied, player. He wouldn't retaliate. His father had told him not to.

Suddenly, a ten-year-old boy, Alfonso, half a head taller than Marcelo and far too heavy for his size, walked up to Marcelo and drummed him into a corner. He hit the younger, smaller boy in the groin with his knee. Marcelo screamed, but the powerful Alfonso dragged him deeper into the corner, one hand over Marcelo's mouth. Then he pulled his shorts down and put his hand in his underwear. "Just wanted to see whether boys with SIDA have balls too." He grinned.

Then he threatened, "Don't you ever again pull my shirt from behind because I run faster. You piece of SIDA crap."

Marcelo cried for help. At that point, friends came to his rescue and shouted Alfonso away. The supervisor looked up but appeared happy when it seemed that the little incident had run its course.

He shouted SIDA twice. SIDA? What is that? Marcelo wondered as he tucked his shirt in his shorts and bravely tried to recover from the attack. Minutes later, he went back into class, his hair still disheveled. He didn't want to talk to his friends about what happened.

SIDA was the Spanish term for AIDS, but it was an acronym Marcelo had never heard in the Lima household. He was the son of Ricardo Lima, a successful entrepreneur in his late forties with several major contracting businesses in the transportation sector. Ricardo was a robust man of average size but heavyset. He sported an impressive white mustache. Even young Marcelo figured out that the mustache unwittingly betrayed his father's hairdo, the black color of which was the product of frequent, thorough dying jobs. Actually, the half inch of white and gray at the lower end of his sideburns conspired with the mustache in the betrayal.

My father looks nice that way, and he doesn't mind my joking about the different colors.

Mrs. Lima was proud of her young-looking man.

About six months before the incident at school between Alfonso and Marcelo, Ricardo had been involved in a serious car accident. He had spent three weeks in the Clínica Abreu in Santo Domingo because of major, mainly internal injuries and recovered completely. He had undergone several blood transfusions in the early stages of his hospitalization. *"Gracias a Díos,"* he would say afterward, "I'm still with Rosita and Marcelo. It was close for a few days, they told me."

Life changed abruptly for Ricardo when a few weeks later a sore throat and strange rashes prompted him to get medical attention. Dr. Barone had to deliver the news that Ricardo had caught the HIV virus.

"Our country's blood supply is safe in principle, but nothing's perfect. You received massive amounts of blood. It's not your fault, but obviously the bigger the quantities, the higher the risk. You've had real bad luck, Mr. Lima. I'm sorry this happened, but I also feel confident that a man of your discipline and means can overcome the health and social issues you certainly will have to confront."

Ricardo had barely listened. He briefly considered filing a complaint against the hospital but dropped the idea. *Futile. They'll blame me with all kinds of insinuations.* His mind was elsewhere, with Rosita and Marcelo. Their lives would be changed too. He sighed. "I know all about it, Doctor. I run companies. I run clean shops; we care for our people, even for those with AIDS. We treat them fairly; those poor souls probably have made a mistake. We help them and warn them not to repeat and take good care of their bodies. But I know what I'll be up against out in the cruel world. I can't say that discrimination and stigma have been rooted out. And you can't tell me that either."

"I wasn't going to. I wasn't born yesterday either, Mr. Lima. Let's get practical," Dr. Barone proposed, his tone compassionate but businesslike.

The discussion went on between two adults who called things the way they saw them. Dr. Barone made an excellent impression on Ricardo and delivered a completely plausible pitch for his proposed treatment and the special assistance he provided, via an organization, to smart and financially strong patients.

Ricardo was impressed.

Later that day, Carla stepped into the picture and then into Ricardo's entire life. Her shoulders would be the ones he would have to lean on for a long time. Dr. Barone spoke very highly of her.

Rosita would be a strong support for her man.

He could face the world.

✿ ✿ ✿

Ricardo almost fell off his chair when, at dinner on March 23, the day of Marcelo's incident at school, the boy timidly asked his father what "SIDA crap" meant. Ricardo put down his fork, wiped his mouth with his hand, sat up, and said angrily, "Marcelo! Who teaches you these things?"

"No teacher. One of the big boys. Alfonso. He was angry with me, jealous of me, I think, and he bothered me. I hadn't done a thing. He's older and knows more words."

"He sure does. Why did he bother you?"

"He said he wanted to see whether boys with SIDA had balls," Marcelo explained. Pointing down at his groin, he said, "And he grabbed me here. It hurt a bit."

"What? *Mierda!*" Ricardo screamed as he pounded the table.

"Ricardo, watch it," Rosita warned.

"Sorry, Rosita. This is cruel and unacceptable," he fumed.

Rosita got up and said, "Marcelito, let's go and see how much homework you still have to do. Don't worry, you didn't do anything wrong. Your papa's tired, I think. He works hard for us."

Marcelo got up and followed his mother. She came back after a few minutes and said, "Don't shout now. He may be listening. He's no fool."

Ricardo noticed the wrinkles of concern on Rosita's forehead. He felt sorry for her and for Marcelo, more than for himself. He said, "He's a poor victim. So are you. And it's Dr. Barone's fault, intentional or not. I counted on him and his people."

"You should discuss with him. Also with the school principal, Ricardo. He shouldn't tolerate this behavior by students."

"You're right. I'll get the principal on the phone, dinnertime or no dinnertime. This can't wait. They're ruining my son. Do we have the guy's home number? Or cell?"

❋ ❋ ❋

Ricardo was lucky. Principal Diego Molina had already finished dinner when he took his call. Ricardo got practical right away. "Would you mind my stopping by in twenty minutes, Dr. Molina? I have something on my mind that can't wait." *I'm sure he hears I'm pissed.*

"I think I already know what it is, Mr. Lima. It's a good idea to discuss it face-to-face. Come on over."

"Thank you. I appreciate it."

Dr. Molina was standing at the front door of his modest house when Ricardo arrived.

"Fine neighborhood, Dr. Molina," Ricardo commented on the way from his car to the door.

"Thanks, but nothing compared to your digs, Mr. Lima. Come in, please. I have a little library where we can talk comfortably." He didn't offer any drink when they sat down.

Carla wouldn't approve of alcohol for me. He knows he can't offer me booze, and he doesn't want to make that too obvious by offering tea or coffee.

Ricardo decided to avoid detours and make it easy for the principal and himself. He said, "Dr. Molina. I have HIV, as you know. Several months already. I know exactly why I'm positive, blood transfusion, and I can handle it. I have it under control. But somehow my status has become public knowledge. Let's not even discuss how."

Molina acted as if taken aback by Ricardo's forthrightness. He coughed for several seconds. Then he said, "I have a problem, Mr. Lima." He stared at Ricardo.

"You?" *The guy seems to think his is worse than mine.*

"Parents are very sensitive and apprehensive when the word SIDA or AIDS enters the room, Mr. Lima. I've received several calls about your boy, most of them late at night. Some parents are honestly scared to death. They suspect Marcelo is HIV-positive and fear he may infect his friends—a little cut here, a little saliva there, you know. Many want him out of the school. I've resisted so far, but it's getting more difficult by the day for me."

"For you. For you! How silly, Doctor. You know that's all bullshit. Marcelo doesn't carry the virus, and even if he did, he'd have a very hard time infecting anybody. It really would have to be on purpose."

Doctor Molina shook his head, his face showing disgust. "I know that, Mr. Lima, and I'm telling them that, each one of them. But they don't accept it from me."

Ricardo got irritated and said, "So my little boy has to suffer because they don't want to hear the truth from you? Have him tested, damn it, and shove the results under their noses. It's pure cruelty what they're doing to my boy, and you must stop it."

"I'm doing my best. Of course, we can have him tested, with your permission, but some parents will never believe me. They'll say that your dollars convinced some crooked lab to produce a fake result. They're unreasonable. Fear blinds them. And they'll say that Marcelo, even though he's healthy now, could get infected by you anytime. That's how they think, unfortunately."

Ricardo stood up, showed all of his body mass, and then pounded the table, screaming, "You know what's unfortunate? That you don't enforce the law. That you don't have the balls. The boy has every right to be in the school, HIV or no HIV, and to be treated fairly. That's the law of the country."

Dr. Molina now had a worried look on his face and lowered his voice. "Believe me, Mr. Lima, I've visited officials, pleaded with them not to throw out antidiscrimination lawsuits lightly. They should do their job, enforce the laws. But I run into stone walls all the time. The officials side with those who want to ban HIV-positive people to some remote island and let them rot. It's smart politics, sadly enough. That's what our officials think, or can be made to think with adequate bribes. I bet you some parents banded together in Marcelo's case and already went to see the officials about him."

Ricardo knew all about officials. "How about the church?"

"The church? … The church … hopeless. The local priests, the older ones anyway, and the bishop, the monsignor. They fulminate from their pews against sinners—I know you're not one. They preach love, all right. But some will say AIDS is a well-deserved punishment. Nuns are much better, but they have no say. They distribute condoms, mostly secretly. I've seen eighty-year-old nuns in action. I always wonder whether they confess these sins of compassion. Good souls, they are."

This spineless ass isn't going to get us anywhere. Ricardo didn't sit down again. He said, "I get the picture. Officials are bigots or they're bought. Some idiotic ones may actually fear burning in hell—as the bishop suggests. I'll have to move my boy elsewhere, to a boarding school far away from me so I don't harm him any longer. He liked your school and his soccer team. And you. Rosita and I will miss our boy." He got emotional, turned, and left without saying good night.

As he drove back home, he didn't bother to wipe the tears off his cheeks. *I must expose the bastards who let this charade go on, or even encourage it. And what about Barone's much vaunted special service that would keep everything under wraps?*

When Ricardo arrived, Marcelo was asleep, and Rosita looked anxious.

"Did he help?" she asked.

"Not there yet, Rosita. I have work to do, but I won't stop before I get to the core of this rot. Let's go get some good sleep now. I'll need my energy tomorrow to whip that Barone's ass."

"Barone? How about this kid who harassed Marcelo today?"

"Don't blame the kids, Rosita. They say and do things they hear or see from their parents. And many parents get their information from bigots. The people in power don't apply the laws to stop this cruel nonsense. Can you guess why? I have a pretty good idea. It's always the same thing—dirty, greasy money … Let's go to sleep."

Rosita bowed her head.

On Tuesday morning, Ricardo Lima stormed into Dr. Barone's building, past the receptionist, straight to the door of the doctor's office. It was 9:00 a.m. Ricardo hadn't taken the time to shower or shave. He lunged into Barone's space, unkempt, in his smelly T-shirt and slightly torn jeans, the ones he would pick up in a hurry when he got out of bed.

"You, big honcho, the master of the so-called care plan, my preeminent protector," he mocked.

Dr. Barone looked as if he had been hit by a truck. "Huh? Hold it, Ricardo. What's going on? Why this rudeness?"

"You dirty leech, you suck the money in and then drop me like a stone."

"Huh?"

"Don't act surprised. And don't say 'huh' one more time. You outed me. You ruined my boy and my family. Got that?" Ricardo fumed.

"I don't know your boy, Mr. Lima, Ricardo. There must be some misunderstanding. What's going on?"

"Cut that shit. I know you talked to Molina. Don't pretend you don't know."

Doctor Barone threw his hands up, looking sheepish. He sounded appeasing when he said, "I was going to look into this with the authorities."

"The hell you were. Bullshit! You haven't lifted a finger for my boy. And you outed me!" Ricardo screamed.

"I outed nobody," Barone said firmly.

"So you think I outed myself? I don't look skinny and sick. I don't let ARV boxes lie around. I don't get drunk. I'm extremely careful when I enter your parking lot late at night for my tests and sneak to the side door behind the bushes. It's you!"

"I didn't out you, and I did my best with the authorities, but my hands are tied. The government officials—"

"They're bought by bigots. And your system stinks, man—stinks! I don't have a frigging piece of paper as proof, but I know you're

the guilty one. You yourself, or your organization. My gut tells me."
"Come on, Mr. Lima, you're a smart man. I wouldn't do something
unethical like that. You know that. And, speaking selfishly, why would
I out you and lose the fee you pay us monthly?"

That argument made Ricardo livid. He shouted, "Shut the hell up!
That's the way it may look. You think you can kill everything with that
fee matter. But maybe one of my competitors offered you a big bribe
to discredit me? Maybe you solicited one? Did you get drunk or high
on coke and talk to a big-breasted babe on your lap? Did your shoddy
operation slip up? You suck heaps of money out of your patients. They
pay you a fortune, but you may have a simple IT guy or an underpaid
secretary spilling the beans. Or a messenger working for peanuts. They
can drop a document, or do whatever, to get an extra buck. They're
ready, underpaid prey for bribers."

Dr. Barone didn't respond. He looked at his notebook and sought
relief in playing with his pen, pushing its tip in and out.

Ricardo raged on. "You're a hopeless, cowardly leech, you scum.
You'd better get your pampers on. I'm going to run this thing up the
political ladder. I have friends too. I can pay bribes too."

"Mr. Lima, cool it. You're blurting out baseless accusations," Barone
pleaded.

Suddenly Ricardo stopped shouting.

Dr. Barone looked up.

Ricardo was figuring out his plan. *If I fight him openly, I lose. Who
knows what powers are behind his system. And how far it stretches, how
high.*

Barone looked surprised, and then relieved, when suddenly Ricardo
said calmly, "The damage is done. I cancel my deal with you and your
system. It failed me. You failed me. I'll have to move to Santiago or
Puerto Plata."

As Ricardo walked out, Dr. Barone looked baffled by his patient's
abrupt change in tone.

*He can't believe his luck. He thinks I caved. Good. I'll make sure he
regrets this till the last day of his miserable life. I have connections.*

CHAPTER

Silvia called Tim on Wednesday. Despite her concerns for Carla, she had had him on her mind since Saturday. "Hi, Tim, how are you doing? How's your stay here? Anything I can help you with? Statistics? I've gathered recent information on the *batey* situation, the politics of it." *Too bad we don't have more common interests.*

Bateys were ghetto-like Dominican compounds housing hundreds of thousands of Haitian immigrants in miserable conditions, with no medical care worth mentioning. HIV was rampant in *bateys*. She knew this was an area of interest for Tim.

"How kind of you to think of a foreign straggler, Silvia. Even one who misbehaves with silly, mischievous questions in serious discussions to embarrass you or make you blush."

He hasn't forgotten I beat him at his game. He still hasn't digested his breakfast of Saturday. She said, "Tim, I'm sure you also remember the very serious part of our discussion on Saturday, about Luis Flores and Carla. I wanted to talk to you about it, and maybe to Jorge later. I received a call from a gentleman by the name of Ricardo Lima. It made me feel strange."

"Why? Who's Ricardo? A friend of Flores?" Tim sounded puzzled.

"No. He's one of Dr. Barone's patients. He was looking for Carla.

Of course, I had to tell him I couldn't help him with that. Ricardo also told me he didn't want to talk to Dr. Barone anymore."

"Okay. So what's the big deal? Falling out with doctors and switching happens all the time."

"Sure, Tim, maybe more here than in France. People are fickle when it comes to their health."

"Not me. I've been seeing the same dentist since I was six. And no other doctors."

"Time for a change, Tim. Your dentist's hands must be getting shaky." Silvia laughed for just a second and then turned serious and added, "Mr. Lima, Ricardo, sounded strange, kind of strangely angry. He's one of Dr. Barone's very rich HIV patients. The man said he needed a more convenient location. I didn't believe his excuse. He sounded laconic, hurried. He said he wanted to thank Carla. He would no longer be in her group."

"Looks like Barone's operation is suffering lately, Silvia," Tim commented, not showing any interest in the doctor's business. "Have you heard from Carla?" he asked.

"No, Tim. She must be in hiding. Dr. Barone doesn't have a clue where she might be." *He's going to ask me, "And you? You really haven't a clue?" I shouldn't have called him.* Silvia now realized she simply had been looking for a reason, no matter how flimsy, to call Tim. She had thought she had found one when she got Ricardo's call.

"The murder case will have to run its course, Silvia. Then she will reappear, when the air is clear again."

"Tim, Carla sounded so scared. I must assume she left the country. The case may be more complicated than we think."

"Have the police questioned you?"

"Not yet. Maybe they won't."

"I hope so. By the way, I'm off to Punta Cana later today."

"You Europeans, always vacation. It's your main employ, it seems," Silvia teased, relieved he had moved away from the Carla-and-Luis topic she had raised herself.

"Work, my lady. Meeting with some Harvard guys who study the impact of the economic development there on the ecological system. A common issue all over in fast-developing countries, many with heavy tourism growth. Good enough?"

"I'll have to take your word for it. You wouldn't make up a sweet lie for me, would you?"

"Would I, for you?"

"Tim, here we go again!" She laughed and wished him a good trip and lots of success in his "work."

He still doesn't take Carla's fear seriously. I trust my uncle will be on the line soon from Kavanayén. Carla must be getting there soon. She kept wondering why Ricardo was leaving Dr. Barone. And whether Dr. Barone would tell her why if she asked him how Ricardo was doing.

CHAPTER

Wednesday afternoon, March 25, Tim was almost halfway into the three-hour trip to Punta Cana in the car of the Alliance, Jorge Riquelme's organization. Jorge had offered him the ride. Tim had done a lot of volunteer work for the NGO in the past, some of it just recently, and was a great friend of all there.

Rodrigo, the driver, asked him a favor, explaining, "In about fifteen minutes, we'll be reaching Higüey. The Basílica Nuestra Señora de la Altagracia there is one of the best places in the world to obtain favors from the Holy Virgin."

"For you? For me too?"

"For anybody. I've read it in our parish paper."

"Wow, Rodrigo. Did you bring a list of the goodies you want from her?"

"I know you like to joke, Tim. You always do. But I'm not talking about goodies. It's about real things. I have my list right here," Rodrigo said, pointing not to his brain but to his heart. "Would it be all right for you to have a drink on the square so I can go pray to the Virgin in the Basílica for ten minutes?"

"Sure. But does the Holy Virgin work that fast? She must have requests from all over the world." Tim laughed. "She must have great bandwidth."

Rodrigo kept looking straight ahead while he answered, "Someday you may need her yourself."

I shouldn't be kidding like that. He's a good guy, a little serious. "You're right, my friend. I could use help right now. I could go with you, but I'm thirsty. I'll get myself a Presidente across the plaza while you pray in there."

Rodrigo still looked a little miffed when, twenty minutes later, he came back from the Basílica.

Tim said, his voice serious, "I hope the Holy Virgin heard you."

Rodrigo now showed a little smile and explained, "I had to keep it short. When I drive back from Punta Cana, it'll be close to dark, and I'll have to hurry home to Santo Domingo safely, before complete darkness sets in. You know about the dangers on this road."

"I understand very well, Rodrigo." *Machetes and guns galore after dark.*

"May I ask you a question, Tim?"

"Not too hard, I hope."

"Do you know Dr. Barone well?"

"I know of him."

"Good things?"

"Good, I suppose. He takes care of a lot of patients." *Where's he going with this?*

"I know he has a huge house in Punta Cana. It looks like a hotel. I've seen it. He must be taking care of an awful lot of patients."

"Why do you want to know whether I know him, Rodrigo?"

"No reason. People think he must work night and day to make so much money. I don't know what you think."

"Hmm. Maybe he often stops at the cathedral in Higüey?"

"So you don't know either." Rodrigo shook his head, frowning, his eyes wondering. Then he started humming a religious song.

I'll listen and try to hum along a little. I've disappointed him twice in the last half hour.

CHAPTER  11

Tim made it to Punta Cana and thanked Rodrigo for the pleasant ride and his wise counsel. He checked in at the Paraíso hotel, dropped his bag on his bed, and headed for the pool.

He swam his laps. The sun was getting low and its glow turning intensely red when he finished. During the ride, his long legs had been forced into different uncomfortable bends for three hours. Now they were grateful for the swim, just as they had been when he had his Presidente in Higüey.

As he toweled off, he looked around. The pool area seemed almost deserted. *Real Punta Cana tourists know their priorities: breakfast, sun, rest, drinks, food, rest, and, number one, dinner with more drinks. After a "hard" day out at the pool, most are now diligently getting themselves manicured, showered, shampooed, perfumed, combed, and dressed to face the dinner chore and what, many hope, comes usually after it.*

In the semi-dark, Tim noticed a pretty blonde in a pool chair, nodding and smiling approvingly at him. Tim walked toward her, just a few steps, while continuing his toweling job. He quickly ran his five-finger comb through his brown mane, pushed and pulled his pinkie in and out of his right ear, and leaned his head to shake some water out. Then he said, "Good evening, beautiful. Best time of the day, right?

Quiet." *Her straps are hanging over her arms. Her tan looks provocatively complete. Very little white left, I bet. European.* He kept toweling.

"You're a good swimmer. I was watching you. I was going to go to my room, but I decided to stay a little longer to watch your beautiful strokes," the lady answered.

"I'm flattered. So now I can have the privilege of greeting you with dry hands? I'm Tim." *She looks gorgeous. And she could be my mother.*

They shook hands.

"I'm Liese, Liese Kung."

"German?"

"Swiss." She smiled. "And you're French."

"I won't deny that." Tim laughed. He looked down at his Speedo and then quickly at her again.

"Why don't you sit down, Tim? Enjoy a few more minutes here. The best moments of the day." She gestured he could sit on her right side.

Her best side? Or her best ear? Great features anyway, from this angle.

"What tour are you with, Tim? I haven't seen you around."

"Just the Tim tour. Two nights only."

"What brings you here?" Liese sat up straighter as she asked the question and tied her straps.

"Well … I knew you'd be waiting for me here," he joked.

"Yes, and you're late at the appointment, darling."

Wow. Shouldn't have started this.

"So you're going to dress up for dinner soon, Tim?"

She wants me to invite her; hungry for companionship. "I don't think so, Liese. I'm not big on dinners. Often a pizza and a beer in my room will do. And I'm tired." Tim rubbed his towel over his hair and then threw it around his neck.

"A Frenchman with a beer?"

"Or two."

"You're just like me. I hate all the chatting and formality, the two hours of fixing your face, and the rest." She giggled.

"Allow me to say I'm sure you don't need much time, Liese. You have the natural look."

"Oh, you think so, Tim? Thank you," she said and kept her eyes on his. "Well, why don't we just order pizza right here? We can have the entire place to ourselves, our own private breeze and quiet."

Tim had to admit to himself he had been studying her. *Great looks for her age. Probably even older than I think, but lively eyes, a vivacious smile. Must have been a beauty. Still is.* "That could be fun. Great idea, Liese, pizza," he said. "How do you like it? Margarita? Pepperoni?"

"Just cheese and olives, dear. And some Merlot? Join me for Merlot? I don't drink beer. I'll put it on my room."

"No, no. Let me be a gentleman. I'll order and pay."

She took his hand and repeated, "Just be my guest. The guy at the desk knows me well. Here's my key. You can show it."

Tim got up. As he walked the short distance to the entrance of the coffee shop, he felt Liese's eyes on his hips. He placed the order, cheese and olives for Liese, anchovies for him. And a bottle of Merlot.

He came back, handed her the key, and gestured to a table nearby. "There? Okay? You get the view."

"The view, Tim? I'll be the one with the view tonight. An attractive, mysterious French view," Liese whispered as she stood up and put her hand on his waist to walk over to the table. "So much better than I could imagine thirty minutes ago." She tightened her grip as she spoke.

Tim didn't answer. He felt her warm hand on his wet flesh. They got to the table. He pulled his T-shirt over his head and chest, and sat down. With arms crossed and his elbows on the rickety metal table, he said, "So how long have you been here, Liese?"

It had to be more than a few days yet; her tan told him.

The Merlot had just arrived, and Liese responded, "Let's have a good sip of Merlot first, to celebrate our getting acquainted, Tim."

As they drank to serendipity, Tim noticed Liese studying a couple of strong, young studs marching by. Her eyes followed them for a few seconds. For a moment, she was somewhere else, it seemed, and then she returned to her French view, her *tableau du jour*. Holding up her glass, she looked at him and curled her warm toes on Tim's long, hairy shin and calf under the table. He didn't acknowledge. She kept smiling and commenting on the wine.

He quickly turned to the pizzas when the discreet waiter served them.

Liese and Tim briefly discussed her business and her occasional writing for *Die Reisenpost*, a magazine in her city, Zürich, Switzerland. Travel stories were her forte. She said she thought the Dominican Republic could be fertile ground for juicy articles her Swiss readers would devour. She inquired about *En Avant*, his magazine. They had things in common. He explained his day job and also his sporadic activity in the AIDS treatment field in the Dominican Republic.

"Now tell me, Liese, if you don't mind, have you been here for a while? And how do you spend these glorious days?"

"First question, quite a while." She immediately added, "And staying two or maybe three more weeks." She waited.

"Wow. Good for you. And the second question? The answer could be interesting," Tim said half-joking.

"So you want to know my little secrets? I'm mysterious too, you know," she said and winked almost unnoticeably.

"Well, you read books? Walk? Swim? Snorkel?"

"All of that, Tim. During the day," she added with another giggle.

"I won't ask further. Don't worry."

"You can, Tim. I'm a little older than you, but I still get around, believe me. I still have my wild moments."

"I don't doubt it, Liese. I really don't," he reassured her.

"Why did you sit down with me?" She kept his gaze as she asked the question.

"You invited me."

"Oh, Tim, be honest. You walked up to me." She took his hand and shook it lightly.

"Did I?"

"Have you forgotten? I haven't."

"Well, I thought you looked like a likeable person."

"And were you wrong?"

"I sure wasn't," he responded jovially and lifted his glass.

"Likeable" she repeated and seemed to think. She didn't giggle now. *Man, this is getting a little tricky.*

Much of the pizza was gone. The bottle was half-empty. And Liese looked more than halfway ready to explore personalities.

"Well, Liese," he said, looking at his Casio, "I should be going now. Thank you for dinner. I have to prepare for an important meeting. This trip is work for me."

Liese waited to answer. She looked at her glass as she responded calmly, "I understand, Tim. Thank you for sharing some of your precious time with me. You're still here tomorrow night, after your meeting, I suppose. You can call me. We may have much more to talk about."

"Tomorrow night I have a dinner commitment with the Harvard people I'll be meeting with all day. I'm sorry. I hadn't expected to meet you here."

"You've got my number. You can call me anytime. And I'll be here for three more weeks, remember? You're in Santo Domingo. We could enjoy a trip into the country side. I'm an adventurer, I told you." Now she smiled again.

Tim got up and said, "There may be a follow-up with the Harvard people next week. Who knows, we might have another drink sometime."

"That sounds good, Tim. I enjoyed your company."

Attractive, witty, good-natured, but lonely. Not fair, Tim thought as he walked to his room and now started to feel his wet Speedo. *Nothing dries here.*

CHAPTER 12

Around the time that Tim was finishing his laps at the Punta Cana Paraíso hotel, Carla Fuentes stepped out of a mud-covered Toyota RAV at the Santa Teresita mission in Kavanayén. The vehicle had a single windshield wiper, on the driver's side, so Carla had been staring at a mud curtain in front of her for much of the last two hours. Heavy rain had actually been somewhat helpful to her.

Carla stretched her legs, took a few steps, and looked around at the area that would be her new home. It wasn't completely dark yet, but close. The place looked dismal, desolate, dreary. No neon light, no sound or smell from a little snack bar or a shop. Not one person, no cat, no old dog. Just this building in front of her, threatening in the quasi-dark. The rain had stopped.

She paid the driver, Antonio, who had yet to take her heavy bag out of the vehicle.

"Wait just a minute, please," she told him. "I want to make sure that this huge, black door I'm going to knock on opens for me."

"Don't worry. If it doesn't, I'm sure you can stay at my friend's house here. I'm staying there anyway; the trip back to Luepá's too dangerous in the dark."

The guy hopes the black door won't open. She chuckled to herself as she waited. In the Toyota she had given herself a fake name, Ana, and said she was Nicaraguan. "I'm going to be a nun at the mission and probably will never leave Santa Teresita again," she had told him.

Antonio had looked askance at her and then down at her long legs. And again.

"You can't tell anybody about my trip here," she had added. "You must swear to that."

"I swear," he answered immediately, "and I hope you understand that I'm feeding a family of six."

"I do," Carla had said. "And I'll pay you another five dollars. But I warn you: the Lord knows who breaks promises."

He had said he already knew.

They may already have called it a day here, she thought as she knocked a second time. *And they don't know when to expect me.* During Carla's escape, Silvia had been her only possible connection, and it had lasted only until the Toyota had left the north-south route from Ciudad Guayana to Santa Elena de Uairén, in Luepá, to go west. At that moment she had lost all coverage. She hadn't needed to contact Silvia since the moment she landed in Ciudad Guayana. That was a good thing, because a call with her would have been traceable. It was still a long, hard drive, three to five hours, from Luepá to her remote destination.

A few moments after her second knock, slow squeaks announced the opening of the huge door. A young monk's face appeared. He smiled and said, "Miss Carla?"

"Yes, sir." *My God! What a beautiful face.*

"I've been waiting since Sunday. Welcome. I'm Brother Marcus."

"Thank you so much, Brother. Excuse me for a second," she responded.

She quickly turned to the driver, who stood behind her and seemed puzzled. She said quietly, "He's got my name wrong, but I'll get in. Thank you, Antonio. Safe travels. Be careful."

Antonio looked a little disappointed as he wished her good night and a good stay. He disappeared in the early night.

Marcus said he would guide Carla to the place they had prepared for her.

The young monk carried her bags effortlessly. He almost ran through the dark hallways. She tried to keep up, her legs stiff from the long voyage and weak because she hadn't seen any decent food the entire day. The monk wore stiff, hard sandals. The clatter of his steps echoed through the building.

"No problem with the noise; our walls are thick, Miss Carla," he explained, looking back at her. "Our brothers sleep well, tired from work, their minds peaceful and undisturbed."

"And I have kept you up late, Marcus. Sorry."

"Brother Marcus, we say, or just Brother. And no problem. I enjoyed listening to choirs sitting near the entrance while waiting for you. My mother gave me some beautiful music on cassettes. I've waited till ten every night since Sunday. Father Francesco will be happy. We can't disturb him now, he's sleeping, but I'll slip a note under his door."

"Good. Let me write it," Carla said.

"You'll find pen and paper on the little table next to your bed when you get to your room. You must be tired, Miss Carla."

"Yes. And happy to find you and your smile, Brother Marcus."

He looked young, powerful. *Nice chiseling job, his face. And he moves like a young pitcher, but under that habit …*

Brother Marcus smiled again.

He acknowledges my compliment.

They walked farther into the building. Then Marcus stopped and pointed to a door about ten meters ahead.

"That will be your place, Miss Carla. The first door. Simple but, we hope, comfortable. The sisters have been expecting you. I can't go any farther than right here." He handed her a key. "Please open the door and carry your bags in if you can. There's water and fruit in the room. Take a look and tell me whether all is okay for the night."

"Thank you, Brother."

Carla took her bags, opened her cell door, and switched on the light. A measly, dust-covered bulb welcomed her. A moth jumped off. Carla saw her cell, all of its hundred to hundred-fifty square feet. *My new home for many moons.* She did a quick inspection. A narrow bed, a table with a drawer, a basin and a can on it, a small nightstand, two chairs, a bench for prayers, a large crucifix, a portrait of Santa Teresita, and a green plastic bucket with a cover under the table. She saw a small window, just under the ceiling. She stuck her head out of the door and signaled to Marcus with her hand that she would quickly write a note. He nodded.

Two minutes later, she went back to Marcus.

"I'm so grateful, Brother Marcus. Thank you so much, again. It all looks great."

As she took the note she had written out of her pocket, she noticed that he looked absent. *His mind is somewhere else. He may never have been in the presence of a woman all by himself.* She felt warmth for this beautiful man. It was almost compassion, although she thought he was probably quite happy.

As she handed him the note, she said, "Thank you," and kissed him spontaneously on the cheek.

Brother Marcus stepped back, seemed startled, and looked around. He stared at Carla and said, "I must thank *you*, Angel Carla, for your presence here." Then he came closer. His hand was shaking as he put it against her back.

She felt his trembling lips on her cheek.

He took a step back.

He can't take his eyes off my body. "I'm so glad you've waited for me, Brother Marcus." Carla was tempted. She decided to get closer and embraced him briefly. *Wiry. Nervous. He clings to me.*

She ended the embrace.

"I must go now. Father Francesco will come and see you early tomorrow morning," the brother blurted and rushed around the corner before she could react.

In her room, Carla prepared for a good night's sleep. She finally felt safe. *I wonder whether I'll see gorgeous Marcus again. I bet I will. Maybe I should postpone my vows for a while.* As she tried to fall asleep, she banned any frivolous thought and considered her precarious situation as a fugitive. She realized that the death of Luis, already so far in the past with the avalanche of events since Friday night, was fast fading from her mind. She was forced to face other issues. She feared for her life.

CHAPTER  13

Around midnight on Wednesday the twenty-fifth, Javier Fuentes and his wife Maria, Carla's parents, were sound asleep at their house in Valencia when they were awakened by several knocks on wood.

"The front door," Javier said as he sat up and waited, his ears focused.

"Yes, the doorbell is still out of order," Maria responded.

"Shh, Maria." Javier's hand gesture spoke volumes in the near-dark.

The knocking continued.

"Yes, front door," Javier repeated. "Quiet. You stay here." He took the baseball bat he kept in a closet near his bedside and slipped into his jeans.

"Be careful, Javier. You know the light in the front yard doesn't work either. Don't fight. They'll have guns. Just give them money. Take some out of your wallet here," Maria pleaded, her voice trembling, her fingernails hooked in the bed sheet she held up to cover her body and half of her face.

Javier took her advice. He had no idea how many people had descended on his house; he hadn't heard men talking. If he didn't open the door, they would make their way in by force, he figured.

He barely heard the last warnings by his terrified wife as he left her and headed for the front door. He held the bat behind his back with his right hand and opened the door ajar with the left one. He hadn't switched on the light inside.

A huge man, much of his face covered by a hat and big, dark glasses, shoved his foot in the door, pointed his gun, and said in a hushed tone, "Open, quick, and don't scream. Drop that frigging gun behind your back."

Javier dropped the bat and showed his hands.

The man pushed him aside, stepped in, and said brusquely, "You just answer my questions. And listen. You scream, I have a gun and friends. Understood?"

Javier saw Maria appear from behind the corner and gestured she should keep away.

But the bandit hissed at her, "You, stay. I'll stuff a towel in your mouth if you scream. Bring me your cell phones. All of them. You'd better not cheat or I'll shoot your man. I already cut your landline. You don't move, mister."

Mrs. Fuentes covered her mouth with her hand and ran away, sobbing and saying, "Don't harm my husband. He's a good person. Please. I get the phones."

She disappeared, and the bandit waited in silence. Mrs. Fuentes came back and handed the bandit two cell phones, her hands shaking and her eyes trained on Javier.

She's asking me what to do now.

"Now unplug your fixed phones and bring them to me," the bandit growled at Mrs. Fuentes.

She left, crying. "We have only one." She came back with one phone.

The bandit turned to her and said, "That's all? Sure? If my men find another one, I'll kill you. Understand?"

Maria nodded.

"Now get the hell out of here," the bandit barked to her. "Go to your bed and keep the windows closed. No lights. And be quiet or else."

The fear-stricken woman stepped back and disappeared around the corner.

The bandit stuffed the phones in a leather bag. He said, "Listen, man. Your slut of a daughter ran away with more than eight million pesos. Hear me? She stole them. She wasn't entitled to them. She works with me. She's a thief, and she ran away. Where the hell is she?"

Javier stared at the bandit in disbelief. "Impossible, sir. Please don't speak that way. I didn't raise her that way. You must have the wrong house."

"Mr. Fuentes, Javier Fuentes, father of Carla Fuentes, I do my homework. Now answer my question. I need the money back, and her ass in jail."

"I don't know where she is. We're worried to death."

The bandit threw his arm around Javier's throat in a stranglehold. He held it for some ten seconds and then released it slightly. "Well, does it help your memory?"

"I can't say, sir. I don't know where she is. She called once, but she didn't say where she was. She was in a phone booth," Javier stammered, terrified.

"When?"

"Monday."

The grip tightened again, and the bandit kept growling, "If you lie, I'll kill you." Then he let go again and said, "Tell me where she is. Five seconds." He threatened with his gun, "This is quick and easy. Where the hell is she?"

"You can kill me, sir, and you still won't know. We have no idea. I swear. Please release me. I have a heart condition. Please."

The bandit pushed Javier away, and the old man hit the wall with the back of his head.

As the intruder walked out, he said, pointing at the phones in his bag, "These babies will tell me everything, and if you lied, I come back and blow your frigging brains out."

Javier didn't have the presence of mind to peer through the front window and try to see the bandit's car in the dark, or whether other bandits were waiting for him. Still shaking, he doddered into the kitchen and sat down for a minute at the table to recover. Maria walked in and hugged and kissed her man, wetting his cheeks and forehead with her tears.

"Good thing I didn't know where she is," Javier said.

"You should call the police, Javier."

"With which phone?"

"Alejandro next door will let you use his."

"Yeah. The police will listen to me? Half-asleep? They'll take some notes and do nothing till morning. This is daily fare for them. I'll go and see them at eight. Let's go back to bed now and sleep, if we can. I need a beer first."

"I don't like Carla's work with the support organization, Javier. It just doesn't feel right," Mrs. Fuentes sobbed.

"But she says she's helping people in need, Maria. We just saw that good deeds don't always get rewarded, not in this life. We didn't deserve this brutality. God will have mercy on us."

"I don't understand why she doesn't call us or answer our calls. She may be dead, Javier." Maria kept sobbing and dropped her head on his shoulder.

She may be. "No way, Maria. We would've heard."

❦ ❦ ❦

The bandit with the big hat didn't need much time to find out who the frequent callers to the Fuenteses were over the last few days, and whom the Fuenteses had called. One number showing up again and again on the phones was that of Dr. Silvia Herrera.

I know of that snitch. Not trustworthy. Kind of works with Barone. Strictly medical. Do-gooder.

The bandit contacted a buddy at Verizon, who told him that Dr. Silvia Herrera had a phone with them. The man agreed to tap it for a small fee. Immediately.

Patience now. I'll catch fish. This is a start.

CHAPTER

On Saturday, March 28, Carla sauntered in the halls of the *Misión de Santa Teresita de Kavanayén*. The thick stone walls provided a pleasant, breezeless afternoon cool. She was reflecting on how much had happened in the last three days.

After her arrival late on Wednesday and her very special welcome by Brother Marcus to the mission, Carla had fallen in a deep sleep. It was halted at six in the morning on Thursday when Father Francesco knocked on her door and embraced her. He thanked her for the message Brother Marcus had delivered to him.

"I've been up since four, but I figured I'd let you sleep in a little," he said.

Carla studied the friendly man, who softly smiled at her, looking over his heavy glasses. *Sleeping in? Six o'clock? He doesn't smile. Is he joking or not? I'd better assume no,* she concluded and said, "Thank you for caring for me, Father. You're very considerate. I don't know how I'm going to pay you back for helping me out this way."

"You just behave well, make me proud of you. That'll be ample reward for me," the father said, with a broad smile now. "And you can sleep as long as you want for the rest of the week, but breakfast is at 5:30."

"Oh. Too late already today. No problem. I have some snacks left in my bag."

"Today one of our sisters will be happy to serve you at seven, if you wish. She can come and accompany you to the room where we take our meals. You can't really call it a dining room," he explained, but he didn't look or sound embarrassed.

"You're being very kind, Father. I'll freshen up and be ready when she comes. Could I call my parents after breakfast? I'll be brief."

Father Francesco scratched behind his right ear and explained, "I have the satellite phone in my cell, and I'll call my niece from there in an hour or so. Silvia will be very happy to hear about you, I'm sure. I'll ask her to call your parents and tell them you're safe and well. The rates on the phone are exorbitant, so I must control its use very strictly. Silvia and I always keep our conversations extremely brief and smartly to the point. The young but very clever brother who does the books here scrupulously tracks all expenses. He won't let me commit grave sins wasting money—our good Brother Marcus, the one who welcomed you yesterday." He snickered lightly and gave her a friendly little nod.

He almost winked, the holy man. I'll have to adapt to the simple life and sense of humor in this remote place. They're so generous. She answered, "Oh, good, Father. Thank you so much. Could you please tell Silvia I'm okay, and give her my best, best thanks? The two of you saved me."

"That's what I heard we would be doing, although I didn't really understand the background. But I believe my niece and you. Some day you can explain it to me quietly, if you like. After breakfast, I'll show you our church. I'll find you in the dining room."

"Thank you, Father."

The old man left.

Just this one phone here. And I must make this one other call myself. She knew from the driver that she wouldn't find another satellite phone in this village, even if she left the mission and ventured into the community. She had already gathered that from Silvia. And there were no lines or cell towers in this region.

60

Father Francesco showed up in the dining room as promised. He didn't want to sit down for a cup of coffee with Carla. She was finishing her breakfast. He'd already drunk his cup for the day.

On his tour of the mission with her, he proudly guided her through the nuns' quarters first, and then the men's, the library, the Ping-Pong room, and the separate guest building. The latter was run hotel-style, for travelers, but it had just rooms, outdoor sinks, and outdoor toilets. Along the way, she noticed sisters and monks and some laborers, all diligently at work. She checked her watch. *Seven-thirty. It's a different world here.*

"We have so much more to show you, Carla, but I kept our jewel for last today. This way." The father gestured, as if unveiling a hidden treasure, in the direction of the church. The structure right in front of them dominated the mission.

She said, kindly feigning surprise, "Oh. I see. Yes. The church there. What an impressive building."

It actually was. A sturdy construction, created with stone from the area, and fully integrated into the complex over which it reigned. Inside, Father Francesco pointed out old paintings and authentic relics, real hair and bones of saints, he assured her, and the beautifully chiseled pew.

Carla noticed six confessionals and just a few people sitting in short rows, apparently waiting their turn for confession. "Masses have finished for today. Some attendees combine confession with Mass in one trip," Father Francesco explained. "Saturday is the big cleaning day. Also for the soul."

Carla was pleasantly surprised when she saw Brother Marcus emerge from one of the confessionals. *My hunk.*

The brother didn't seem to notice her. He spoke to the parishioners waiting at his confessional and gestured apologetically to them that he had to leave. He pointed at other confessionals.

Carla heard some confessants grumble that they would have to start at the end of another queue. Some walked out of the church. She caught a couple of curse words. *In the church.*

"Of course you know our Brother Marcus," the father said, pointing at him. "I had him wait for you every night till you arrived. He's done with confessions for the day now. He finishes them just before eight so he can get to his accounting work. His office is next to my place. You can see some parishioners look disappointed that he's leaving." The father chuckled as he went on, "They know he's very young and hears well and speaks softly. That's good for the discretion we all need. We're all sinners, but our neighbors don't have to hear the details. And he goes light on penances, I discovered. He argues that people have 'real' work to do. That's one way to look at it. He's, of course, still inexperienced."

"Does he hear confessions every day?"

Father Francesco looked pleasantly surprised by Carla's interest and quickly answered, "Yes, every brother does, except on Sundays. From seven to eight a.m., and also by appointment for emergencies, of course."

"What's an emergency?" Carla asked, trying to conceal her feeling of slight amusement.

The father lowered his voice. "Some people may have a special, urgent need, Carla. Good souls like you wouldn't know about that." He threw his arm around her shoulders and shook her softly, with a friendly grin. Then he retracted his arm and added, his tone serious, "Many people come to the confessional in a crisis. I can understand you don't know that. They may pretend they're confessing, but they often are just looking for a shoulder to cry on, unseen. Most of them don't realize I can recognize all my parishioners in the dark confessional. I see their faces. I know their voices and whether they use toothpaste. They may have just run away from home after a fiery argument and be looking for advice. Or shelter, protection sometimes. Who knows?"

"So they just come running in and knock on the brother's cell door in such a case?" Carla wondered, still incredulous.

"Oh no. Of course not. No visitors are allowed there, in the brothers' quarters. The brother on duty at the front door must be given a paper, in a closed envelope. He has pen, paper, and envelopes available at the desk. He then has the note delivered to the particular brother the sinner needs to see. The confessor shows up in a short time ... but maybe not in the best mood." He smiled.

"Any time of the day?"

The father responded proudly. "In principle, yes. The Lord loves his people every minute of the day. We assist anytime. Sometimes even in the middle of the night."

"But this can get very difficult. It means brothers can never be sure they'll have a good night's sleep." Carla's tone had become slightly argumentative.

"You're right, in theory. And we're here to help anytime to take care of real emergencies. But they don't happen that often. Very seldom, actually. Who will have a brother awakened for a bagatelle? I know from experience that it's a very rare parishioner who will rush to confession in a panic during the night, fearing he'll die and go to hell before morning confession hours," the father said as he winked rascal-like at Carla.

"I see. And you, or any brother, could raise the penance if a night call were for a trifle." Carla now laughed.

The father frowned lightly and said, "Let's not dwell on this. I know you'd go to heaven if you were to die now or during the night."

I'd like to bet he's wrong, but I won't disappoint him. "And I'd see you there later, Father—much later, I hope. I'd hold a good seat for you."

"Okay, okay. Now ..." The father checked his watch. "I suggest you go to the kitchen and see how you can help, if you like. It'll be good for your mental state, I think."

The next day, Friday, Carla had breakfast at 5:40 in the dining hall. She sat with the sisters, young and old, who asked her friendly, supportive questions and encouraged her to take a robust breakfast, the basis for a good day's work. It would be a long morning; lunch would be at 11:30.

She wore a white blouse, buttoned up high, and a decently long skirt of blue jeans cloth. Carla looked around and thought, *I should get myself a habit and a small veil, just as a practical hair matter. The nuns look good in light brown cotton habits and nonsensical, fake leather shoes.* Carla joked to herself that she could be a novice. *But I won't go the next step.*

When she finished breakfast, it was still too early for confession with Brother Marcus. She helped in the kitchen, not just with the cleaning up, but also with peeling vegetables and washing, cutting, and putting them in salted water, ready for the cooking. At 7:15, she dried her hands, smoothed her skirt, and headed for the church. The sisters said they were grateful for the help she had provided.

Arriving in the church, she noticed two parishioners lined up in front of Brother Marcus's confessional. She took a seat in the row and waited for her turn. It came after ten minutes. She lifted the curtain that shielded confessants from nosy parishioners, stepped in, and kneeled down. All was dark.

After about fifteen seconds, the confessor slid a wooden cover away, leaving just a thin sheet between his face and the confessant's. The sheet had rows of very small circular openings in it. He made a cross in the air with his right hand, barely discernible by Carla. His space was darker than hers. Carla knew the confessor wasn't supposed to look at her face but straight ahead, at the confessional's door.

She spoke first. "Good morning, Brother Marcus. I don't really have to confess. It's me. Carla. I wanted to thank you for your generous reception on Wednesday. I felt so welcome. Good to see you. I looked forward to hearing your warm voice again. How are you?"

The confessor coughed and said, "*Señora*, I heard about your arrival, and I detect an accent. Brother Marcus left for Santa Elena very early this morning. He'll be back late tonight."

A torrent of blood rushed to her cheeks. *He can't see it.* "Oh, well, my apologies, Brother. I didn't want to misuse the confessional, but I had little time to thank the brother when I arrived here, late at night and very tired. I'm embarrassed now. I was the last person in the row in front of your confessional, so I didn't bother anybody else."

"Nobody will know, so you won't have to be embarrassed. I'm

bound by my vow of silence. And you didn't bother me. Go in peace. Unless you have to confess."

"I went to confession just before I left my country. I knew my trip could be dangerous." *How many years has it been?* "I won't take more of your time now. Thank you."

She exited the confessional, kneeled down in the back of the church, crossed herself with big gestures, steepled her hands to pray, and put her lips on her fingertips. She pretended to say her self-imposed penitence prayers. Ten minutes later, she proceeded to the front door of the mission.

A young man, barely twenty, manned the welcome desk there.

She addressed him with an upbeat voice. "Good morning, *caballero,* I wonder whether you could help me. I'd like to write some letters. Would you happen to have some paper here? And envelopes?"

The youngster looked very pleased with the way his visitor addressed him. He pushed his shoulders down to accentuate his firm but still skinny chest. He said, "I'm just substituting for a few minutes, *Señora.* Let me look. A minute, please."

He opened the various drawers and soon came up with what he was looking for. He gave her six or seven sheets and more or less the same number of envelopes. Then he volunteered a pencil, but she said she had her pen. She held up one of the envelopes to the sun and noticed it was made of very thin paper.

"Thank you so much, *amigo.* Someday you'll be a great monk."

"I hope soon, *Señora.*"

She walked away in the direction of the church. When she took a ninety-degree turn after twenty meters, she saw him wave at her, just a hand gesture.

When she arrived at her place, she carefully locked the door and lay down on her bed. It was still early morning. Staring at the ceiling and the dirty lightbulb, she wondered how she would spend her second full day here. *Cleaning? Maybe tomorrow.* She started drafting a message to Brother Marcus, just in her mind. She heard herself pronounce the words she would write on paper soon. She wanted to hear how they would sound to Brother Marcus when he would receive, read, and recite them to himself in his room just before midnight. *I must talk to this man. I need him.*

Half an hour went by before she pushed herself off the bed and sat down at her table. She moved the water can and the soap to make room for her elbows and the paper she was going to write on. Then she wrote her message. When she finished writing, she folded the paper so it would fit in the envelope. She took a second sheet and folded it over the first one. Then she put both in the envelope. She closed it, licked the glue, and pressed. Then she wrote words, not on the front of the envelope, but on the back, and so that the top half of each character was on the flap, and the bottom half on the envelope body. She used as poor handwriting as she could manage and wrote two mistakes intentionally. Her words said that this envelope was for confessor Brother Marcus.

At 9:00 p.m. Carla slipped quietly into a dark, little corner close to the front door of the mission. She started observing the desk, where a monk on duty sat reading. She heard heavy rain. *Marcus's trip back home will be atrociously difficult.*

After she had waited about ten minutes, she heard a hard knock on the big front door. The monk closed his book and walked away from his desk. He let in a brown-haired man in shorts and a T-shirt who rubbed water off his arms and legs. He wore light sandals.

She saw the brother start a conversation with the man, take two umbrellas, and walk out with the visitor. *The tourist must have his wife waiting in the car.*

Carla ran toward the desk—there was nobody around—and slowed down to a normal stroll once she got out of the dark section and close to the desk, pretending to just walk by. She put her envelope on the desk, walked away calmly, and switched over to a quick, forceful march as soon as she was out of sight from the desk.

At twenty minutes past midnight, Saturday morning already, Carla walked to the church of the mission. She carried her shoes in her hands and walked barefoot. She avoided the front desk, where a small light was on. She opened a small side door of the church, lifting the knob slightly to limit the squeaking as she turned it. In the dark, she put her left hand on the end of bench after bench so she could follow the walkway to where Brother Marcus's confessional was. She lifted the curtain to step into the confessional. She did not kneel down, but sat down. She waited for the brother, her confessor tonight.

"Why don't you kneel, so I can see you, Angel Carla?" It was little more than a whisper.

Carla jumped up and kneeled. She couldn't really see Brother Marcus's face in the dark, but she heard his fast breathing. *I smell him. His heart may be beating even faster than mine.* "Brother Marcus …"

"Please call me Marcus, Carla."

"Marcus, I'm sorry for the inconvenience."

"I'm glad I got back on time. I haven't slept yet," he whispered nervously, panting. "I arrived at eleven. I saw your note for an urgent confession. I couldn't rest—not because I feared something was wrong with you, or thought you had sinned gravely, but because I was so happy. I wished your note had said 11:15, not half past midnight. I read your message a thousand times."

"I have trouble hearing you, Marcus. Can we speak just a bit louder?"

"Just step out. I'll open my door. We have space for two here on my bench." His voice trembled.

Wow. He's reckless. So young, of course. That'll be a first for me.

Carla heard a little click as she stepped out and saw the little door of the confessional ajar. She slipped in and, in the dark, landed in the arms of Brother Marcus.

What got into him?

He smelled sweaty from the long trip. His skin wasn't smooth because he was perspiring, and his hands were shaking. *Fear? Excitement?*

Never been close to a woman. Carla felt the strong arms around her waist, his hands all over her hips, his lips rough. When he tried to speak, he had to swallow several times to be able to make a sound. She squeezed her breasts against him and whispered, "How long has it been since they've called you a hunk? I saw you are one, Wednesday, and again yesterday morning when you stepped out of your confessional just before eight. You didn't see me. Now my hands can feel my eyes didn't deceive me. I'm glad you received my message."

Marcus sighed. "I didn't know angels could feel so divine. I wish we could stay together for a long time."

"We can't here. But the world is big. Dream of other places. Nobody has chained you to this place. Think about it. But we shouldn't rush things. This is only the second time we've spoken to each other."

"I want to be with you, Carla. I know it. In the car today, I pretended to sleep for hours so I could dream about you," he whispered passionately. "I hoped you would stay with us in the mission for a very long time. Will you?"

"Let's meet again and reflect together on what you just said." *The speed of light. All that testosterone bottled up. And going to waste.*

"Tomorrow? Same time?"

"Same time. I'll wear a silky blouse." *And a short, thin skirt. I need this man.*

"Please dress decently. You may run into somebody." Marcus now sounded a bit concerned.

She put two fingers on his right cheek and whispered, "No worry, my hunk. I'll walk like a repenting sinner, head down, badly in need of an urgent confession. A big one. Do you need another message from me asking for a confession, just in case?"

"Your message of today will do, Carla. It has no date."

"I know."

CHAPTER  15

It was Saturday, the twenty-eighth, when Tim got a call from Liese around 10:00 a.m.

He turned the TV down and asked, intrigued and somewhat amused, "How did you find me, Lady Liese?"

"Lady? How about foxy? Tracking you down was a piece of cake. Everybody knows you in Santo Domingo. I tried a few hotels—and bingo. Here I am." She laughed triumphantly.

"A detective's nose."

"And your special cologne, Tim. So unique, so easy and exciting to trace and track."

"Yeah. Sure. So how are things out there in Punta Cana?"

"I've been having a blast the last couple of days. I went out late with a couple of friends I'd met my first days here. We renewed friendship and … had a ball. Again. We still are. We're on tonight again. Come and join the fun," she suggested enthusiastically.

"But you're telling me you don't need me there. Isn't that the message?" Tim joked.

"To the contrary, Tim. I'm waiting for you here. You promised, right? More or less anyway."

Less, I'm sure. "You have all those friends there. I'm sure their meringue moves are much better than mine. And their hips a lot looser."

"That may be true." She giggled. Then she changed tone as she said, "But there's more than meringue, Tim. Brains count too. You and I get along well. The young kids here are nice, and fun, but …"

"Kids? Dancing with kids?"

"Almost, Tim. But hunks." She sighed. "Sometimes I long for more mature conversation."

My mother talking. My editor should hear this. Mature? Me?

"Well, I'm not sure yet, Liese, but maybe I'll come to Punta Cana this Thursday or Friday."

"Oh, good. Let me know. I'll cancel everything."

"I may bring a friend. About as mature as me."

"Great. I can't wait, Tim."

He hung up.

Silvia called Tim around 10:30.

"Good morning, *Monsieur*," she said softly.

"*Buen día*, Silvia. Are you still in bed? You sound a bit sleepy. Are you okay?"

"No giant breakfast for me today, Tim. Jorge must be stuffing himself all alone at Café Barahona. I just got up—10:30. A shame, I know."

"No, it isn't. You must make sure you get your beauty sleep."

"You think I don't?" she said, half-teasing.

"I didn't say that. Sorry," he said. "Can we talk without question marks today?"

"Do I hear you pleading with me? Do you realize you just used your third one, Tim? Don't blame me."

"Touché. So I'll ask you a question in the form of a statement: I was just going to call you to invite you to join me for next weekend in Punta Cana. I found a good place."

Silvia felt simultaneously happy and hesitant. She answered, "Just like that, Tim? A giant leap to … well, to where? This must be the French way, with the speed of French trains, or of that nuclear collider on the border with Switzerland. I don't know you very well."

"True. And vice versa. But that doesn't mean we can't be good friends for the weekend. I can be the perfect gentleman."

He's pleading his case with robust confidence. He must have seen through me at breakfast last Saturday.

"Tim, before we get into that, I'll have to confess something."

"That you have a crush on me. Shoot, I was going to be first, but you beat me to it."

"That I haven't told you all I knew about Carla."

"I had a hunch she wasn't the angel you said she was."

What does he know about her? Nothing, she thought. *But I did kind of lie to him.* "Tim, believe me, she *is* an angel, and … I helped her flee to Venezuela."

"You did? Venezuela? Wow. That's news. Why didn't you tell me? Why did you decide to tell me now?" He sounded puzzled.

"I had promised her not to tell anybody," Silvia explained, feeling like a little girl. "She was so concerned that her plan would leak out. But she's safe now at her destination, so I can be a bit more open. I must be able to talk to somebody about this, Tim. I can't sleep at night. I know you won't harm her, and I trust you can keep a secret. I apologize. I'm sure you'd help her if you could."

"She had to flee that far," was Tim's only comment. He sounded wistful.

"She's in a remote area. She'll be completely safe there. One of my uncles lives in that region and made arrangements for her, for a place to hide. He called me very early Thursday morning to let me know she arrived safe and well. I'm grateful to him."

"That's great news. How did she get there?"

"That I don't know. I only did the lodging. She didn't want any other help. She wanted to keep it all very secret. Even her parents didn't know where she was till I told them she had arrived at her destination. They were very worried about Carla, and they feared for their own safety too."

"More threats? How are *they* involved in this?"

He thinks I'm dramatizing. "Not involved at all, I'm sure. But Wednesday night very late, when they were in bed, an ugly intruder burst into their house and demanded all their phones—at gunpoint. Then he threatened her father, Mr. Fuentes, with strangulation. Not just threats. He held him in a stranglehold 'for an eternity,' Mr. Fuentes said. The bandit tried to pry the name of Carla's hiding place out of him. Of course, her father didn't know it. The scoundrel eventually took off with their phones, still shouting threats."

"This is starting to look serious, Silvia." Now Tim sounded concerned.

"The bandit accused Carla of stealing a big amount of money and having fled with it. A big lie, of course."

"Still stranger … I wonder … She traveled alone in a remote area … Which area?"

"Kavanayén, in the Canaima National Park. South of the Gran Sabana, close to Brazil and Guyana."

"I know the region. I traveled into Brazil that way once, through the Gran Sabana. Never to Kavanayén, but I heard of it, in almost mystic terms."

"I was so relieved to hear she'd made it. But I've been worrying since last Saturday that I should've told you." *What will he think of me? We had a very long breakfast. Talked about everything, except …*

"You didn't have to. I'm not involved in this."

Whew. Off the hook. "I wanted you to know I'm sorry about it, Tim."

"Good," he said, speaking slowly, his tone serious. "I'll forgive you. And I understand why you sinned: you had a good reason. Therefore, the penance will be minimal: a weekend with me in Punta Cana. *No más.* You're getting off easy. Or am I being too harsh?"

"Oh, Tim." Silvia laughed but hesitated briefly before she answered, "Well, okay, I'll accept my punishment. And I appreciate your magnanimity."

"You need a break, Silvia."

"Yes, Tim." She let her voice fade softly.

Tim said he would come back with details.

CHAPTER  16

Silvia had finished her morning yoghurt at her desk and was taking a last sip of coffee to start her day at the office with a decent dose of energy. It was 8:00 a.m. on Tuesday, March 31. She looked at an old hiking picture from Central Chile, her shorts unreal, so short, her legs showing longer than they actually were, and she wondered how it would be to go there with Tim. Then she felt she was being silly, getting ahead of herself. *Let's see how things work out in Punta Cana over the weekend.* And she thought of Carla.

Suddenly Dr. Barone burst into her office, startling her and waving a piece of paper. He was fuming.

She reflexively righted herself on her chair.

"You know where Carla is!" he shouted angrily. He pointed at her, flung the sheet on her desk, inches from her face. "I know it too. Just heard it. Ten seconds ago. Kavanayén. Venezuela. I'm so angry I could kill. She ran away with a ton of money, the thief. Never thought she could be like that. And you were in on this too. I feel like strangling you." He quickly took the sheet back, put his hands on his hips, and stared at her, looking ready to pounce.

Silvia recovered from the surprise. She absorbed the flood of words that came over her and stated calmly, "Slow down, Doctor. Watch your heart. And you're wrong. Carla's no thief. I know that, and you know it too. Who tells you this nonsense?"

"I know where she is. The end of the world. But we'll dig her up from that place, wherever she's hiding with the loot. And you're colluding with Timonier to keep her in hiding. What's your cause? What share of the haul did she promise you?"

Somebody must have overheard my conversation with Tim Saturday. "Dr. Barone," she said indignantly, "you're insulting me. And Mr. Timonier certainly isn't involved in this."

"You're lying. I know. And I know about this French wimp. He's the one who caused all the trouble for Enrique Cuevas a while ago in Santo Domingo—puts his nose in everything and throws around baseless accusations. Mr. Poison Pen. Besmirching decent people."

Silvia put her index finger in the air as she responded, "He's an honorable man. His reputation is stellar, and I don't appreciate your listening in on our personal conversations."

"I didn't, lady," he said scornfully, his face telling clearly that such a thing was beneath him.

It must have been the bandit who attacked the Fuenteses. He has their phones and must know I call them sometimes. Silvia went on the offense, mocking Barone, "Oh? Who did? Do you know? Do you? And just like that? Through my closed window? Mr. Timonier's window? From under my bed? Somebody dropped a listening device under my sink? Or is it just good old-fashioned bribery of a Verizon employee?"

"Why don't you tell me what you're up to, lady? Are you still a team player here? Or just working for a paycheck? We care for our patients, and I despise people who try to get in the way of that effort. Particularly if they steal money. Where's the dough?"

"Dr. Barone, you're leaving a few things out. Things have happened. Luis died. Carla fled. Her parents were savagely attacked in their house. Would you happen to know about that? What's going on?"

Barone swallowed. Then he said, "Things happened, right. But what the hell have I to do with the unfortunate death of poor Luis? I do my physician's job. I care for my people, and they need my help and the guidance of a support group for the rest of their lives. That's all.

Understand? I know Carla's your friend. She was mine too, until she robbed us. I know that right from the source, from the person who does the books. We'll miss her in our group. Somebody must have talked her into this stupidity. Money …"

"Doctor, I'm simply a low-ranked physician taking care of patients. I'd like to keep it that way. Yes, I have helped Carla because she was scared to death, and I know she's a good person." *I should ask him whom she should be scared of.* She saw that Dr. Barone was taken aback, and she wondered, *Was it the word "scared" that I used for the first time?* She was convinced that "theft" was just a pretext they were using to chase Carla. *Somebody wants to shut her up.*

"Hmm. You better grow up, open your eyes, and see the world for what it is." He turned his back to her, stared at the hiking picture, and looked sad when he turned again to her. "Look," he said calmly, "I appreciate your work here. You're a reliable resource for us. Just stay out of these Carla matters now. Justice will have to be done, sooner or later. Now that Carla's so far away, it can take a while, of course. You'll have to accept whatever the eventual verdict in this theft matter will be. We should trust it'll be the correct one."

Silvia kept listening and staring at Barone, who seemed to get uncomfortable. She enjoyed dominating him for a few short moments.

He went on, "Whisper in your friend's ear that he'd better mind his own business. He can find plenty of problems to solve in France, I'm sure. I have connections, you know. Tell him. I know you can get close to his ear." He patted her on the shoulder and forced a knowing smile.

Silvia gestured she had a pile of work waiting and said, "I've heard your suggestions, Doctor. Please also respect my privacy. And I'll change my cell number."

"Your cell is none of my business, Silvia. I wouldn't stoop that low."

Sounds like Nixon saying he's no crook. "My apologies for my inappropriate presumption, Doctor." *And I will change my number.*

✳ ✳ ✳

As soon as Dr. Barone had left her office, Silvia picked up the fixed phone on her desk. The hiker in the picture from Chile seemed to watch her. *I was young then and unencumbered by concerns over money, greed, and deceit.* The air-conditioning blew too-cold air on her bare feet and neck. She threw a shawl over her shoulders but still shivered. The goose bumps on her arms weren't from the air-conditioning. She dialed Tim's number.

"Good morning, this is Tim."

He doesn't recognize my office number.

"Tim, I don't want to ruin your day …"

"Silvia? You can't make it Friday?"

"I can. I think so." She laughed softly. "There's something else. I wanted to make sure you were available to talk. I'm at my office now. I'll call you in fifteen minutes. Not from my office. And not from my cell."

"Okay …"

"I'll explain."

She jumped in her car, drove to the nearby gas station, and said to her friendly attendant, a good acquaintance whom she always tipped well for cleaning her windshield and checking her tire pressure, "I just discovered I left my phone in the office, Ignacio. Can I use your cell for a second while you fill up my tank? I forgot I have to make an urgent local call. Very urgent. Just local."

"To a boyfriend the office shouldn't know about, I bet." The young man laughed. He reached into his right pants pocket and took his cell out. He handed it to her and warned, "My secrets are sacred. No log checking, *amiga.*"

"Would I do that?" She laughed and thanked him. She walked away, just a few meters. She knew Ignacio was evaluating her gait. He had the not so unpleasing habit of complimenting her on her better physical attributes. She called Tim again.

"Good morning. Ignacio? This is Timonier …"

76

"Tim, it's me, Silvia. I'm back. On Ignacio's phone. Can't use mine."

"Ignacio who?"

"You don't know him. A good friend at the gas station. Listen, somebody's been hacking my cell phone. I bet it's the creep who beat up Carla's father last week. He took the Fuenteses' phones. He must have found me in their logs. He then must have had my phone hacked and heard about our conversation of Saturday."

"Are you sure?"

"Barone basically told me so without saying it. He spoke to me minutes ago. He screamed. I can put two and two together."

"He screamed at you? If he knows about our private conversation, I can understand why he's angry: he wants to be the one who parades you in Punta Cana this weekend," Tim joked.

"Am I a good enough reason for that anger, Tim?" she teased with weak enthusiasm, not really in the mood to play along. She got serious. "That bandit who manhandled Mr. Fuentes talked to Barone. I just know, from the brutal words Barone hurled at me a minute ago."

"Poor thing."

"You remember we discussed Kavanayén on Saturday. The hacker must have heard me tell you where Carla is." She sighed. "Barone's furious about the money he says Carla stole. That's a lie of course. He's also furious with you. He ordered me to tell you to get out of the country, that we don't need foreigners who meddle in our business, as you did with Dr. Cuevas."

"And he was enough of an idiot to tell you that he knows where Carla is? I don't get it."

"He was enraged, out of control. He wasn't thinking. An animal."

"So Carla's no longer safe there?"

Silvia was already planning. "I'll have to talk to my uncle Francesco. He'll have ways to handle this in that wild part of the world. She's in his good hands. He runs a convent, a mission, in Kavanayén. The bandit and Barone don't know she's at the mission. I'm pretty sure I didn't mention that to you during my 'confession.'"

"You didn't. I didn't know till now."

"It's a vast, wide place, Kavanayén, with lots of places to hide. But any stranger arriving there to trace her would be noticed by the locals in no time. I've started thinking that maybe the criminals are happy she's gone—far away. Then again, I may be naïve." She spoke in a tone that solicited his comment.

"You're sure she didn't take money?"

"Never, Tim. She'd never do that. I bet the real reason they want to know where Carla went is they want to make sure she doesn't talk. When they say they need to know her whereabouts so they can recover the money she stole from them, it's just a cover, a pretext."

"Wow. So you think they had Luis murdered? Right?"

"Yes. Somebody they knew did it. When I yelled at Barone that I was sure Carla ran away without that money and simply because she was scared to death, he suddenly backed off and turned into a soothing diplomat. I must inform my uncle—not scare him, though. No panic."

"Silvia, the bastards may want to make sure she doesn't talk ever. Know what I mean? Not ever."

"You don't have to repeat it. My uncle and Carla will have to be very careful and smart. For a long time. Actually till the day the murderers of Luis are caught. I must go now. Don't try to phone me until I call you from my new phone. I look forward to Punta Cana, Tim. I need a break."

"Me too, darling."

"Hasta pronto." *Darling? Presumptuous … Maybe not. How do French hormones work? And a French brain? How does mine work? Easily overruled? By …?*

She went back to Ignacio and thanked him with a smile and an extra hundred pesos after he had filled up the tank of her Jetta with regular.

"Thanks. Did you have a nice chat? Good guy, I'm sure, Dr. Herrera."

"A sweet guy. Almost as sweet as you, *caballero*."

Just before closing time, Silvia walked out of the small Codetel shop close to her home and started memorizing her new cell phone number. She called Tim. He didn't answer, but she left a voicemail. *I must warn my uncle.* She looked at her watch. It was close to 8:00 p.m. She decided to postpone the call till tomorrow. Her uncle would be in bed by now, and she felt it was in fact better to think things through before alarming him and her friend Carla.

CHAPTER

Wednesday morning, April 1, Silvia received a call from Ricardo Lima.

"Dr. Herrera, Ricardo Lima here. You probably remember," he said with a chuckle, "that we spoke briefly, a week ago. I told you then in no uncertain terms that I didn't want to see Dr. Barone's face ever again."

"Yes, Mr. Lima. I remember that call well; you spoke in 'no uncertain terms' indeed," Silvia answered.

"Okay. But I didn't explain to you last week *why* I was breaking with Dr. Barone. If I can have five minutes of your precious time, I can make it clear why I did that and why I'm calling you again."

"Believe it or not, I was expecting your call, Mr. Lima; Dr. Riquelme of the Alliance called me last night and briefed me on your sad situation. He said that you had called him minutes before and that he had understood you very well. But please go ahead." She sighed softly and switched her recorder on.

"It's a long story, but I'll spare you the details. You must have heard most of them from Dr. Riquelme anyway. What I have to say is that every day and night since last Wednesday, I've been brooding about the injustice my wife and son and I have to deal with. I want to, *I must*, exact revenge on Dr. Barone for a misdeed I have no proof of. I'm convinced, my gut tells me, that he's responsible for this injustice, directly or not, willingly or not, and I'll prove it someday. Today I know one thing without any doubt: Barone is a man driven by greed, the dirty fuel feeding the 'engine' that keeps discrimination alive and kicking in our country, our paradise."

Sounds like a politician's stump speech. Silvia was shocked by the blunt talk from a person who barely knew her. She asked, "What makes you so sure about that engine?" and looked at her watch. "For starters, Dr. Herrera, I know very well that some government officials charged with upholding the law look the other way as long as their pockets keep getting lined by criminals profiting from stigma and discrimination."

"Some newspaper articles say so, but they don't really offer much proof," Silvia retorted, trying to have Mr. Lima back up his claim.

"I, Ricardo Lima, will prove it, but we don't have much time this morning, so let's just talk about Barone. I loathe the man. Nowhere do I detect any redeeming trait in this person—no guts, no natural grace, no warmth, no soul. I see a cool, calculating person who doesn't care about his patient's unnecessary suffering."

Silvia felt it was time to get practical but had kept listening because, just like Dr. Riquelme, she felt sympathy for Ricardo. She asked, "So what can we do? What are you thinking of doing?"

"I've contacted authorities, social counselors, and specialists. No bragging, I have the means to spend days on my effort to unveil the truth about the network Barone apparently is involved in, the network that sucks money out of rich patients fearing discrimination. That despicable prejudicial treatment of citizens still flourishes although the law prohibits it. My businesses will hum along nicely without my full-time presence for a while, and I have the financial means to engage, buy if necessary, ears and hearts for this cause. I want to get to the bottom of this cesspool. Barone's."

"Hmm. I understand. Tell me how I fit in this, if I do."

"At some point in the conversation last night, Dr. Riquelme fell silent for a few seconds. Then he mentioned you, Dr. Herrera. 'I'm trying to connect some dots as we speak,' Dr. Riquelme said. 'Could you give me permission to speak in confidence about your case with

Dr. Silvia Herrera at Barone's office? She's a good friend of mine and can be fully trusted. Maybe she can help.'"

Silvia didn't say whether she could or not. She watched the time. "What is it that I can do for you?" she asked, impatient.

"Carla. Your colleague. On my way home last night, my thoughts went back to her. I just know her disappearance is somehow part of my puzzle. Last week you told me that you had no idea where Carla was. I kept wondering whether you might have some new information. And here I am!"

Silvia had started believing in Ricardo and said, "Okay, I'll be open with you, Mr. Lima, in confidence. I know you're a good man."

"Thank you. And Dr. Riquelme thinks highly of you."

"She ran away," Silvia told him. "It was fear for her life. Simple as that."

"Hmm." He didn't sound that surprised.

"I've always known why she ran. From the moment she disappeared. Even before. And I've also known from the beginning where she was. She's in Venezuela, in the south, in a village called Kavanayén."

"You knew? How come?"

Silvia didn't answer the question but said, "I kept it a secret to protect her, of course. Until recently, till the day my phone got hacked and some really bad people got their hands on my information. They're now aware of her whereabouts and may try to track her down there. Kavanayén is a rough place, a very small village, remote and hard to reach by car. It does have a short landing strip. I feel I can tell you where she fled because I know you're grateful to Carla and don't wish her harm. To the contrary, you've convinced me that you're trying to help her."

"You sure got that right, Dr. Herrera. We must protect Carla. A landing strip, you said? There might be a chance that I would be able to help you find that ugly crowd that's chasing her."

"Could you? Really?" Silvia couldn't help sounding skeptical.

"You think I'm bluffing? Listen, I'm not sure of course, but I'm going to work like hell to track those criminals down, and also the higher-ups who're in cahoots with them. I'm so grateful you're playing open cards with me. Where exactly is this Kavanayén?"

"It lies in the Canaima National Park, in the south, close to both Brazil and Guyana. A hellish drive, the last thirty or forty miles."

"I see. But how long is that landing strip? You see, I know a couple of things about planes, small ones. I'm a 50 percent partner in a company providing private flights."

"Oh? I've heard it's about 700 meters. I visited Kavanayén once but didn't see the strip. It's probably not a pool table," she laughed.

"Why would you think that? You're not being kind to Kavanayén, and you're going out on a hell of a limb with that guess," he joked.

"Okay, I'll agree: not kind," Silvia admitted, amused.

"The bastards must have some ugly reason to threaten Carla like that."

"She stole money, they say, a ridiculously dumb accusation, of course."

"Right. I bet you one of their goons will try to silence her there. She better hurry out of that little spot."

Silvia went on, "I must add that the 'goons' don't know *exactly* where she's hiding. Or with whom. And I have my uncle there, a monk who has a strong grip on the village. He's helping her to stay safe. He used to tell me that intruders with bad intentions are spotted in no time and dealt with 'swiftly and appropriately.' His words."

"That man of the cloth, so low on the totem pole, has more guts than the high-up monsignor I pleaded my antidiscrimination case with yesterday morning," Ricardo said, sounding bitter. "But how did they know that bugging your phone would lead them to Carla? And who are 'they'?"

"A bandit who manhandled her parents, the Fuenteses, one night and took all their phones. I was a regular caller and listener to them since the moment Carla disappeared. He must have noticed my name in the logs. Easy. And got me bugged. Also easy."

"Any description of that scum?"

"Carla's father said—"

"Hold on. Taking more notes. Carla's father?"

"He said the brute was over six feet, huge, big hat and dark glasses, raspy voice, fat, crooked nose, a light lisp. 'Ugly too,' Mrs. Fuentes added."

"Thanks. Exactly the kind of guy I'd like to have a leisurely glass of rum with." Ricardo laughed. "The description isn't much to go by, but you never know. Maybe it's a little piece in the puzzle. What car?"

"We don't know, Ricardo. It was pitch-dark when he made his friendly house call."

"Thank you, Doctor. Count on me to help you get to the bottom of this. I have my ways. I'm not kidding. I think you should tell your friend Carla to hurry to another place."

"Hold on, Ricardo. Please note my cell number. It's better to call me on that one. My God! I should've thought of that earlier." She whispered the number.

After Barone's outburst and her discussions with Jorge Riquelme and Ricardo yesterday and today, Silvia felt she couldn't wait any longer to inform her uncle about the almost certain threat to Carla. She would count on his knowledge of the area, his connections in Venezuela, and his wisdom to protect Carla. She decided to call him now.

When Father Francesco picked up, he said he was in a small meeting. "My little niece? Good morning!" he exclaimed with great enthusiasm. "We're discussing here the different types of beans we buy. My accountant, Brother Marcus, and Sister Cecilia from the kitchen are giving me a real lecture. It's not just a matter of finances, but of smart nutrition. Colors count, just like in the case of birds and ladies' dresses. We're getting sophisticated here. I'm learning." He laughed. "But go ahead."

"Your 'little niece' also wants to know about the beans, Uncle. Some other time. First, this is my new phone number. Got a pen?"

"One second. From colors of beans to phones. Ready."

"It's 8837189, with Codetel."

"Cheaper?"

"No. To be safe again. They hacked my phone. It's the reason I must call you this morning. A bandit is chasing Carla. He's the one who hacked my phone, had it hacked, almost 100 percent sure. I know he found out that Carla's in Kavanayén. More people may be involved."

"My God! Oh, no. The bandits know she's here?" Father Francesco shouted, panic overtaking his voice. "Is that true, Silvia? Are you sure? What can I do? My God," he lamented.

"Relax, Uncle. Please relax."

"But what shall I do? I must hurry. I don't know where to move her to. Whom can I entrust her to? What do you think? You know our place a bit."

"Uncle, let's be calm. I'm sure they know the name Kavanayén. But that's all. I'm absolutely certain they don't know she's in the mission. Of course, they might guess it. On the other hand, they probably wouldn't expect Carla to hide in the most obvious place or in one fixed place."

"Just Kavanayén. Nothing about the mission, right?" the old man asked again to confirm, sounding a bit more hopeful.

"Correct. But don't forget, the man may well have murdered. Almost sure. He accuses Carla of stealing a big amount of money."

"Shameful. A murderer." The father sighed. "I already know Carla. She would never steal. Sister Cecilia sits here and shakes her head, convinced. She and Brother Marcus praised her behavior just twenty minutes ago, here in the office. Why is that bandit pursuing such an innocent woman?"

"I have no idea. But I know she's no thief. She's a good person. I don't know what's really best, Uncle. I'm sure you know better than anybody else there how to protect Carla, in Kavanayén or in another village or mission in the area. I hadn't expected this kind of complication. Carla went so far away, to such a remote place, that I thought nobody would ever find her there. But I talked too much over the phone. My fault. Stupid me. I'm sorry for causing so much trouble."

"Don't feel guilty, my child," Father Francesco said much more calmly. "I sit here racking my brain for ways to hide Carla somewhere else, immediately. But I don't see a way. I'd like to say let's in the first place not put the burden on Carla. We don't have to. Not yet, anyway. She's safe with us here but still so vulnerable. And she's in touch with you, through me, if she wants to. Our villagers are alert and perfectly reliable informants about anybody who sets foot in Kavanayén, except for our own sporadic hotel guests. We keep good tabs on those ourselves. I'll keep an extra eye on Carla. Our mission is a fortress, so to speak, as you know, with guards on duty around the clock. We don't talk to outsiders about her presence here. We'll give her all the peace and quiet to get her stress level down. The poor girl."

"I understand. I can describe for you the person I suspect. He may or may not show up there. I hope not."

"Okay, Silvia. Brother Marcus, could you write down as I repeat what my niece says? The details of the murderer who may be headed here to threaten Carla. We'll have to watch out."

"Ready?" Silvia asked. Then she said slowly, "A huge guy, over a meter eighty. Heavy. Big hat and dark glasses. Raspy voice. A lisp. Ugly. Big, crooked nose. Mean-looking."

Father Francesco repeated verbatim and then said, "I wouldn't like to meet him in the dark. Anything nice about him?" He laughed. "Dominican accent, right?"

"I suppose so, Uncle. So there you have something nice about him."

"Indeed, and easy to notice. We'll spot him as soon as he sets foot in the village, but let's not bother poor Carla with this now. In fact, we don't know whether the man will ever risk coming out here. How would he explain his visit? That theft story wouldn't hold water for long. The whole threat may slowly evaporate."

"I'd hope so, but I'm not sure. I'm glad I called you, Uncle. You ask good questions." *Maybe I exaggerate the gravity of the situation?*

CHAPTER 18

Silvia expertly unleashed the power of her Jetta's manual transmission to blast by a truck just before a curve.

"Good move," Tim exclaimed from the passenger seat. He turned to his left and lifted his right hand for a high five.

Silvia took her hand off the shift stick to respond, relieved. "Whew. If I didn't put the mastodon behind me here, we'd be stuck for a long, winding stretch at thirty kilometers per hour."

She sat back and handled the routine traffic hazards as they came. She felt relaxed.

Tim sporadically put his left hand on her right one when during a discussion she had to handle the shift stick.

Hmm. Warm. And his convenient French way to emphasize a point.

Silvia and Tim were on their way to Punta Cana. It was 9:30 on Friday, April 3. Tim had an afternoon appointment there with the Harvard folks.

"Thanks for the ride, Silvia. I invited myself."

"You do know how to beg friends for weekend rides to the beach," Silvia teased.

"You think so?" He laughed and explained, "Yes, I sometimes really beg. A rental car means a lot of money in this country, and even

French driving expertise is no match for the challenges of DR traffic. I appreciate your generosity, Silvia."

"*De nada*, Tim. You're welcome."

"We're cleared for an early check in at the Paraíso. I'll have to leave you there for about three hours for my meeting. It's a terrible place for you to be stuck alone, but I'll hurry back."

"Your initiative, *mon ami*. I just follow orders," Silvia joked. "I'm on French auto-pilot."

"Good. And we don't answer questions with questions this weekend. And let's block out all that Father Francesco, Carla, Luis, Barone, and who-else stuff for a couple of days … and nights," he added, sounding like a nine-year-old rascal.

"Right. Got it," Silvia replied. "But you should add Ricardo Lima to your list. He's really getting involved. I spoke to him yesterday. He wants revenge on whoever outed him or on whoever let him down—and on those in the government who refuse to move a finger to combat discrimination. He says he just knows Barone's a crook."

"Okay, I just added Ricardo, and now we forget them all. And Barone's a crook."

"Yes," Silvia said. She briefly touched Tim's leg without looking away from the road ahead of her. Then she asked, "What arrangements have you made? Beach view or tropical garden? They always make it sound nice."

"Back parking lot view. Including the garbage bins. Exactly what you like, I know." He laughed and put his hand on hers. "I wormed my way into a suite overlooking the beach. I think you won't mind. You can sleep in your bed or on my couch, whichever you prefer."

"We'll have to have a good drink before we start that discussion, don't you think so, Tim?" she asked softly.

"Don't you already know exactly what I think? Oops, question mark. Two of them, one each."

"You …"

"You …" Tim burst into a loud laugh.

Silvia joined.

They arrived at the hotel at 11:30 and entered the lobby through the wide open-air entrance hall.

Tim said he would try his luck to check in before noon and went straight to the reception desk. Silvia started looking around, and up at the three huge fans that adorned the high dome. They emitted slow groans as they worked their hearts out to bring relief from the midday heat. A couple of times, looking out of the corner of her eye, she caught Tim glancing at her as he turned his head.

"Tim," Silvia said as she stepped closer to him and pointed discreetly with her thumb close to her stomach, "that lady keeps looking in our direction. I don't know her. She's a tourist, it seems."

Tim turned, looked, and nodded in the lady's direction. He waved slightly at her and pointed with a big gesture at the computer on the reception desk.

He said to Silvia, "It's Liese. She knows me. She's staying here. I chatted with her last week at the pool. A lovely lady. Witty. Out for a good time, she said. I told her I might be back this week. We could have a drink with her sometime."

Liese slowly put her hand up, acknowledging his greeting, and stayed in her chair.

"She's lost her smile," he said to Silvia.

"Sir, it'll be about forty minutes. I can take your credit card information, and I'll call you when your suite is ready," the receptionist told Tim while taking an inquisitive look at Silvia.

"Okay. Let's go ahead. Here's my card."

"Your friend looks depressed, Tim. You said she likes a good time," Silvia remarked quietly, keeping her eyes in Tim's direction while she spoke.

"She's not my 'friend,' Silvia," Tim whispered, keeping his eyes focused on the domed ceiling. "She's Swiss. She could be my mother. But you're right; she looks sad, worried."

The check-in done, Tim suggested to Silvia they walk over to Liese. As they got close to her, Liese didn't get up.

"Liese, this is Silvia. Silvia, meet Liese."

Liese put her hand out to Silvia and Tim and said, "I think you're going to have a beautiful weekend with your friend, Tim." Her tone was flat, her voice almost powerless.

"We'll have to get together for a good drink, Liese. Right now we're waiting for a room, and in a short while I'll be picked up for a meeting outside the hotel. But later …"

"I'm not sure I should have drinks, Tim. Or that I want to."

"What's the matter, Liese?" He turned and looked at Silvia.

Does he expect me *to answer his question?*

"I know I look sad, Tim, but I'm so glad to see you again. I need help." She pulled an envelope out of her purse. She held it up and sighed. "I found this slipped under my door this morning."

"And? What does it say?"

"Please read it. You're a person I can talk to. I must discuss this with somebody. I didn't have breakfast. I couldn't. I've been debating with myself all morning what I should do. I didn't leave my room until twenty minutes ago to sit down here."

"No breakfast. Why don't we get some coffee and cookies for you?" Tim proposed.

He feels sorry for her.

He pointed at a little coffee table nearby.

"Read, Tim. Please read," Liese asked again.

Tim opened the envelope. He ran through the text, stopped reading, exhaled, and said, looking perplexed, "Wow. Can Silvia read it too? She may be able to help. She's a physician."

Liese studied Silvia for a moment and then said, "Yes, she can. Please."

Silvia thought, *I have a hunch,* as she accepted the sheet. When after fifteen seconds she looked up, she just nodded. *Careful. Liese is Tim's acquaintance, not mine.*

"This must be a scam," Tim whispered, his teeth and lips barely moving. He looked around and pointed at a far, empty corner in the entrance hall. "Why don't we move over there?" he suggested.

Once they were seated in the quiet space, Liese opened up. She said, "It may not be a scam."

Tim looked at Silvia, who nodded again.

Liese went on, "I've told you, Tim, that I met people here, that I like a good time. It's my vacation. My body is still young. I enjoy life. I did anyway, till this morning."

"I understand you very well," Tim commented, his voice compassionate.

"I met this person who called himself Humberto. A lively person, friendly. And very good-looking. Lost his job, he said. Young, maybe twenty-two. He and I spent several nights together. He was very sweet. I gave him presents … cash too. Quite a lot, actually … several nights. We used protection. Always, I think, but we drank too … I haven't seen him recently, not for six or seven days."

Now Silvia spoke, "Yes, Liese, such attractive, friendly young men do roam here. I know the infection rates for people who try to make a living Humberto's way. They're not low figures." She turned to Tim and whispered in almost inaudible Dominican, "Jorge Riquelme has scary statistics about this phenomenon of older female tourists infecting young men and vice-versa."

Tim nodded, his eyes closed.

"My God. I should've known. Too late now," Liese sobbed.

"It's not too late, Liese," Silvia assured her. "You can deal with this matter. And it could be a scam, as Tim just said."

Liese looked at Silvia with trusting eyes and said, "Can you help me?"

Tim glanced at Silvia and then at his watch.

His Harvard guys. Silvia asked for Tim's opinion. "I must test Liese," she said. "We just passed the Verón clinic on our way here. It's less than fifteen minutes away. We could take her there for a Rapid test. They know me there. Two years ago, as a weekend volunteer, I helped them start up their HIV activity with Jorge Riquelme."

We're looking at a situation that won't end with a simple Rapid test. If Liese's HIV positive, we'll see more drama and sadness, and more testing to confirm.

"Let's go to the clinic together," Tim proposed.

In the car on the way to Verón, he called one of the Harvard guys to postpone his meeting with them till 3:00 p.m.

When Silvia, Tim, and Liese arrived at the clinic, the receptionist embraced Silvia warmly. Silvia informed the friendly woman she wanted to visit Doctor Moreno. The receptionist dialed the doctor's number and said, holding the phone, "I'm sure he'll be happy to see you, Dr. Herrera. And your friends, if you like."

They all went to the doctor's office, where Silvia briefed him. The doctor nodded. He didn't look surprised at all and proceeded with the first Rapid right away.

All waited in suspense. The Rapid was negative.

Liese showed a big smile.

"Hold on, Liese," Silvia said. "We need a second one."

The second one was also negative.

Liese jumped for joy. The tests had taken only a few minutes.

But she still needs confirmation. More finger pricks in a few weeks, several weeks.

Liese sounded jubilant; she was free of HIV. Her face told the story, and she exclaimed, "Thank you. Thank you." She embraced all, even Doctor Moreno, who smiled. She tried in vain to wipe her tears off his cheek with her Kleenex, which was already soaking wet.

Silvia calmly cautioned Liese that she wasn't completely out of the woods yet. "But I'll keep an eye on you and personally repeat the tests in another two or three weeks, if you're still around. The virus can hide for several weeks."

Liese heard her but seemed confident she had beaten the odds.

The doctor and Silvia then went into a conversation of the pros and cons of the boom in the tourism industry. Then they strayed into the politics of the business.

About thirty minutes after they had arrived at the clinic, Silvia thanked the doctor. She was ready to go. She shared in the happiness of the moment, but in the car on the way to the hotel, she sank into less pleasant thoughts. *This story may not end here. I want to know what crook or crooks sent Liese this ugly message. Bye-bye tanning on the beach.*

When they arrived back at the hotel, Silvia asked Liese, "Could Tim and I accompany you to your room? Would you mind? Tim can order some food for there. I'd like you to make a phone call to the number in the message that has started your misery this morning. And I'd like to listen in, with Tim."

"I want to help clinch the bastards," Tim said.

"Me too, *die Schweine*. The pigs," Liese said and translated.

Silvia and Tim laughed when they heard the expression of raw Swiss determination.

Liese went on, "I write stories for a travel magazine. This one qualifies, and maybe we're just at the beginning."

"Yes, we must get the *Schweine*." Tim laughed. "Can you say it, Silvia?"

Silvia shrugged and didn't try.

CHAPTER

Ricardo Lima drove his Lexus to a hangar adjacent to Santo Domingo's Las Américas International Airport. It was a hot afternoon this Friday. He carried a light briefcase and had loosened his necktie when his early luncheon meeting with Scotiabank ended on Avenida Lincoln, in their building just next to the Piantini building. In that part of the city, he had to be dressed properly. Now, just minutes later, he felt like a man newly freed from shackles as he entered the hangar. He liked this place. Here he could walk as a farmer on his field and speak folksy language. And the weekend lay ahead.

This was the place where he had his "toy," together with his partner Gonzalo. They both enjoyed the excitement and almost youthful enthusiasm they could put into the small private-plane airline they ran from here.

Gonzalo was the engine of the little business. Ricardo was a coinvestor and supposed to be a quasi-silent partner. But he had to admit he spent more time here than the relative size of this business in his portfolio actually justified. It was fun, and it didn't hurt that it had become recognized as one of the better companies of its kind in the DR.

Once in the hangar, he went straight to the door of a small office. It was constructed with light, wooden panels painted white, and it sported a noisy little air conditioner he could hear humming from far. Cigar fumes often tickled Ricardo's nostrils before he even opened the door of the office. Not today.

Gonzalo's huge, new Greca coffee brewing machine, right behind him, competed with its owner in the scene that met Ricardo as he opened the door. Gonzalo greeted the visitor with a loud, *"Buenas tardes."* A heavenly aroma, strong enough to supplant the traces of any cigar Gonzalo might have finished in the last half hour, enveloped and invaded Ricardo.

"Gonzalo, what's wrong? No coffee yet today?" Ricardo joked as he patted his partner on the upper arm.

"I think you're jealous, *amigo*. Sit down and relax. Tomorrow it's golf. So you just saved Scotiabank, and now you're here to whip things up."

"Right. I knew I had to," Ricardo joked. "But, on a practical note, can I have some of your joe?"

"Of course. You talk so much, I had no chance to offer any yet."

As they drank a cup, Gonzalo started opening the log book and mentioned some of the typical challenges of a plane-leasing company. Maintenance was an issue. Every day, all kinds of new requests popped up from ever more demanding customers. Taking care of spoiled brats called pilots was another topic.

"That's all? Nothing else? I see I shouldn't have come," Ricardo commented, trying to keep a straight face as Gonzalo concluded his litany, "except for the coffee. But I have one thing for you." Now he turned serious. "This is confidential." He glanced back at the door. "I'm looking for a guy, a murderer. And I know he plans to murder again. In Venezuela. A woman who's very scared of him fled to Venezuela and I'm 99 percent sure he's chasing her. I'm trying to help her."

"A woman. Okay ... That's it? Do I know her? Can you narrow it down a little? 'A woman' can have disappeared in a crowd in Caracas or Maracaibo like a needle in a haystack," Gonzalo remarked, sounding skeptical.

"I know the woman. She's under protection in a remote area in the south of Venezuela. That's a fact. The nearest airport with scheduled service is Ciudad Guayana, a very, very long way from her place. Chances are—a long shot of course—the murderer is trying to fly directly to the remote spot with one of our kinds of planes, a small private plane. In the middle of the night, so to speak. Or literally. The place, the village, has a short landing strip."

"A guy with that kind of plan wouldn't go commercial; you're right. That wouldn't be too practical, certainly not with weapons," Gonzalo commented, his face showing he was getting intrigued. "What kind of a guy, your murderer?"

Ricardo repeated the description of the bandit that Silvia had given to him. He described how the Fuenteses had been robbed.

Now Gonzalo was all ears. He had different kinds of customers who didn't want to be seen on commercial flights. Some found those too ordinary for their taste, with too much hassle and arguing about bags and spoiled dogs. Some were in a big hurry. Some wanted to show off. Some didn't want to be seen because they shouldn't be seen. The latter was the type of private plane traveler Ricardo was after today.

"Well, I had a guy in here briefly yesterday," Gonzalo said, rubbing his chin, "who seemed to be in a real hurry. He was bald, didn't wear that hat you mentioned, but he sure was big and wore glasses. His nose was a real piece of work."

"How about his voice? Any lisp?"

"It was particularly raspy. He may have lisped slightly—not sure. He perspired heavily. I just didn't like him. He looked nervous and in a big hurry."

"That could be him. He has the look of a guy who robs and murders," Ricardo said. He saw Gonzalo wanted to explain.

"He knew nothing about planes. He wanted a Cessna. Immediately. Maybe the only small airplane name he knew. He didn't know which Cessna. I asked him where he wanted to fly, and with how many passengers. He wouldn't answer!"

"Sounds like him, a murderer straight from the rough alleys," Ricardo said. *I may be getting ahead of myself, but my gut …*

"I have more. I wanted to get rid of the creep, so I asked him whether he could pay cash in advance. That did the trick. He mumbled something I couldn't understand and then said he'd come back today and would take any plane with a radius over 700 miles. 'One that can fly 700 miles,' to use his words. 'The cheapest,' also his words. He didn't give me any destination. Out the door he went before I could give him our rate schedule. And … I haven't seen him today. It's 2:30 now. It's always possible that one of our not so choosy competitors picked him up yesterday or today. Could be tomorrow, next week. Fine with me. But if I'd known about that creep yesterday …"

Ricardo was riveted. *It all fits. And I bet he had a lisp, but Gonzalo didn't listen for it.* "Yeah. I should've come yesterday. And I agree we shouldn't do business with such people. Other customers would frown if they'd see him around," he said. Then he abruptly apologized to Gonzalo for rudely having to break off their discussion, explaining, "I must handle something private in a hurry."

"Okay," Gonzalo said, looking surprised. "I'll make a few calls to some of our friendly competitors to see whether that piece of crap made it out to Venezuela yet. Doubt it; he had no money. May have to rob another old couple so he can pay."

Ricardo rushed to his Lexus, sat down, and called Silvia from the parking lot.

CHAPTER  20

It was Friday, April 3, in the early afternoon at the Santa Teresa Mission in Kavanayén.

By now Carla had taken up knitting. This afternoon, she sat practicing her new hobby in a quiet, cool corner in a semi-dark hallway that on one side looked out on a garden where vegetables and flowers were grown by an old monk devoted to his "children."

Until Wednesday night, her life had been simple. She had felt protected and cared for by her hosts. At times, when she reflected on how calm and peaceful life proceeded at the mission, she would think of a small pond surrounded by tall, thin grass. The surface of the pond was free of wrinkles, the grass blades motionless, hot air loitering over the still water and undulating softly.

A smile would come to Carla's face when she thought about the little pebble she and Marcus cautiously would drop, now and then, in the pond, around midnight. *Almost every midnight since Friday, March 27.* The pebble disturbed the pond only slightly, near noiselessly and for a short time, and in the dark, nobody saw the little, slow, and short-lived little waves it caused. All in the mission were asleep at that time, except probably the guard who was supposed to be awake and watching the front gate, not the church or the confessionals.

She had kept wondering how Marcus could be so smitten with

her so instantaneously. She imagined he had been raised in a quiet, religious, small-town family that had sent him to a pre-seminary school at a tender age, where he had been shielded from outside influences, particularly the attractions of the flesh.

Her life had taken an abrupt turn for the worse on Wednesday around midnight. At that time, her hips were lovingly warming Brother Marcus's quadriceps in the confessional. Suddenly she had started shivering when Marcus told her a bandit was probably on his way to kill her in Kavanayén. Marcus had sounded nervous and said he wasn't supposed to tell her. "I was in the room with Father Francesco and overheard his conversation with his niece. Sister Cecilia was there too. Father Francesco decided not to bother you with the news."

"What? My life is in danger, and I'm not supposed to know?" Carla had reacted angrily. But she quickly recovered and whispered, "Thank you for telling me. I won't mention it anywhere. But what do I do? I must flee."

Marcus pulled her closer, caressed her hair, and explained, "It wasn't that clear cut, my angel, not 100 percent sure that the bandit had indeed left for our village. Father didn't want to prematurely add to your stress and anxiety; he felt he had your protection organized and didn't see an immediate possibility to get you to a better place. He thought your best spot was here, inside the mission."

"I must get away from here," Carla had repeated nervously, impervious to Marcus's words.

"The bandit doesn't know you're with us here, with me, in the mission. And I don't want to see you run away in a hurry, not knowing where to go. You'd be lost out there. You'd end up in a worse place. And I'd miss you," he whispered passionately.

"But if he comes to Kavanayén, he'll find out I'm here. I'll have to flee."

"If he finds out, I'll go with you," Marcus assured her, squeezing his arms around Carla. "I'll protect you. But we would have that man tracked down long before he can find out where you are. All the villagers are Father Francesco's friends, and mine. We'll run the bandit out of town the moment he sets foot on our soil."

Carla had one secret. But now she had to tell Marcus about it—some of it anyway. She said, "Since I arrived here, I've been racking my brain how I could make a phone call to a person in Santo Domingo who helped save my life."

"Father Francesco's niece?"

"No. Somebody else. It's very personal." She looked away from Marcus.

He touched her cheek, softly turning her face back to him, and said, "Maybe I could make the call for you on the phone of the mission? I do the books. I'll make sure nobody finds out about the cost."

"You're very kind. But I must make the call myself," Carla insisted.

Marcus sounded slightly irritated and somewhat helpless, as he sighed. "Then the call must wait till Father Francesco is out of the mission for a few hours or busy doing something he doesn't interrupt," he said.

"Like what, Marcus? Sleeping? Doesn't he sleep every night?"

She felt him wriggling on the wide, hard seat of the confessional. *He's afraid.* She moved her body off his legs and slipped next to him on the seat. *So hard, this bench. What a difference.* She stopped arguing and rearranged her clothes. Then she said, "I wish you good night, Marcus. Time for some rest. Sleep well. I love you, and we'll find a way, won't we?"

"I'll try my best, angel. Maybe we can."

I need him. But I can't scare him. She said, "We must." Her tone was grave but soft.

She kissed him, stepped out of the confessional, and walked slowly, head down, hands folded as if she was praying, to her cell, her face showing godliness and devotion, her dress modest and looking unwrinkled in the near dark. Her shoes squeaked lightly as she gingerly put her feet down one after the other and waved off mosquitoes with small gestures. She was sure nobody noticed her. She didn't look back to check whether Marcus had stepped out of the confessional yet.

He'll wait his usual five minutes.

CHAPTER 21

Silvia raved about the view as they all walked into Liese's room.

"What a place to receive such an awful message, Liese. Relax now and enjoy," she suggested jovially. *She must pay a fortune for this room. That kid Humberto knows how to pick his prey.*

They had stopped at the reception desk when they got back to the hotel, and Tim had placed an order there from room service: papaya, lime, and shrimp with toast.

Silvia was a woman in a hurry. "Can we go ahead? Can you make the call now, Liese? And put it on speakerphone?"

"You just said you wanted me to enjoy. Was this one of the things you had in mind, Silvia?"

She's recovering fast. "We all might enjoy it," Silvia responded with a wink.

Liese picked up the phone.

"Looks like a Valencia number," Silvia commented as she watched Liese dialing the numbers.

Tim looked up and frowned, seemingly puzzled.

"Hello, can we help you?" a woman answered, with a smooth, polished voice, almost warm.

"I hope so. Good afternoon. My name is Liese Kung, and I'm responding to the message you had delivered to my room, 302 in the

Paraíso hotel, this morning. I appreciate the help you offer. But it would've been better if you or a colleague would've come to my room and explained to me in person what exactly it is you can do for me under the circumstances. The news is so devastating. I need all the help I can get. I feel abandoned here—lost."

Liese hides her relief and exuberance well. Neutral, lifeless tone.

Tim made a wild thumbs-up and then encouraged Liese with a fist to go on. He also whispered to Silvia, "These *Schweine* of Liese's can grunt nicely over the phone when they have to."

Silvia put her index finger over her lips.

"Our sincere apologies, Miss Liese," the voice on the speakerphone said. "We assist lots of patients and really can't provide the service you suggest. I have our report on you here. Our mission is to limit HIV infections and its ravages. Our surveillance group identifies persons who may run serious risk of infections. The bar scenes at hotels are fertile ground for that purpose."

"Good. I think I understand that. But how can you help me?" Liese winked at Silvia and Tim but kept her voice flat and monotonous.

"We have a building in a quiet street in Higüey where we can welcome you for Rapid testing, even over the weekend. If you happen to be found HIV-positive, and we hope you won't, we can suggest the appropriate medical treatment right away. We can also provide additional testing and a wide range of assistance to guide you emotionally and socially and, above all, to help you maintain complete confidentiality. That's very important to every HIV patient."

"I appreciate your concern, young lady. I really do. May I ask you how we arrange payment?" Liese looked at Silvia and Tim for approval.

Tim started scribbling something on a sheet of paper in big capitals and put it in front of Liese. Silvia read it and nodded.

The lady at the other end of the line answered, "We assume you have a good limit on your credit card. The folks in the Paraíso usually do. An initial three thousand dollar payment will be fine. We trust you'll be a reliable patient when it comes to paying additional bills later."

102

"What a sum. Three thousand," Liese sighed, sounding helpless. She added, her voice turning indignant, "That sounds like extortion to me."

"Miss Liese, you should realize the stakes are high. Maybe your life, maybe your reputation," the silky voice said. The response sounded artificial, as if read from a sheet in a manual.

Liese ran through the note Tim had put in front of her. She held her hand over the microphone and asked Tim, "Who's Barone?"

Tim whispered, "Just do what I wrote. No worry."

Silvia smiled.

Liese went ahead. "Miss, since it's so much money, just for starters even, I'd like to think this over and respond in half an hour. I may have another solution. A friend I consulted this morning suggested I go and see Dr. Barone. Do you know him? Would he be a good solution?" She looked at Tim, who nodded.

The silky voice now said, "Well, oh, I think I've heard of him. He's in Valencia, I believe. He is, well, he's a good doctor, they say. He is. You'd probably have to wait till—"

They heard a knock on the door. Tim let the waiter in with the lunch.

"Hold on a second," Liese said to the lady on the phone.

"Miss Liese," the lady quickly cut in, "I think we'd better end this conversation. You can always call me back. I hear plates and cups being put on a table. This call is no longer confidential."

"Oh yes, it is. Don't worry. I'm fine. They're just delivering my lunch. It'll be just a second. Hold on," Liese said again.

The lady ended the call.

For a couple of seconds, nobody spoke. They just looked at each other.

Then Tim said, "Yep. My scribbles worked, Liese. We got it."

"Got what?" Silvia asked.

"The connection of Liese's case with the network Barone is involved in. As soon as Liese mentioned his name, the lady on the other end froze. She started stammering. Why did that name have to throw her off like that? She had sounded so smooth and confident until then.

Barone is in on this, and she felt we suspected it. She froze exactly the moment we dropped his name on her."

"Tim, you're making dangerous jumps," Silvia said. She didn't hide her skepticism. "She didn't hang up when Liese mentioned Barone's name, but when she heard the plates. It's very possible that she may have feared a setup. Police, maybe. A sting operation."

"Right, police delivering plates. I'm always the expeditious one, too cavalier and too swift for my own good. Listen, I may be wrong," Tim said, "but my gut … She used the plates as a convenient excuse to hang up and get off the Barone topic. People get room service all the time."

"My gut tells me the same thing as Tim's," Liese said. "I don't know anything about this Barone, but I hit a nerve with his name. I could tell; I make my living as a detective. In Switzerland I do surveillance and tracking of wayward husbands, wives, boyfriends, and what have you. Tricky sometimes. I detect lies."

Tim frowned and asked, "You do?"

Liese smiled as she said, "And I carry a gun on the job, but I …"

At that moment, Silvia got a call and looked at the screen of her phone.

"It's Ricardo Lima," she said to Tim and Liese.

"Good afternoon, Ricardo. This is Silvia."

She listened and then responded, "No, I'm in Punta Cana. With friends."

The phone conversation went on for half a minute. Then Silvia said, "Let me put you on speakerphone. My friend Tim is here with me and another friend, and I'm sure he'd like to hear what you're telling me. He knows about the situation."

"Okay. Hi, Tim. Ricardo here. We never met, but I've heard about you from Silvia."

"Oh, no. More bad press for me. Hi, Ricardo." Tim winked at Silvia.

"No worries. Nothing but good stuff from her, Tim. I think she likes you. Wild guess," he said with a laugh. "I just told Silvia that that piece of crap who tormented the Fuenteses awhile ago tried to get a plane to Kavanayén. I'm pretty damn sure it was him. I have my connections," he added, sounding very proud.

"When did he leave, Ricardo?" Silvia asked.

"Don't know. He may not have left yet. Seemed to be a bit short on cash. These things cost money. I'll keep checking, but he's definitely planning to get to her there. Poor thing, our Carla. That whole network of bloodsuckers, they make me sick to my stomach."

"It's disgusting what's happening," Tim said.

Silvia added, "I've informed Carla, through my uncle there, that she could face a serious danger, almost certain. This is big news, what you now tell us, Ricardo. The threat's getting real."

"We must get the bastard. I'll leave no stone unturned," Ricardo declared, sounding solemn. "I'll find out when and how the creep went there, or will go there. Count on me. I'll get back to you with more soon."

After the call, Silvia, Liese, and Tim tasted some shrimp and took a slice of papaya, although none of them looked very interested in food.

"I love that Ricardo's vocabulary," Liese commented with an eye roll.

"Yeah, graphic and clear," Silvia said. "But anyway, now I know I must go to Venezuela and help Carla. I couldn't look in the mirror anymore knowing I didn't do all I could to save my dear, innocent friend. I don't know whether or exactly how I can help, but I'm going to Kavanayén."

Tim nodded. "I understand your feelings, Silvia. I'm intrigued too. What happened to Liese was bad enough in itself, but I see it connected to the bigger operation involving Barone. The death of Luis, Carla's flight, the harassment of the Fuenteses, the hacking of your phone, Ricardo's shameful treatment, the scam on Liese, it's all converging in my mind. On Barone. But I have no real proof. I'm going with you."

She took his hand and squeezed it hard.

"And I want to go with the two of you," Liese joined in. "I know how to handle a gun, how to hack phones, spy, and even how to write about it. I don't know Carla, but after what happened today, I feel like her sister. Maybe I should say aunt." She giggled. "And I promise you, I won't be baggage for you guys."

And better not chaperone either, Silvia thought. *On the other hand, neither Tim nor I could handle even a Swiss knife.*

"I'm taking the rest of my vacation in Venezuela. I can't believe it," Liese cackled.

"The Punta Cana tan will have to wait," Silvia concluded, shrugging.

"The Harvard boys too." Tim sighed and picked up the phone to call them.

CHAPTER  22

On the Las Lagunas golf course in Santo Domingo, Dr. Barone toweled off his forehead and hands as he prepared to take a break after the ninth hole. He wasn't happy with his score—his card said forty-nine—and he looked forward to a five-minute chat with the servant who kept the iced tea and the guava juice cool. It was Sunday, April 5, more than two weeks after Luis Flores's brutal voicemail had catapulted the doctor into a series of actions he wished he never would have had to take. That call jerked a thread out of the smartly knitted network the doctor had joined, and that was active in the HIV treatment system. This thread, one loose filament, threatened to unravel the entire network. And he blamed it for his poor halfway score.

He sat down on the bench, and after some small talk, he felt he didn't want to continue the chat. He found it hard to joke or brag, even on a beautiful day as this Sunday when a welcome breeze was taking the sting out of the midday sunrays. He saw that the nearby servant kept checking on him, his eyes and thumb combination at some point asking the respected doctor whether he was okay or might want another drink. Dr. Barone forced a weak smile. He waved the man off and mumbled about sinus headaches and pollen. *That guy's frigging job's serving tea, not playing psychologist.* He was happy that two men of his foursome had gone to the restroom and the fourth one was on his phone.

"Ready?" one of his golf buddies asked when all looked set to proceed with their tee shots at the tenth hole.

The doctor was actually relieved that the rest pause was over. The game took him away from his somber thoughts.

When they finished, he said he didn't feel like playing the nineteenth hole. He called his driver, who came to carry his clubs, and they went to his BMW.

"Just turn the engine on, and let's get some cool air in the car," he told the driver. "Give me a second before I get in. I have to make a quick call."

He remembered that Silvia had said she was going to take a weekend trip to Punta Cana with a bunch of friends, but he decided to call her anyway on this Sunday, friends or no friends. He had been getting restless over the weekend. He had been wondering for two weeks now where exactly in Kavanayén Carla was—whether she still was there, in what condition, and with whom. He knew she liked that Luis Flores. *That dirty-mouth Flores.*

Silvia had told Barone several times she had no idea of Carla's concrete whereabouts in Kavanayén, of her condition, or of any town or village she might have fled to. *She must be lying. She must have told Carla that I know she fled to Kavanayén. Silvia likes to switch subjects awfully fast when I mention Carla.*

It was about 2:30 when he dialed Silvia's number. He was going to corner her.

Her phone was off. *Shit. Still broiling her buns on the beach. She tans like a damn Yankee. Comes back red as a lobster, painful to look at for days.*

"Let's go," he said to his driver, Fernando, as he opened the right rear door and took his seat. "Home."

"*Sí, Señor.*"

Dr. Barone never felt a social obligation to talk to his driver, but he closed his eyes anyway, pretending to be on the verge of a well-deserved nap.

As they drove to the city, stop and go through long stretches of clouds of dirty fumes despite it being Sunday, he thought to himself, *Traffic. Nowadays, every janitor drives a damn car.*

He started making an inventory of his involvement in "the system."

He was just one of several heavy hitters in the group. Its tentacles reached all over the island and even into Jamaica. Charles Montenegro ran the show in the DR, coordinating financials, policy, tactics, and enforcement of the system's behavioral code. He had the extremely critical contact with the government official, Decker was his name, who pulled the strings on discrimination cases.

These strings were the most important element of the operation. Discrimination had to be vociferously condemned publicly, officially and with outrage, but largely ignored and tolerated privately, or the entire business premise of the system would be gone. The system would collapse as a house of cards.

Besides Decker, local politicians were important too, but they were almost automatic, natural allies for the system. They said they hated and condemned discrimination, but deep down, not even that deep down, they favored it because it allowed them to play on it for votes. In the case of many, it was even an animalistic, instinctive reflex. All of that meant that longevity was almost assured for the system.

The doctor's involvement in it was very lucrative. The properties he was able to buy were spread out over several countries, lest he raise eyebrows. His patients were taken care of in extraordinary fashion. Complaints were rare.

All patients had been carefully selected regarding resources. The importance to them of total discretion had been meticulously verified for each case. The stakes were highest for politicians, the doctor assumed. And almost all of them were rich. Money was obviously the real reason most had chosen the profession. Many openly admitted that after a couple of drinks. Also actors and actresses were juicy targets for the system. So were well-off tourists. Special recruitment cells had been set up for that target group in Punta Cana and Casa de Campo. Samaná would follow soon.

On and off, there was a problem. The recent incident with Ricardo

Lima was unfortunate, but it looked manageable. After he had given Mr. Lima a chance to rage for a while, Barone had seen him walk out calmed down, a reasonable man who had come to his senses and would not cause further trouble. A couple of tourists had raised hell about fees, but they eventually would leave the island after a few days, not having any connections in the country, and take their fury somewhere else. A bothersome article in a newspaper or magazine about the misadventure of an unnamed tourist might follow sometimes, but it would all blow over.

The death of Luis Flores was different and something Dr. Barone had no direct involvement in or concrete knowledge of, although he had more than hunches. And he had no sympathy for that loud nouveau-riche. Barone had contacted and briefed Charles, and that was that. He had his hands full as a physician, and Charles had his own folks to take care of people who became a pain in the ass, like that meddlesome Luis Flores.

What particularly bothered Dr. Barone were the strange, accusing glances he lately had to endure from Silvia, even when he wasn't explicitly inquiring about the whereabouts of Carla. But then again, he told himself, this was just his imagination. *She's just a simple physician who thinks there isn't much else in the world than her narrowly defined job. Leave her where she is.* But now, in the car with Fernando, he started wondering whether Silvia was playing him for a fool. *Did she decide, fifteen minutes ago, not to push the green button on her phone because she saw my name on the screen?*

He decided that he would call her into his office first thing tomorrow morning. He would compliment her on her tan, inquire about any good luck in the guy department over the weekend in Punta Cana, and then he would catch her off guard with a pointed question about Carla.

As they arrived at his residence and Fernando started to take the clubs out of the trunk, he asked Fernando whether he knew with which group Silvia had gone to Punta Cana for the weekend. "Just curious," he said. "None of my business actually." She and Fernando chatted sometimes, he had noticed.

"I don't know," Fernando said. "I'm not sure she went, because I saw her from a distance yesterday, sometime before noon, shopping in La Sirena in Santo Domingo. She was with an older blonde lady. She seemed to be in a hurry. I didn't want to bother her and her friend. And my wife wanted to buy shoes."

CHAPTER  23

A few hours after Fernando had lifted Dr. Barone's golf clubs out of the trunk of the BMW at the doctor's home on Sunday, Silvia, Tim, and Liese checked in for one night at the Caracas Hilton. Tim asked for a double room while Liese looked at Silvia, who searched for something in her purse.

Silvia and Tim had one bag each, but Liese pointed to two big suitcases when a bellboy came to show them to their rooms.

The youngster had his left foot in the hallway of the fourth floor and held the elevator with his right one as he gave "Mr. and Mrs. Timonier" directions to their room. Liese and her impressive luggage stood right behind him, inside. As she walked away with Tim and looked back at Liese, Silvia managed to suppress her urge to smile. "See you at the Orinoco Lounge, Liese," she said. "At 7:30, as agreed."

"Don't forget to check your watch, Silvia," Liese responded as the elevator door closed.

Early in the evening, the threesome sat down for a light dinner. The restaurant, adjacent to the Orinoco Lounge, was quiet this early Sunday night. Silvia felt they'd better keep safely tucked away in the hotel tonight. She and her friends had heard their share of horror stories about Caracas, even in its best gated neighborhoods on selected hills.

"Tomorrow we must be ready to get on our way at five," Liese said. "We'll take Aeropostal 342 at 7:45 a.m. Once we set foot on the ground in Puerto Ordaz, Ciudad Guayana, we're halfway to Kavanayén. According to my map anyway," she added jokingly and looked at Silvia.

"Oh, yes. Halfway! Sure," Silvia said. "And then even the best driver will need seven hours to get to Kavanayén. And fasten your seat belts." She rolled her eyes but produced a smile as well.

"I'll take the wheel. I'd like to," Liese said. "Okay? You guys trust me?"

Silvia already knew Liese couldn't wait.

Puerto Ordaz was part of greater Ciudad Guayana. That city lay indeed a good distance, one hour's flight, southeast of Caracas. From there, the main road south would lead them to Kilómetro 88 on the border with Guyana, and then farther south through the Gran Sabana, direction Brazil.

Good thing we have a "manager" with us for this adventure, Silvia thought. *One who doesn't feel uncomfortable with a gun to boot. And she looks unconcerned about the Rapid tests she still will have to take in ten days or so.* She knew Liese had been on the phone with two of her staff in Zürich all day yesterday, from her hotel room in Santo Domingo, and had found a contact person in Ciudad Guayana. That woman would provide Liese with binoculars and a weapon and had arranged for an SUV upon their arrival by air at 8:45 a.m.

On Monday, after they had stocked up on water and food at Kilómetro 88, Silvia and her two companions soon entered the splendid Gran Sabana, situated at an altitude of 1,200 meters. Almost every ten minutes, its scenery changed abruptly from beach-like sandy, yellow-pink-orange plains dotted with lush palm trees to mountainous, seemingly impenetrable tropical forests. *Tepúis,* very old mountains with broad, flatted tops, would pop up left and right.

From their Montero, with Liese at the wheel and Silvia in the passenger seat, the travelers admired the spectacular scenery perpetually unfolding in front of them and all around. Millions of years ago, some say two billion, this was ocean territory.

"Too bad," Silvia said, "that we don't have the time to take a few of the wild side-paths to discover the spectacular waterfalls you can find all over. The *saltos*."

"Never mind the waterfalls," Liese commented. "Let's make sure we find the *Schweine*. I can't wait to see what their snouts look like."

Tim lay on the backseat of the Montero, his long legs stretched diagonally.

He's taking mental notes, his eyes more on the smoke-tainted roof of the car than on the splendors of nature. "You're so quiet back there, Tim," Silvia said as she turned to him. "Sweet dreams, *caballero*?"

"I try, but nothing, Silvia. I always return to wondering where the top of the system is in which Barone works his dirty trade. Who the top is. Who calls the shots. Who ordered the murder on Luis Flores. Who sets the fees, and who again and again frustrates the forces that want to end the bloody discrimination."

"Wow." *That's a load*, Silvia thought as she sighed.

As soon as they took the right turn in Luepá to go southwest in the direction of Kavanayén, life in the Montero changed drastically. *Tim's mental excursion is over.* Liese no longer simultaneously joked around, admired nature, and did the driving. The road had changed into an obstacle course. Mud, enormous, gaping holes, little river crossings over unstable pieces of rock, forks in the road baffling first-time visitors fearing they might make a wrong choice, trees lying across the roads, the feeling of being in a place where no help could be found—it all conspired to make Liese's job look almost heroic. Fighting nausea, Silvia raved about how well Liese was up to the challenge. Tim now sat straight up, holding on to the back of Silvia's seat. He complained about his spine.

A lonely farmer waved them down. He was standing, without obvious purpose it seemed, in a spot three hundred meters away from what looked like a little hut. Nothing else in sight. He was dressed in what had been pants and a torn, faded shirt.

He survives on simply flagging down the sporadic tourist who, hopefully, can spare a few pesos. Most are happy to see a living soul. "Good afternoon, *Señor*," Silvia said with a friendly voice as Liese stopped the SUV. "This road leads to Kavanayén, right?"

"Yes, *Señora*, if you don't get lost farther down. We got a lot of rain the last few days. You'll see a lot of new forks. People have to get around the biggest flooding one way or another. Would you have any sardines with you?"

"We do," Silvia said. She reached in her bag and, turning to Tim, she said, "I knew it. That and coke."

"How far to go?" she asked the man.

"I never went by car. I can walk it in less than a day, back home very late at night," the man responded, already opening the can of sardines.

Silvia caught the smell. *I had forgotten about getting hungry.*

They continued their journey, and around 6:00 p.m. they noticed a plume of smoke far ahead of them. Then a couple of huts appeared on hills a good distance away from the road.

They were nearing Kavanayén.

The three visitors had communicated their approximate arrival time to the Misión de Santa Teresita; Silvia had made a very brief call to her uncle on Sunday to inform him. He sounded relieved. He said he wouldn't tell Carla yet.

When Silvia, Liese, and Tim reached the front door close to 7:00 p.m., darkness was setting in. They didn't have to look for a doorbell or knocker; the door swung open when they were still a few steps away, and a smiling brother welcomed them, his hand stretched out.

"Our home is your home. Hospitality is our rule. I understand there's a relative of Father Francesco among you."

"That's me, Brother. I'm Silvia, one of his many nieces," Silvia answered. "Allow me to say that I know my companions very well and that they will be very grateful guests in your home."

"Very good, Miss Silvia. Unfortunately, Father Francesco had expected you somewhat earlier. At this moment, he's leading an hour-long prayer session with our sisters. It started only ten minutes ago. He told me to welcome you and guide you to your rooms in our guest building. He goes to bed at eight."

"Sorry to be so late."

"We know it's very hard to find decent food between here and Kilómetro 88, so we put fruits, bread, and water in the three rooms. You'll find restrooms, sinks, and water close by, outside in the yard of the building, in case you want to freshen up."

"How kind of you, Brother," Silvia said. "We understand about the prayer session. We'll see my uncle tomorrow. We're all tired and want to rest. I do, anyway. We got up long before dawn. But could we meet Miss Carla? We came to see her too. Or is she also in the prayer session?"

"Not this time, Miss Silvia. Today's session is strictly for our sisters. I'll send a sister-novice with a message to Miss Carla's room," the brother volunteered. "Please wait here. Miss Carla can't go to your rooms. Father Francesco doesn't want her to. Her safety. You understand."

✳ ✳ ✳

Silvia told Tim and Liese, as they waited for Carla in the entrance hall, that she was happy that her friend was under such strict control.

"Your uncle takes his role of protector seriously, Silvia," Liese said as she kept her eyes on the simple but sturdy-looking wooden construction holding the roof above their heads. "That's very good. I know a couple of things about such situations."

Carla appeared, dressed and walking modestly in a light gray skirt and blouse. When she got close, she gasped, ran toward Silvia, and threw herself in her arms. Tears flowed, and she wouldn't let go of Silvia's hand.

"Liese, this is our Carla," Silvia said.

"And I recognize Tim. Tim, right? Thank you all for coming. What a surprise. The brothers and sisters are all awfully nice to me," Carla said. Then she lowered her voice and added, "But it's so good to see other faces too."

"We rushed over, Carla. We couldn't make it any sooner. We're glad we made it on time," Silvia responded.

"For my birthday? That's next week. You're early! Where are the presents?" Carla laughed loudly and then covered her mouth with her hand and looked at the brother, her eyes apologizing to him for her clamor.

She jokes? With a murderer on her heels?

"So there's no trace of any bandits yet. Carla?" Tim asked.

"They won't come here. Nobody will find me here." Carla sounded surprisingly confident.

"Does my uncle see it that way too?" Silvia probed. "I'm sure there's little time to be lost. They might be on their way now. That's why we rushed over here."

Carla threw a glance at Silvia and then shrugged. She didn't seem to understand how serious and immediate the threat probably was, and she just said, "Silvia, your uncle protects me very well."

Strange. I'll have to talk to him as soon as possible. He still hasn't explained the situation to her. I made things very clear to him. Fortunately, he keeps her under close control. She should know the real danger she's in. But he must have his reasons.

"Well," Silvia said, "we should get some good rest, and maybe we can meet for breakfast?"

"Mine is at 5:30," Carla responded, and looked at her visitors' faces. Then she smiled.

"In that case …" Tim said.

"Guests have breakfast in the village," Carla went on. "Sisters tell me travelers can buy their eggs and plantains in a store, and in a little restaurant close by the owner will fry the food for them. Silvia may remember."

"Good! A new version of *à la carte*," Tim commented.

The visitors wished Carla good night and proceeded to the guest building. Father Francesco had assigned the rooms himself, the brother explained as he walked next to Silvia the short distance from the mission's front door.

Silvia and Tim looked at each other as they received their keys.

They all thanked the brother and wished him good night.

"Now to our Ritz Carlton digs," Tim whispered to Silvia and Liese when the brother was a few steps away.

They called it a day.

In her bed, Silvia could not fall asleep. She kept hearing every little groan of the building. The springs in her mattress were merciless as they found new spots to poke her, whatever position she took. The mosquitoes were worse. Her worries about Carla grew more serious by the minute. Around midnight, she got scared as the building groaned louder and longer, and then, between groans, she thought she heard mice. She jumped out of her bed and ran out of her room to Tim's, her purse in her hand. She knocked on the door. *Quick, Tim, quick please.* She had to knock two more times, harder each time, before Tim opened the door. At that moment, a second door opened. Silvia saw Liese looking out into the hallway and noticing her.

"I'm so scared, Liese," she explained sheepishly.

"Just go in, Silvia," Liese said, pointing at Tim's door. "Together, both of you will be less scared."

"You have no rats?"

"I have my gun," Liese whispered with a serious face and big eyes, and then she winked. "Just go in there and close the door well. Hurry."

CHAPTER

Carla had exchanged awkward good-night wishes with her visitors and returned to her cell. She felt silly because she hadn't wanted to betray Brother Marcus, and she had wondered whether Silvia and Tim and Liese had seen ignorance or irresponsible nonchalance when she acted as if she wasn't anxious at all.

She felt she had to play ignoramus because Father Francesco didn't want her to know how serious the threat to her life was. He knew the threat was imminent. But he still kept silent. He hadn't even told her about the visit of Silvia and her friends. What had gotten into him? He was supposed to protect her. She knew he wanted to and that she should be grateful to him. *Maybe he thinks the threat isn't as bad as it really is. Nobody can really know it because I told only one person all that happened, and that person wasn't Silvia. The father is afraid he'll have to tell me there's nothing he can do.* She felt compassion for the old man, who knew she would be looking at him, her eyes begging like a helpless child's. *Maybe he's hoping things will clear up, that the threat will subside.*

She felt she should be grateful to Silvia and her friends for their concern, but when, minutes ago, Silvia had tried to subtly point out that the real situation was bad enough to prompt her and Tim to rush to her help with Liese, Carla had concluded that she had to take matters in her own hands. *They don't know my real situation. Neither does the father.*

She looked at her watch. Eight o'clock. Midnight couldn't come soon enough. And she knew she would have to be on her best game tonight with Marcus. Time was running out.

❄ ❄ ❄

As Marcus approached the confessional shortly before midnight, he had strange premonitions.

Fear had been building in him that the encounters with Carla would make him the subject of the wrath not only of the Almighty, who knew everything, but also of Father Francesco. That man seemed to be blissfully unaware of the sins Marcus and Carla were committing. And they kept repeating them.

Marcus had sporadic bursts of guilt, but he hadn't confessed anything, not yet, and he thought Carla probably hadn't either. In his mind, no penance could fully counterbalance their sins. He felt an unspoken compunction deep inside his heart. He didn't want to discuss that with Carla. *I keep trying to believe that hell exists. But if it doesn't, this inner torture must be close to what it should be.*

Lately, Carla kept saying that she really had to use the father's telephone to make one absolutely necessary call, as soon as possible, to a person she wouldn't name. As she lovingly taught him step by step to discover his and her body, her courses would leave him close to breathless. But lately they were followed, and often accompanied, by a request for the phone. He had become hooked on Carla, on her presence and her body, and he felt that someday he would have to pay the price for his addiction.

The phone she wanted to use was kept jealously by Father Francesco, mostly in his own cell, but sometimes in the little office next door that served as office for the mission. Marcus was the accountant and office manager for the mission.

He had his head down as he arrived at the confessional. He put his hand on the little doorknob and caught a waft of a perfume that almost smothered him in excitement.

I wonder whether she's wearing the blouse with only two buttons.

Carla welcomed him on the bench with a passionate kiss and moved close.

He forgot about hell, the real one and the one inside him, and got swept up in the whirlwind Carla unchained. He submitted eagerly to its twists and turns. He started perspiring heavily, and he felt Carla's skin welcome the sweat covering his body. "I'll do anything to save you from your nightmare, angel," he whispered, almost out of breath. "I'll flee with you, if you must, to the end of the world."

"Oh, Marcus. You make me happy and confident, despite my fears. There's one person in this world who really cares about me; that's my Marcus. Yes, let's flee. We must." She squeezed her body against him and held her arms tight around his waist.

"We must plan, angel. We can't just run away without knowing where to go."

"We will, *amor*. But I do need that phone for a few minutes. No later than tomorrow."

Fear now overtook Marcus's passion. He started shaking. "Tomorrow?"

"Tell me you'll bring the phone tomorrow, Marcus. Or where I can come and see you and use it. Father Francesco won't need it at midnight."

Marcus sighed.

It was getting late. Carla buttoned her blouse and started putting her hair in order.

"Tomorrow. I'll bring it, angel. I promise."

"Very good, Marcus. I know you're a courageous person. I'll be waiting for you. Same perfume," she whispered.

As she slowly walked away, an elegant woman seemingly deep in religious thought after a heart-wrenching confession, Marcus already regretted his decision. But at the same time, he couldn't entirely suppress his excitement. *So beautiful, this woman. But I risk the Father's punishment and hell. This must be what some people call living on the edge. But if we flee together …* He tried to imagine what life with Carla would be like.

He checked his pocket to make sure he was carrying her note. *It looks a little wrinkled after nine days.* He trusted Carla would have a good plan once she'd made her phone call.

CHAPTER  25

Tuesday morning came, and Silvia woke up to a glorious morning in Kavanayén. The air felt pleasantly dry. The temperature was mild at 6:30, in the low twenties, Celsius. It offered a welcome respite from the oppressive heat of steamy Santo Domingo and Punta Cana.

As she stood on the tips of her toes to peek out of the small window of the room, she felt her calf muscles flexing slightly. She turned to Tim and saw his approving glance. She told him she noticed only a deserted little road, probably paved many years ago, if ever, and an old man pushing a cart. She knew the village was a few hundred meters away. She rejoined Tim in the bed and curled up to him. He caressed her legs. Her calves didn't flex any longer.

As the sun started piercing through the little window, Silvia said to Tim she would awake Liese and discuss breakfast with her. As she stepped out of Tim's room, she was met by her uncle, who embraced her warmly.

"Welcome, Silvita! I'm so glad you made it safely. I was on my way to your room, ready to knock on your door to greet you. Let's go back in and have a chat. We put food in your room yesterday, and I've asked for coffee," he said jovially.

He proceeded to the door of Tim's room.

"This way, Uncle. That one is Tim's room. I went there to suggest to him we have breakfast together in my room. I still must ask Liese, Miss Liese Kung, my other companion. She's in the room next to mine."

"Yes, I know."

And what does he think? Silvia wondered as she opened her room and let her uncle in. This was the first time she saw her room with daylight seeping in through her little window. *Thank God my bed has clearly been slept on.* The room was sparsely furnished, without restroom, a midsized, brown-painted table dominating the place with the narrow bed that had four black metal posts, one of them slightly bent inwards. The wooden floor's cracks appeared to have been avid collectors of rather sizable dirt particles for years.

Father Francesco served himself a banana right away and said, "Go ahead, get Miss Liese too, Silvia. We'll have the coffee soon." He disposed of the peel on the table.

Tim and Liese met the father a few minutes later and started telling him stories about yesterday's quite amazing trip. They sat down. Silvia had asked them to bring their chairs, and she sat on her bed.

A bit later, while Father Francesco and Tim were in discussion about the well-published border issues with Guyana, Liese pulled Silvia by the sleeve and asked with a twinkle in her eyes, "Not too many rats in that other room, I hope?"

"Let's listen to my uncle," Silvia said. "He's explaining the negotiations about the disputed area between Venezuela and Guyana. He's a local. Tim can learn from him. So can we."

"Good." Liese giggled. "He can publish in French, I in German. My article will mention rats too. His won't, I bet," she added, whispering.

Silvia had had enough. She elbowed Liese slightly in the side and then smiled.

They heard a knock on the door and opened it. A female servant came in, bowing and greeting, a wrinkleless face. Her youthful hands looked entirely smooth as she poured coffee and spooned generous quantities of sugar in every cup. She offered powdered cream and left.

The door was barely closed when Silvia said, "We must have breakfast, but I want to clear something up right away, Uncle. I think

Carla should be told how precarious her situation really is. We're picking up rumors that make it more so by the hour."

The father looked a bit defensive as he said, "I try to take care of Carla. Shield her from threats and evil. She's so vulnerable under the circumstances. I treat her like my child. And frankly, I don't really know what else I can do right away." He glanced silently at his guests and held his coffee cup motionless, as it seemed to wait for answers with him.

Silvia felt uncomfortable and said politely, "I understand you very well, Uncle. But I think it's time to brief her fully, for her own good. We rushed over here because we may be able to help. Miss Liese has experience in similar matters, and she has a keen personal interest in unraveling the mystery of exactly who, or what group, is threatening Carla, and why. None of us really knows, but we plan to find out soon. Right, Tim?"

Tim seemed impressed by Silvia's summary. He held his palms down in front of him and swung them apart rapidly. He declared, "That's it. No need to waste more words."

My Frenchman is talking with his hands. Good hands. Silvia came back to the business at hand and said, "I can talk to Carla, Uncle, and explain. I will, if you don't mind. I may be able to define better what she knows or has experienced—why exactly she's had to flee. She may be hiding something she's too afraid to mention. I'm her friend. She wouldn't tell me more over the phone than what we know at this point, but in person it may be different."

The father looked relieved. He answered, "I'm glad you came. It will be good to share this responsibility, and you know much more about the rest of the world than I do. I have become a Pemón, a local. All I know is Kavanayén, the souls of the good people here, and a few things about the Gran Sabana and *tepúis*. Go ahead, my child."

"We'll try to set up a plan together, and help her implement it, Father," Tim intervened. "Would you have any immediate suggestions, just from your gut? Now that you have us here, you can maybe think of other approaches than when you were facing the problem alone. We have a vehicle. One of us even has a firearm. Liese."

"Oh," the father exclaimed, his arms in the air, "I pray the Lord it never comes to that."

"We pray too, Father. Well … I mean, we feel the same way," Tim quickly clarified as he looked at Silvia.

That clarification wasn't necessary.

The father went ahead and said, "You're smart people. I can help you with the area. We do have a Capuchin house with security in Santa Elena de Uairén. The monks there would certainly take good care of Carla. It's about five or six hours from here. You must go back to Luepá first, then south on the highway till you're practically on the Brazilian border."

Tim nodded.

Liese looked like she was studying a map in front of her, a frown indicating concentration.

"In Santa Elena, she could use a regular phone to get in touch with me in Santo Domingo, I would think," Silvia commented.

"And be tracked by bandits," Liese quickly added.

The father looked up, surprised, but he continued explaining, "If she's discovered there, we have our own ways to get her over the border into Brazil. We get along very well with the border agents. We've helped them catch diamond smugglers a few times. And they halt plenty of suspected criminals at the border crossing. That could include the ones threatening Carla. Controls are strict going from Venezuela to Brazil. The other direction is much easier. It's like the situation between Mexico and the US, except that the orientation is reversed; here it's easy from south to north. I digress, sorry, and that's just my own point of view, of course. I don't do politics, so I may be a little off. But not too much."

"That's helpful, Father," Tim said, "and quite revealing."

They continued their simple breakfast.

It was the second meal of the day for Father Francesco, who clarified with a broad smile that, of course, he just wanted to be social. When he finished and got up, he said to Silvia, "You stay here, child. I'll have somebody look for Carla, and I'll send her here with a couple of brothers to guard her. This is going to be her first visit outside the mission proper.

All her trips so far have been in the hallways of our Capuchin quarters, and of course to the adjacent church where I see her praying frequently. I now must go. My flock awaits me. And that means the entire village. I know them all by name." As he walked out, he turned around and said, his index finger in the air, "And all attend church on Sunday, except for a couple of lost souls. You're welcome for Mass every day, of course. Even Protestants." He glanced for a second at the voluptuous blonde with the guttural Teutonic-sounding accent and smiled.

A shy smile.

CHAPTER  26

Dr. Barone was having a tough time Tuesday morning. It hadn't been easy yesterday, but today his concerns started weighing even heavier.

More than two weeks ago, Charles's hit man, Mickey, had handled the Luis Flores matter. Barone actually had no concrete knowledge of this, but he had more than a hunch that the bullets that pierced Flores's body came from rough Mickey's pistol. He knew Mickey; months ago he had treated him a couple of times for superficial wounds from a car accident.

Right after the Flores shooting, Carla had disappeared. A few days later, Mickey had called him to tell him that she had fled to Kavanayén, with the help of Silvia, another of his employees. Minutes after that call, Barone, in extreme anger, had blown his stack at Silvia.

Now, a week after that confrontation with Silvia, Barone was no longer able to find Mickey.

On Sunday night, Fernando had told Barone he had seen Silvia in Santo Domingo on Saturday, when she was supposed to be in Punta Cana. Barone couldn't wave off this discrepancy and blame it on the whimsical nature of women or on Silvia's reputed penchant for dropping boyfriends without much of a reason or notice. *That picky broad will never get hitched.* Yesterday, Monday, she didn't show up for work, without notice. She didn't answer phone calls. The doctor had to invent excuses and offer apologies to patients who came to see Dr. Silvia Herrera. Today again, there was no trace of her.

At 8:15, he decided to call Charles. He informed him that Mickey had had the phone of Silvia Herrera hacked and had discovered she helped Carla flee. "He felt he had to let me know what my dear employee Silvia was up to. And now Mickey himself seems to have disappeared."

"I don't know either where Mickey is, Doctor," Charles answered, sounding embarrassed and defensive. "What I do know is that when I spoke with him a few days ago, he sounded overly concerned about the Flores case. He didn't say so, but for some reason, he seemed to fear that somebody could accuse him of the crime. I'm not sure about that fear. We're of course making sure we always cover his tracks. But he sounded adamant that he needed to silence possible accusers. He didn't mention any names. He also asked me for an advance. I have another project for him, next week. He wouldn't say why he needed the extra money so soon. Normally we settle bills after the goods have been delivered. I assured him the system was fully protecting him."

"That's all as it should be. Mickey is of course not *my* problem, but now Silvia Herrera's gone too. I won't bother you with a long list of reasons or arguments, but in my view, the chances that her disappearance has nothing to do with the Flores case or Mickey are less than my getting hit by lightning today. What the hell's going on?"

"Doctor, my own bet is that Mickey is chasing that Carla. Wherever she's gone."

"So we agree. Good, but what do we do? Mickey seems to be freelancing and spending money he hasn't even earned. That's dangerous."

"I didn't give him the advance, Doctor."

"Then it's even more dangerous; he may have seen the need to 'find' money somewhere else, exposing us to another risk. We need absolute loyalty, discretion, and discipline. Discipline! Freelancers complicate matters."

"I'll halt his escapades as soon as I can get hold of him." Charles sighed.

Charles never sighs. His ego doesn't allow him. This is unusual, worrisome.

"Shouldn't you contact Decker, Charles?"

"I'll handle it," he said, ending the conversation.

CHAPTER

Charles knew that Decker hated calls regarding "organization." They lay below Decker's pay grade. He knew Decker was rock solid when it came to operating principles, but he wasn't the man who could be bothered with details; that man hadn't made it to up high on the political ladder by fiddling around with little issues or disputes. He had built himself a reputation of a clever politician who was clearly headed higher.

Charles had found him to be always reliable and predictable, something that provided a measure of comfort to whoever dealt with him. One just had to know that Decker liked ever more political power and more money. Also more women, who seemed to flock to the lanky, sixtyish man with the ready smile, sharp features, and graying sideburns. In discussions with friends and speeches to voters, he wasn't bashful about his exploits in the female department.

The women and the money were a major interest of Decker's, and not just because he simply enjoyed both.

"Both help me bolster and protect my career, my power," he once told Charles, who understood the money angle and the power but had trouble figuring out the women part. He didn't want to admit that to Decker. Sometimes he was tempted to tell Decker he thought it might hurt his electoral potential. But Charles had just nodded, assuming he had to accept that Decker's brains and insights were of another class than his.

"What do you expect *me* to do when *your* guy runs away and runs a little business on the side? It's your problem," Decker grumbled after Charles had summarized his suspicions about Mickey, that he could be chasing Carla.

"Also Dr. Barone thought it was necessary to contact you," Charles politely interjected.

"He should keep his own house in order. Does he think he can tell me what my job is?"

"He didn't say so, but I felt Barone believed you should be made aware of the situation, and he probably hoped you would agree to some effective action or suggest one."

"Like what?" Decker sounded irritated.

"Like sending a team out to nab Mickey before he can do more harm—putting the word out to border agents, immigration officials."

"Border agents?"

"He may be in Venezuela," Charles explained.

"Come on! Mickey? He can't find Venezuela on a map," Decker mocked.

"Barone told me he hacked some phones and found out that Carla Fuentes went to a place called Kavanayén in the south of the country. Close to Brazil."

"Mickey the globetrotter." Decker laughed. "Impossible that he'd find his way to …"

"Kavanayén."

"Right. With a C or a K? I never heard of the place. I hope Mickey the hacker heard correctly."

"It's written with a K. He had the hacking done by a friend. I know the place exists."

"I'll Google it; I'll find out what godforsaken place we're talking about. But I'm not sending any goddamn team there. I have other fish to fry. You do what you've got to do and let me know when you've fixed the mess. You'd better get it done soon. Thank you for informing me. And tell Barone to watch his shop."

Charles hadn't realistically expected anything more from Decker. But Barone had wanted him to call the big honcho. *Decker's right. Barone should run his own show a hell of a lot better. We have so many problems with his patients.* "Yes, sir. One more thing, of lesser importance, but since you just mentioned Barone, one of his physicians is missing too. And he sounds like he's missing her. Her name is Silvia Herrera. She's the one who suggested to Carla she flee to Kavanayén. It's her phone Mickey had hacked. 'Cute face,' Barone says, but he doesn't know what got into her."

"Well, what's one more? I told you, Barone has to run his shop the right way—lock the revolving doors and make sure his physicians aren't just cute, dammit. If his place keeps making so much trouble, we'll kick him out of the system."

CHAPTER

"Come on in! The more the merrier," Silvia exclaimed as she opened the door of her tiny room for Carla. "Tim and Liese are already here." It was a few minutes past nine.

"Thanks, Silvia. What an experience: my first trip outside the missionary complex. It feels like a liberation. I still have two pleasantly chatty protectors with me, though."

Without turning her head, she winked at Silvia and pointed with her thumb at the two young monks standing behind her. She whispered in Dominican dialect, "I've been reborn as a curious, nervous doggie on two invisible, short leashes. Good leashes." She then turned to the monks and said, "Thank you, *amigos*. I'm in good hands now. I'll see you later."

One of the guards addressed Silvia. "*Señora*, would you or your friends be kind enough to accompany the lady back to the front door of the mission when your meeting ends?"

"Not a problem. We'll take care of her. Thank you."

The monks bowed and left.

When Carla entered, Silvia apologized for her room. Too small, too full, too many chairs in it. "I haven't had the energy yet to clean up the leftovers or make my bed."

"This Hilton suite looks great," Carla said, sounding upbeat as she greeted her friends. "And we have food."

"Coffee? We have some left," Silvia suggested.

"Do you mind if I have a banana too? It's been four hours since I finished my breakfast. But I must confess I have a sister two cells down from me whose family secretly keeps her stocked up on cookies. I share her secret and sin with her sometimes," she added with a wink. She carefully peeled the banana and removed a few dark spots, keeping her pinky far away from the action. "How are you guys doing?" she asked, looking a little nervous, her eyes still on the banana.

"We had a good night's sleep in this serene, quiet area," Silvia said.

"Young people. I envy how well they sleep, like lambs." Liese didn't hide her little smile.

Carla sounded slightly uncomfortable as she said, "I must tell you off the bat that I've known all along that I was in more danger than Father Francesco let on. His glances and the excessive restrictions he imposed on me spoke volumes. He did it for my own good, of course. I just couldn't bring myself to tell him what I simply knew and always had feared. My apologies for putting on that act yesterday. I didn't want to embarrass the good father when he would first speak with you. He's the generous man who has taken it upon himself to protect me. Forgive me. I did what I thought was best."

Silvia said calmly, "We understand your concerns, Carla; you wanted to be a good guest, and I know you've been. My uncle is full of praise for your behavior. Let's just get practical and see how we can help you. Father Francesco already gave us some ideas for a plan B, one that takes you out of Kavanayén. I thought this village was the perfect place for you. And apparently it has been, until the day I mouthed off about your hiding place to Tim over a phone that was hacked. Too bad and too dumb, but we're lucky we soon found out that we'd been overheard. I feel guilty, and I'm here to help repair the damage I've done."

"You've saved my life already, Silvia. I owe you big thanks. And I also appreciate Tim's and Liese's efforts. I feel I'm imposing on you, heavily."

"Not at all, Carla," Tim said. "We all have our own reasons for being here. What we all have in common is our intention to get to the bottom of this, to expose the people who are behind all that's happening to you and to some others."

For a second, Carla stared at the wall in front of her. Then she nodded but didn't comment.

"Let's all get practical," Silvia proposed. "We can get Carla out of here under cover. We have a vehicle and a weapon. And we've got four good brains here in this room. We could of course smuggle Carla into a big city in this country, where she could disappear in the masses. Ciudad Bolívar comes to mind, and I even thought of Maracaibo, very, very far away from here." She turned to Carla. "But you'd be really on your own there, Carla ... Another plan could have us sneak you over the Brazilian border, just south of it. You might stand out a bit there, of course, not even speaking the language. But you're smart, and the bilingual Capuchin brothers in nearby Santa Elena could help you with the language initially. Also with the border crossing. Brazil is a stone's throw away from their place."

"So there are Capuchins in Santa Elena too?" Carla asked.

Silvia explained, "Yes, they have a Capuchin house there, but I understand from my uncle that it's rather small, with only a few monks. I'm a little worried about that idea. The house is located in a regular street, one of the major ones. It has a guard most of the day, but you'd be much less hidden or protected than here."

"Well, yes, but ... I like that Capuchin house idea. I wouldn't be that far away from Father Francesco and could maintain contact with him through his colleagues in Santa Elena. I could come back here. And I could easily flee into Brazil from Santa Elena if the bandits discover I'm hiding in the city."

"True. And as Silvia's uncle told us, bandits couldn't just simply pursue you over the border. The Brazilian immigration officials are strict, he said, and I read that their jails aren't much more fun than the ones in Venezuela or the DR," Tim explained, rolling his eyes.

Every Latin American knows that. No need for a Frenchman to rub it in, Silvia thought to herself.

Carla gave Tim a look but then simply repeated she felt good about Santa Elena. "Can we take a couple of days to think this over?" she asked. "I don't think we should rush this. The bandits aren't here yet. We should plan and fix the details: the time; the route; the coordination with the house; assurance that the Capuchin order in Santa Elena accepts me; how I'll get out of the mission unseen by the villagers; who will be my adviser or main contact in Santa Elena; how much I'll be paying if I stay for a long time, etc."

Tim had been listening and frowned. Now he spoke, glancing at Silvia first. "So much detail, Carla. I don't think it's all that complicated. Strangely enough, I get the impression that your three visitors are more rushed and nervous about your well-being than you are. But I understand that for now you feel safe where you are, and that you don't want to risk your life by too much improvisation."

"Exactly, Tim," Carla said. She sounded grateful to him and looked at Silvia.

"I'm prepared to stay as long as it takes," Silvia said. "And I agree we must avoid undue haste. We must think it over and plan. But we can't waste time."

Liese and Tim nodded.

Time had gone by fast, and the clock said twelve. That was a little early for a Venezuelan lunch, or any lunch, but Tim let it be known that he couldn't sustain his tall frame on just bananas, coffee, and some old crackers.

"The village has a little restaurant, the one where they fry your plantains," Carla said. "You could go there."

"And you can go with us. You won't stand out too much; you're in our group, a bunch of tourists staying in the guest building. You'd be safe," Tim suggested.

Carla looked at Silvia.

Is this smart? What will my uncle say? He doesn't have to know, and she's safe with us. Half an hour. She nodded.

Liese said she had to get her camera from her room.

"Why don't you grab your gun too and tuck it under your skirt, Liese? We all need your protection," Tim half-joked.

"So you didn't notice yet, Tim?" Liese shot back.

When she returned from her room, she showed Tim a couple of big eyes while pointing at the little bulge visible on the inside of her upper thigh, and handed Carla a huge hat.

After a five-hundred meter stroll from the guest building, Silvia and her companions found the Roraima restaurant with all of its four metal tables, twenty-four plastic chairs, a small Formica-covered counter, and a ceiling fan that, it seemed, had eagerly been collecting grease and dust for ages. The short, more-than-rotund owner, Omar, welcomed them and switched the fan on as they entered, helpfully pointing out where it would be spreading most of its relief.

Silvia asked Omar where they should go to buy their eggs and yucca.

"I have it all here," the man assured them, "still cool and fresh."

"Oh. Good. We don't have to go to the store then."

"Only when my stock runs out, usually around six or seven in the evening. I can serve you a local *pabellón*. I have a freshly prepared casserole."

"*Pabellón* here has black beans and rice with tomato-soaked steak, Liese," Silvia explained. And she whispered, "You have a good dentist, I'm sure, so I can recommend the *pabellón*. And it will make us instant friends of Omar. He could come in handy. Who knows?"

"*Pabellón* for me!" Liese shouted as she plumped down on a chair. "And a good beer."

"Sorry, no beer, *Señora*. Coke?" Omar looked embarrassed.

"Okay then, my friend Omar." Liese laughed.

"Father Francesco would frown upon alcohol," Silvia explained quietly to Liese, "and Omar doesn't want to get on his wrong side. My uncle runs the town, if you know what I mean."

"But I understand the father drinks wine every day, as much as he wants. Sometimes twice a day. He can simply tell the choirboy how much to pour. I once had a Catholic boyfriend who'd been a choirboy." She laughed again and rolled her eyes.

"I don't think we want to argue that alcohol issue with my uncle. We need a unified team, him included, Liese," Silvia joked.

"We do. I'm in. And ready for Santa Elena." Liese gave a thumbs-up.

"So am I," Carla chimed in. "Although I feel safe here, even in this little restaurant almost out on the street."

Carla seems to take it all in stride. She's so relaxed. At times, though, she looked a little absentminded this morning. I may be exaggerating the threat. Or was she in a crazy panic when she so frantically asked for my help that Saturday morning when they found Luis Flores dead?

The lunch was a simple but delightful affair.

After a jovial good-bye from Omar, the group walked back to the mission where they met the guard on duty.

CHAPTER

As soon as he had finished his unpleasant conversation with Charles, Decker went into action. He had to prevent Mickey from going rogue and creating all kinds of fuss, confusion, and suspicion by going out of his remit. *The worst thing he can do is go after Carla Fuentes, an innocent person whom he suspects of knowing more than he thinks she should.* Harming Carla would be highly unfair, Decker felt, and it could have very unwelcome reverberations, such as more questions in the media regarding the circumstances of Luis Flores's death. Indeed, Luis had been a patient of Carla's and there were published reports saying that she had been observed dining with him at the Vesuvio just a couple of hours before he died.

He ordered his staff to alert the Department of Justice and Immigration Services at airports and ports about Mickey. He knew Mickey's real name was José Mora.

"Mora must be arrested immediately. Maybe we can spot him as he attempts to obtain a passport or leave the country," he told his direct staff. "And by 2:00 p.m. I want the details of his rap sheet. Get some ugly pictures of him out of our files. He may already have fake passports under several names."

At 2:00 p.m., the head of the Antidiscrimination Task Force, Dr. Juris Mauricio Decker, signed a cover letter. Two attachments came

with it: a two-pager describing Mickey's—Mora's—criminal history
and a sheet with copies of four unflattering pictures of the suspect. The
documents were sent out by e-mail a minute later.

Wanting to plug a major and well-known leak in the immigration
system, Dr. Decker then paid a personal visit to a number of hangars at
Las Américas International Airport. Most of the private flight business
was run from these hangars, from small offices tucked into them. Many
of these private airline operators worked on shoestring budgets and
competed for every scrap of business. These fly-by-night outfits wouldn't
mind accepting a neat sum from someone like Mickey, papers or no
papers, even if the pesos or dollars he offered were blood-drenched, so
to speak. Decker knew this very well. He himself had "escaped" a few
times from press and nosy voters via this route. These operators could
land their little planes in places where visas could be bought on the
spot.

One of the visits Dr. Decker made in the hangars was to Ricardo
Lima's partner, Gonzalo, who immediately looked with interest at the
pictures the high government official and politician handed him a
minute after he walked in. The man had identified himself as Mauricio
Decker from Justice.

"Pin them up on that wall people look at when they walk in here,
sir," Decker had politely suggested. "His name is José Mora."

"I sure will," Gonzalo said, continuing to look at the pictures. He
didn't pin them up right away and seemed to check his memory as he
studied them, tapping his forehead with his left index.

"You know him? Saw him?" Decker asked.

"Hmm. It's possible … I may have heard of him."

"Recently?"

"A few days ago. Of course, odds are high I'm thinking of somebody
else."

"Right," Dr. Decker said. "Verbal descriptions are sometimes
nothing like the real thing. Even pictures can lie."

"Yes, Doctor, but meanness shows." Gonzalo kept studying the
pictures.

"Keep me posted. Thanks."

"No problem. But you may want to see my friend Firmín of API too, the Aerolínea de Pilotos Independientes," Gonzalo suggested. "He has quite an operation, much bigger than mine. I'll go with you. I know a shortcut. We have quite a mess around here."

Decker nodded and the two men went to Firmín's office. A detergent odor hit Decker's sensitive nostrils as they entered. They met Firmín's receptionist, Gloria, and Decker spotted a cleaning lady in a far corner.

"Our manager will be back in thirty minutes," Gloria told her visitors and asked, "Can I offer you a cup of coffee?"

Decker shook his head as he looked at his watch. "Thank you, very kind of you, but I must go now," he said. *The manager apparently can't stand the odor either.*

Outside Firmín's office he thanked Gonzalo again and walked out to the parking area. As he prepared to step into his green Jaguar, he looked back at Gonzalo and saluted him with his hand. Then he drove the fifteen kilometers to Valencia.

Now I'm going to give Barone a piece of my mind.

CHAPTER

Gonzalo called Ricardo as soon as he got back to his office. *The guy in the photographs looks exactly like the one Ricardo and I discussed on Friday, the one Ricardo is after,* he thought. But he hadn't wanted to jump to a conclusion in Decker's presence; he barely knew him. *What kind of politician is he?*

He called Ricardo, itching to brief him. *Why does it take four or five rings?*

"Ricardo! Remember the creep we discussed last week?"

"Sure do. How are you? You sound excited, man," Ricardo said. "Did he come back to bug you some more? Did he show you his fat wallet?"

"No, but I got pictures of him, I think. Pretty sure."

"How's that? Did somebody activate a security camera?"

"No, but what I'm going to tell you is *big*. Listen. A Dr. Decker from the Ministry of Justice was making the rounds here with pictures of a guy named José Mora. Decker wants Mora arrested if he shows up here. The official visited several companies, not just ours."

"Wait, Gonzalo. Are you talking about Decker the politician? The guy heading the Antidiscrimination Department?"

Gonzalo felt proud as he answered, "Yep. It was him, from Justice anyway. One of our men here told me seconds ago he's indeed the antidiscrimination honcho. The distinguished gentleman wanted our help. He wants Mora in prison—said he had a thick file on him. I decided to call you right away. Decker just left. I saw him step in his Jaguar seconds ago." *Quite a vehicle for a man on a government salary …*

Ricardo sounded unconvinced when he said, "We're talking about coincidences, Gonzalo. Maybe just that."

"Maybe. All we can do is keep looking and inform Decker if we spot the scum," Gonzalo said.

"Hold it, Gonzalo. Do me a favor; in that case, please call me first. We have no proof that the ugly visitor is the guy I described to you. I doubt he is. But if your assumption is right, we could pull a real stunt with this one. Let's keep our mouths shut about this."

I have no idea what he means. So many words to say he's not sure? "Okay. But someday you'll have to explain to this dummy why all of a sudden you sound so skeptical and mysterious at the same time."

"Okay."

Ricardo knows more.

※ ※ ※

Gonzalo hung up but didn't feel satisfied. He had to share his excitement with somebody else. He called Firmín's assistant.

"Glorita, could you give me a buzz as soon as your big boss gets back? I must see him right away."

"No problem, Señor. My pleasure," the sweet voice came back.

"Señor? My name is Gonzalo, and you know it. When was the last time I called you an angel, Glorita?"

"It's been too long, Señor Gonzalo," she giggled.

He got the call from Gloria half an hour later.

He hurried to Firmín's hangar. His friend waved him into his private office. Gonzalo immediately pulled the pictures out of his hip pocket. He had been perspiring heavily, and the pictures already felt damp as he handed them to his friend. They seemed to have quickly decided to adopt the curve of Gonzalo's buttocks. He studied Firmín's reaction to the ugly face staring at his friend from the photo paper.

Gonzalo took the pictures back and said, "Firmín, I wouldn't want this guy on any of my planes. I couldn't ask a pilot to put up with him for hours. He looks like bad news."

"Where did you get them?" Firmín asked. "Why do you show me them? Are they the reason you came to see me? Or did you just want one of my Puros de Hostos?"

Gonzalo laughed and explained, "A man called Decker, from Justice, came to see me. A big shot. He wants this man arrested—for very good reasons, he said. He had more pictures. He wanted us to look for this kind of person. That Decker looked like a man on a mission."

"He must be. A big shot from Justice doing this kind of grunt work. Hmm," Firmín opined. "We don't see too many of those getting their hands dirty here in our luxury suites."

"I came with him to see you. But you weren't in."

"Good. I don't need any Decker wasting my time, Gonzalo. I have enough of a job the way things are," Firmín declared. "And I don't want any jerks or crooks like the one in your pictures on my planes either. And I want clean money, good banks, certified checks."

"Let's keep an eye on this creep, buddy. I don't think you'll forget that face easily. And thanks for the cigar."

"That face will keep me awake at night. No, I take that back; I can think of something juicier," Firmín joked as they shook hands.

"I have no idea what you mean," Gonzalo said with a wink, and he departed.

CHAPTER

The dust flew as Decker raced into the parking lot and came to a screeching halt in front of the entrance door of Barone's offices. He slammed the car door, marched into the building, and brusquely approached the receptionist desk. "I must see Dr. Barone."

The girl jumped up.

"Good afternoon, Dr. Decker," she said. She immediately headed in the direction of Barone's office, saying, "I'll let Dr. Barone know. Excuse me for a moment." She disappeared but came back, rushing to her desk.

Thirty seconds later, Barone came out of his office and greeted Decker, who had started a conversation with the receptionist. "What a pleasant surprise," he said, walking up to Decker.

The receptionist listened, looking anxious.

Barone frowned as soon as he saw Decker's face, and he started sounding insecure when he said to his unannounced visitor, "Welcome. How are things?"

"Let's go in your office," Decker said curtly, pointing to Barone's door with his head. "Sorry, no politics today, purely medical issues," he courteously apologized to the receptionist for proceeding after so few words with her.

Barone closed the door. "Always the vote-counter, Mauricio. I don't blame you; every single one counts."

"But I should blame *you*, Barone. We're in a heap of trouble. And you know damn well it's your fault. It all started with you and that bloody Flores."

Barone looked dumbfounded and argued, "Mauricio, you agreed with Charles that action had to be taken; that Flores was a walking time-bomb. It was of course Charles who fixed Flores's new fee that set this steamroller in motion."

"You could've given Charles decent input regarding the fees. You're supposed to know what a patient can take, at what level he'll revolt. You did a half-ass job. Charles couldn't know Flores had financial trouble. You should've known. And now we have rough Mickey chasing Carla."

"Yes. That's probably true. If he can find her he may … Carla's my employee, and a good one. I'm still trying as hard as I can to stop him. That's why I asked Charles to speak with you. Maybe you could find a way."

"I have no idea whether he left the country or not and went to that place …"

"Kavanayén."

Decker had calmed down somewhat. "Right. With a K. I think we, just the two of us, can make some progress, get our butts out of this mess. Kavanayén is a small place, barely a speck on a detailed map. It should be possible to go there and find out in what house or hut she's hiding. Then we can protect her—maybe move her. We should be able to get that done before Mickey can reach her, the poor girl. And of course, we must try to keep him from leaving for Venezuela in the first place."

"That's right. If he harms her, it's another PR disaster for all of us. But I have no idea how we can find and stop Mickey. And I don't think it's going to be a cakewalk to find Carla in Venezuela. I don't see how I can help. It's not my area of expertise, and wouldn't know where to start. Charles doesn't either. You, your office, must have some ways or means or connections …" Barone sounded plaintive.

Shit! He's trying to wash his hands of the mess he created. Dump it on me. Decker was furious. "We're stuck, Barone. We're stuck! And you refuse to take responsibility. Carla will get killed, and the shit will hit the fan! We're toast!" he screamed. He felt his face almost bursting from anger and the veins in his temples swelling. Suddenly he had to hold onto the armrest of his chair. He felt weak. He fell off his chair.

✼ ✼ ✼

Barone immediately took Decker's pulse while screaming at the receptionist, "Dr. Decker fainted! Get me a stretcher so we can bring him to the care room. The defibrillator. Quick!"

Barone and a nurse rushed to the care room with Decker on the stretcher. Barone drew a vial of blood for the enzyme test and ordered the EKG equipment in.

"You stay here," he told the nurse. "I'll run to the lab for his enzymes."

"Oh, no, Doctor. I can do that if you want. Maybe you want to watch Mr. Decker yourself," the nurse suggested.

"No, Teresa, I'm in a real hurry. Do as I say. I'll be back in no time." He ran out.

In the lab, he handed the blood specimen to the technician and said, "Take half of this and test it. Quick."

The technician did as ordered and handed the vial back to Barone, who put it in his coat pocket and went back to Decker.

After about five minutes, Decker regained consciousness. His heartbeat was then still very irregular, and the EKG still all over the place. He seemed to grasp the situation.

The enzyme test showed no heart attack.

About fifteen minutes later, Dr. Barone told Decker, when they were alone, that he would be just fine. It probably was fatigue and maybe a little too much anger, which could easily be avoided in the future. The mystery of Mickey and Carla would be resolved.

Decker looked resigned, grateful, and slightly embarrassed. "First time ever," he said. "Never happens to me. I can go an entire day without food."

Barone instructed his secretary to accompany Dr. Decker to his home.

"Take a taxi," Barone told her. "We'll take care of the doctor's car. On the way back, don't tell the taxi driver a word about what happened. Politicians don't like these stories," he whispered. "They must look strong."

He checked his coat pocket and felt the vial.

CHAPTER

A minute after midnight on Tuesday, Marcus's hand trembled as he handed Carla the old satellite phone he had just produced out of his boxers and from under his habit.

"It feels nicely warm and heavy," Carla whispered as she cradled it with two hands.

He quickly took it back, explaining, "It's not easy to operate, angel. Let me do the dialing for you."

Carla dictated the number, and he dialed. When he heard the phone ring on the other side, he handed it back to Carla. *I should move out of the confessional, but I can't. She can't want me to.*

They both heard a weak, tired midnight voice answer the phone. "*Dime*, say it."

Brother Marcus sat next to Carla, their legs touching, his shaking. He signaled he could hear the voice on the other side. He put his middle fingers in his ears and looked for approval from Carla. She smiled and nodded, a grateful expression on her face.

"It's me, *amigo*. Carla. I'm safe in Kavanayén. Safe, yes," she said over the phone. She listened for a few seconds. She winked at Marcus. She continued, "Don't holler so loudly. There's a loud echo ... You'll awaken the monks ... You don't hear the echo?" Carla listened again and then said, "Yes, please go and get her. Sorry to call at this horribly late hour."

"He's getting his wife," she whispered to Marcus, who had reflexively taken his fingers out of his ears as she leaned toward him.

A conversation between two women. This can stretch out for half an hour. It spells trouble on the monthly statement. "Keep it as short as you can, Carla," he pleaded softly, making the money sign with his right thumb and index finger.

She nodded. He put his middle fingers back where they had been. She smiled again.

I can hear most of Carla's words anyway. She knows.

"*Hola*, Ana, so good to hear you. Finally I can talk to you." Carla pressed the telephone hard against her left ear. Marcus sat on her right side. Carla frowned as she listened to the answer and then said, sounding surprised, "I don't sound enthused? Believe me, I am—of course. But this is a quiet place of piety and devotion. I can't shout here. My happiness is inside me. All's very well here. I'm safe. Tell me about you and your husband …"

Another frown appeared on her face as she stopped talking, listened, and then spoke again. "They could be hacking us? I'll be careful. Don't worry. Tell me."

Carla concentrated intensely and reacted with sounds of approval. At one point, Marcus coughed. Carla looked up. Then he coughed once more, his fingers still in his ears.

"Hold on, Ana." Carla turned to Marcus—his fingers got another rest—her hand over the microphone, and whispered, "Please cover your mouth when you have to cough. Okay? Sorry."

Then she spoke again into the phone, explaining, "No, it wasn't really anybody's coughing. I have these sneezing bouts, tried to cover my mouth. Sorry. Please, tell me more about the birthday party you're having there, Ana."

Sneezing?

For the next two or three minutes, Carla just listened. Then she said, articulating well, "I'll follow your good advice, Ana. Thanks so much. I have understood you well."

Carla looked at Marcus, rolling her eyes, and whispered quickly, "She always thinks she can give me hints about my diet. About sinus sprays too."

She turned back to the phone, listened, and answered, "No. Ana, that visitor hasn't shown up. And sorry, I don't think I can call back anytime soon. I must make this short. I'm glad you said you'd all be thinking about me ... Bye. Say hello to your *caballero*."

The call ended.

She turned again to Marcus and said, "I love her."

Marcus had been wondering why she made up a lie for the good friend she loved. He said, "You didn't sneeze, Carla."

"I know, my dear Marcus. When you coughed, I didn't want her to think somebody was with me. She was concerned that somebody might be hacking us or listening in. She secretly helped me to get here. She has lots of money. You're now the only person other than Ana and me who knows how I fled here. Nobody was listening in from our side, right? Your fingers did the job, right?"

Marcus smiled, and so did Carla as she went on. "I had to come up with something not to alarm her." She paused, handed him the phone back, and whispered, "And I couldn't tell her how happy I was to sit here together with the man I love and who's going to flee with me." She kissed him passionately and said, "Your poor fingers must be tired. I'm sure they like this better than plugging your ears." She took his two hands and put them on her bosom. "Right? I love those hands. I feel them tremble from excitement," she said as she brought them to her face and put her cheeks against them. "I'll calm them down, your loving hands."

"I'm ready to go with you, Carla. I've made up my mind," Marcus said. He was happy and scared.

"We must escape, Marcus. I know my friends who arrived yesterday want to move me soon to another place. But I want to go with you, not with them."

"Why was this call so important, Carla?" *I must start learning how women think. I had to get the phone out of Father's office for this call, but the conversation didn't sound like the biggest deal.*

"My friend Ana once literally saved my life, Marcus. I'll explain someday. She was terribly worried that I might not have arrived safe and well. But I couldn't call her, as you know. Till today. Now she knows I'm just fine and well-protected. I have peace now. And she gave me good advice. Thank you so much."

CHAPTER

Silvia hadn't slept well Tuesday night. Tim had come to her room and shared her narrow bed. They both had felt impeded in their movements by the old springs and couldn't help noting the repeated coarse comments signaled to them from within the mattress. After their lovemaking they discussed Carla's situation until Tim suggested that a good night's sleep would work wonders; things would look more clearly outlined in the morning. In the end, Silvia was happy to agree.

After they kissed good night, Tim had several hours of good sleep, but Silvia didn't. Not only did Tim's long legs take awhile to get accommodated in the narrow space, his elbows made themselves felt from time to time too. Silvia wasn't exactly petite, but she did find a curve here and a little open space there where she could curl up and listen to Tim's slow breathing until she fell asleep for short intervals.

She was happy when around 7:00 a.m. she found a message under her door. *From my uncle. Better than a knock on the door—and the end of his illusions.*

"My uncle proposes we meet in the dining hall at eight. All of us, including Carla. He says he'll personally serve us breakfast," she whispered to Tim as she curled up to him. *Another two minutes.* Nights and early mornings in Kavanayén weren't overly warm. The village lay 1,200 meters high.

"My poor uncle probably didn't sleep any better than I did," Silvia said to Tim.

"Worse. Maybe on a better mattress, but all by himself … I think. We both vaguely, remotely remember how that feels." He laughed loudly.

"Shh, Tim. The novices cleaning the hallways know this is my room."

"And you don't want them jealous."

"Don't push it, Tim," she teased. "I bet those young women couldn't care less about your hot looks. They have devoted their life to a higher calling."

"You're probably right about my looks. How about my charming character?"

"Too hard to unearth, Tim."

"Okay," Tim conceded, and he changed to a serious tone. "Back to work. How about *our* calling, Silvita? Getting Carla out of this village safely?"

"I'm sure my uncle won't leave the dining room before we've got that planned. It's gnawing at him. His face is exactly my father's when he walks around worried. And then my mother gets concerned too. I must inform Liese about the breakfast invitation."

At eight sharp, they all met in the dining hall, from which all traces of the 5:30 breakfast had been swept.

Big, old but shiny stoves and aluminum containers created an atmosphere of too much light in the huge room. In a far corner, silent novices seated at metal tables cleaned vegetables. They looked up as the visitors entered, and down again as soon as they saw Father Francesco with them.

"They know you're the people for whom I ordered breakfast at the unusually late hour of eight," the father explained with a smile. He pointed to a big tray sitting on a table in another corner of the hall, a good distance away from the novices. "You have corn bread there, plantains, eggs, papaya juice, and coffee," he said.

Father Francesco stared compassionately at Carla as she sat down at the dented table. She looked tired but assured her friends she felt just fine. She had gradually taken to invigorating naps in the afternoon, she said.

"That's smart," Silvia commented. She felt good about that.

Silvia and her uncle had had a short conversation in the early evening the day before. She had briefed him on the preliminary ideas and discussions the group had had after he had left her room; she didn't think it was necessary to scare the man by telling him the discussions had continued, with Carla present, in *Roraima*. Now the concrete planning had to start.

"Do we still think that the Santa Elena house option is the best?" Silvia asked, looking around.

All nodded. The father glanced at Carla and said apologetically, "I've been so happy to take care of you, Carla, and I'd love to continue. We'll miss you here. But this looks like the best step we can take."

Carla nodded, expressionless. "I do understand, Father. And I won't be far away. I'm sure you'll visit Santa Elena from time to time."

Is she on Valium? Every word in the same tone?

Liese signaled she wanted to speak. She directed her attention at Father Francesco. "I don't know about all of you," she said, and threw a quick glance at Tim, "but, Father, I spent most of my night thinking about the plan we more or less had agreed on yesterday. We badly need your further assistance to detail it, so we can execute it."

"Good. Tell me how I can help, Miss Liese," the father said. He wiggled on his chair, looking for a comfortable position. Then he looked ready.

Liese now spoke to all. "In Zürich, I deal with these situations on and off, and one thing is evident to me in this case: danger may lurk from many corners, because the bandits have money, means, and connections. That tells me we need complete secrecy to fulfill our mission. And we need deception. Don't worry, Father, it's not as bad as it sounds. What I mean by deception is that we must create the impression that she's still here long after she'll be gone, actually as long as we can. If we succeed in doing that, we're done. The bandits will be looking for their target in the wrong spot. And the police can wait for them in that spot."

"But the bandits don't know she's in the mission," Silvia cautioned.

"Not yet," Tim intervened. "I'm sure the father can 'mistakenly' and 'inadvertently' mention she's there days after she's gone."

"Yes," the father laughed. "That sounds good. Anybody can make a mistake or two. I could 'forget' she's gone. Consider it done, Tim."

My uncle has many confessionals in the mission. I wonder which confessor my uncle uses for little sins like these. For bigger ones, he probably travels to a non-Capuchin church in Santa Elena or Luepá. But very few trips, I bet.

Tim went on, "The deception may not last long; once you're gone, Carla, some of your new friends in the mission might be missing you and, unaware of your problem, talk to other visitors or villagers about you and tell them that you're no longer in the mission."

Father Francesco sat up straight and said he could speak in confidence to the three or four people in the mission who had more or less close contact with Carla. "We've kept her quite isolated," he explained. "I assigned two older sisters to her for the meals. One is also her neighbor. I'll talk to the other neighbor as well. She's her knitting pal. Does any other person come to mind as a regular contact, Carla?"

"No, Father. You covered it well. Thank you. And I have deliberately kept to myself a lot, for my safety. It wasn't always easy." She looked at her sandals for a second but then quickly lifted her head.

"But we should confess, Father, that yesterday we dragged Carla to Omar's place for lunch," Tim said, looking a bit embarrassed. "It wasn't Carla's idea; it was mine. A very short lunch. She hid her head under a big hat."

"She was under my protection," Liese added.

Father Francesco looked shocked and shook his head. He remained speechless as he looked at Silvia.

We disappointed him. "I apologize, Uncle. But at no time did Omar think she wasn't a tourist, one of our little group. There were no other guests in the restaurant."

The father threw his hands up and said, "My brain doesn't work as fast as yours anymore, so …" He looked away.

"I've another question," Carla interjected. "A concern. We can't use the front door, obviously. The guard will notice us, and also, any bandit who comes or has come to Kavanayén to get me will be smart enough to have one of his guys observe the mission, its front gate in the first place."

"That front door is verboten. That was on my list, Carla, believe it or not," Liese proudly said. "And let me tell you about something else on my list: I love to drive that Montero. But, don't take me wrong, I don't want to drive you to Santa Elena, and—"

"I can drive," Tim jumped in. "It must have tired you out, that hellish road. No worry."

"Yes, worry, Tim," Liese shot back. "Nobody should drive her. Unless we can put her in the trunk of a car and wrap her in big layers of polystyrene for the shocks and bumps. At least for the first ten miles or so."

"Yeah," Tim jumped in, joking. "And we'd better have the trunk cover tied slightly ajar for air …"

"And provide her with fifty sickness bags—isn't that what you call them?—for … whatever," Liese played along. "We'd have to leave her arms out of the polystyrene wrap so …"

"Enough already. We get it," Silvia said. "Let's get serious. I agree she shouldn't sit in the car, visible to villagers and even to the few other people driving down to Kavanayén. But it could be done in the dark. Or with a disguise. No?"

"The drive in the dark is life-threatening, even for locals," Father Francesco warned. "And disguises? I don't like them. I can hear it already. 'Somebody who never entered the village is leaving it? Did Father Francesco perform a miracle? Another one?'" He laughed jovially.

Oh my, did he recover from the Omar intermezzo.

Tim agreed, smiling broadly. "The last thing we want to do is ruin your reputation with baseless rumors about fictitious miracles, Father. And we must look for a realistic plan."

Smooth talker.

"I see a solution," the father said, still visibly enjoying his miracle, "but it costs money. We have a short runway here, not great, bumpy—but anyway, nothing like the regular dirt roads. The Capuchin order uses planes sparingly, of course, but we have a decent price agreement. A flight from Santa Elena to here, and then from here to there, would be a little over 1,100 dollars. It's quite a sum, but so were your flights from Santo Domingo, I guess."

"I have the money for that," Carla quickly volunteered.

Wow.

"And that could be done in the dark," the father suggested. "The strip is a twenty-minute walk east of here. The dark could be your cover. The area is quite isolated. Maybe Tim could walk there with you for protection. Not too many can go, if you don't want to get noticed. Making that short trip by car is impossible in darkness. I guarantee you'd get stuck, and then the whole village would know about the escape."

"Tim shouldn't go," Liese said categorically. "He's too tall—a strikingly tall, brown-haired, pale-faced gringo. I'll go. I'm normal size, height-wise anyway. I'll wear a cover over my hair, so nobody will see a smashing blonde sneak out of the mission and the village." She smiled and made big eyes.

"You're too modest, Liese." Tim laughed and then turned serious. "And I worry; you'll have to come back alone then."

"Me and my gun, Tim. Don't you worry. I've done taekwondo too, for your information." She showed two fists. She added, "Maybe you can come and look for me if I don't show up back at the guest building within an hour or so. We'll have to set a time schedule."

Father Francesco also made big eyes but didn't speak.

A woman. A lady. Alone. Taekwondo. This is out of his world, Silvia mused.

"Okay, Liese. That would be great. If you're not scared," Carla said and then turned to the father. "Could you order the plane, Father, at that good price?"

"I can, Carla. Do we all agree?"

He looked around and saw nods, one slower and less deep than another. "How about sometime after midnight tomorrow? Say 2:00 a.m. That would be a good time. Everybody will be sound asleep then," he suggested.

He wants to get her to safety pronto.

"It'll be a bit more expensive because of the hour," the father said.

"I still have one concern," Liese said. "As I mentioned a minute ago, when Carla and I leave the mission, we can't use the front door. We'll need another route. Father, I'm afraid we must rely on you for this too."

Father Francesco rubbed his chin. "All right," he said. He leaned forward over the table and started whispering, "I'll show you the exit from our sacristy, behind the altar. A narrow staircase leads down from there to a heavy outside door that's always locked and opens on a little open space outside, at the rear of the mission. That's the route we hope to use to save, in case of fire or other disaster, our people, of course, and also the sacred vestments and books and the relics we store there. From that heavy door to the path that leads to the airport, it's maybe forty meters through a grass field. High grass, uneven, soft surface. The key to that heavy door is hidden close by, just under the lock, because in a panic situation, every second counts. I can find it with my eyes closed."

"And the sacristy? Can Carla just walk in there?" Tim asked.

"It'll be locked. I'll be there at 1:00 a.m. to let her in. Liese can go straight from the guest building, unnoticed and avoiding the front entrance, around the mission proper, to that heavy door. She can wait there, outside, for Carla. We have a code to enter the sacristy. Only brothers, and not all of them, know it. We have gold stored in there, not just sacred items of high religious value, and ..." He suddenly stopped speaking.

My dear uncle. He said too much already, he knows. "But that means you would have to wake up in the middle of the night, Uncle. At your age ..." Silvia was concerned.

"No problem, *primita*, my little niece. I think it'll be just as hard for Liese as for me; we're about the same age. Right, Liese?"

"Huh. Yes, Father. I hope so. You look so young," Liese responded without batting an eye. Then she waited, her lips pressed together.

There was no response from the father.

He's so pure and innocent.

Tim looked at Silvia.

She broke the silence. "You don't want to give me the code, Uncle? And tell me where the key to the exit door is? I'll open the door for Carla and lock it after she's left with Liese. I won't copy the code of the sacristy door, and I'll give you the sheet back on Friday morning. I'll return the key to its place. I want to save you some good sleep."

"I can't do that, Silvita. Don't you worry about me."

Suddenly Liese sounded a little afraid for the first time since she left Santo Domingo. She sighed. "I hope I'll be able to find my way to that door in the dark. I must get there on time."

"I'll go with you this afternoon, Liese," Silvia proposed. She turned to her uncle and asked him, "Can you draw a little sketch so we can find the door from the outside? Liese and I can go and look for the place."

The father nodded.

Liese then also wondered whether, from the mission area, they would be able to hear or see the plane come in. "That would help us with the timing. We don't want to stand around at the strip for hours."

"We normally don't notice these little, very low-flying planes from the village at night," the father explained. "The strip lies in a heavily wooded area. But I'll make sure by phone that all is on schedule. I'll stay in touch with the airline operator in Santa Elena so we'll know for sure that the plane will be waiting."

Liese sighed. "Good. Thank you, Father." She turned to Silvia and said, "Great, we can explore that little walk together later today, with the father's sketch, but for the real thing, right after midnight, I'll go to the door below the sacristy by myself. No need for you or Tim to get in trouble on your way back; you don't have a gun. On my return, I can go straight from the strip to the front door of the guest building. I'll have to check out that route too. Well, my legs will have their work cut out."

Silvia noticed the father look at Liese's legs. *That skirt doesn't leave much to his imagination when she crosses her legs.* "I'll be waiting for your return in front of the guest building," Silvia said. "With Tim. Okay, Tim? We can give you signals with a flashlight."

Tim didn't look overly enthusiastic about Silvia's suggestion. He said, "Better yet, we can leave the light on in our room. You'll notice it from a good distance in the dark, Liese."

"Right, we'll leave the light on in our rooms," Silvia corrected.

Tim looked away.

"Good," Liese said. "I'll leave mine on too when I leave. Then I'll have two lights guiding me. Three, Silvia."

Carla showed a slight smile.

Silvia rolled her eyes and quickly said to Carla, "Do you feel all right with this, *amiga*?"

"I don't know how to thank you all, and especially Father Francesco," Carla said. "I feel like I'm asking too much."

They agreed to meet again the next day at 5:00 p.m., and the father said he would order the plane immediately.

CHAPTER 34

The day after Dr. Decker visited the hangars of the small airlines at the airport, Gonzalo's friend, Firmín, saw a big, heavyset gentleman enter his office. He presented himself as passenger Manuel Delgado. His passport seemed to be in good order.

A moment later, Firmín looked again at Mr. Delgado, attentively this time, and instantaneously thought of the man in Gonzalo's pictures. The ugly man started searching for something in his sizable travel bag that stood on the floor.

His shave is better than in the pictures, his bald head clean and smooth, but that ugly nose … Firmín asked, "Could I have your passport again for a second, Mr. Delgado? I forgot to note the expiration date for my log." *It must be a fake. Brand-new.*

"No problem, sir," Delgado answered.

Firmín studied the picture. *Shit, it's him.* "Let me check, Mr. Delgado. Emilio booked you a small Cessna, I see here on my screen."

"A six-seater," Delgado said.

He speaks funny too. First the lisped "sir," now the "six" and "seater." Bad teeth?

Firmín made a quick executive decision. Juan, the pilot booked for the Delgado flight, would have to be ill.

"An hour ago, your pilot asked me for a postponement of one

day, maybe one more," Firmín said as he shook his head and feigned disappointment and embarrassment. "You see, Mr. Delgado, we have a little problem. The pilot is a real pro but also a migraine sufferer. Is your timing flexible?"

"It isn't, sir. And this isn't a little problem. I've had many delays, and my mission is extremely important. I have the money right here. Even the extra for a good deal of waiting time."

"I'm not concerned about money, Mr. Delgado. I trust you're an honorable person, but there's nothing I can do. Our pool of pilots is stretched to the limit. Business isn't bad. Could I call you later tonight? Maybe I can work something out."

"The hell you'll work something out!" Delgado screamed. "A bunch of frigging lies you're telling me. On my way here, I was greeted by Juan in the hangar. He walked up to me. He'd already figured it out that I'm the passenger he's flying to Venezuela!" He stopped screaming, pulled a gun, and pointed it at Firmín. "Listen, mister, I know—I can see you're peeing in your pants. Good. Just don't wet my shoes. Hands up."

Firmín hit the button under his counter with his knee, his eyes trained on Delgado. *He didn't notice. I must keep him talking.* "I promise you, sir, you'll have your plane tomorrow. Juan didn't know he'd been assigned another plane tonight. We ..."

"And he's ill?" Delgado mocked.

"I misstated that. I didn't want to admit the screwup. I apologize." *I need another thirty seconds.* "Those bloody computers mess up everything nowadays, sir. We just made a change—"

"Stop babbling nonsense! You damn liar. Get me that plane right away. Speak! Get me the plane, I said. I can blow your brains out just like that." His words were ice-cold, almost whispered.

"If you do that, you won't be able to fulfill your mission, sir," Firmín tried to reason.

"None of your frigging business, you liar."

Through the glass door of his office, Firmín saw three security agents line up to rush in.

"You'd better put that gun down, Mr. Delgado. Put it away. You're surrounded," Firmín said as calmly as he could. He pointed with his index finger, his hands still up, at the door behind Delgado.

Delgado turned. He looked again at Firmín.

Pale. Furious. Helpless.

The agents rushed in, guns drawn and shouting, "Drop your gun and raise your hands!" Then they ordered them behind his back. They handcuffed him and took him away.

"I was just making the point I got cheated," the bandit kept arguing as he was led out, looking back at Firmín in anger. "I didn't lay a finger on anybody," he lamented.

Firmín took a last look at Delgado's impressive nose.

❋ ❋ ❋

After his eventful encounter with Mr. Delgado, Firmín needed a few minutes to get his heartbeat down. He took a cup of coffee, walked a few circles in his office, and then called Gonzalo.

"I think I had your beauty queen here at my counter, Gonzalo. Just a few warts, I noticed." He was still breathing fast but happy enough to joke.

"What? Our darling from the pictures? The one with the great legs?" Gonzalo joked.

"Yep. I'll bet my house on it. The security guys roped him in. You should call that politician. He'll be happy."

"Decker. Yes. Wait, Firmín. Roped in? What happened?"

Firmín explained, "I turned him down for his Cessna. He pulled a gun. I called the guys with my knee. Done. You know our system."

"Good. Great! Wait. One more thing. Did you hear a lisp?"

"A lisp? Yeah. I sure did. It got heavier after he pulled the gun."

It took a couple of seconds before Gonzalo calmly stated, "Between you and me, this guy is a murderer, Firmín."

"Sure? So I should tell the authorities? Or the guy who came? Decker?"

"Do me a favor; don't do anything. We're onto something really ugly. I'm going to make the connection right now to get this guy's ass in jail for life for murder, and we'll save another life in the process. Believe me. He's out to kill a woman in Venezuela."

"You're shitting me. Venezuela?"

"You caught the big tuna. You just stopped a murderer and maybe a murder," Gonzalo repeated.

"Let me know what's next, buddy. This is exciting."

"Of course. Got to run. Thanks! You're in on a big frigging deal."

❋ ❋ ❋

When Ricardo saw Gonzalo's name lighting up on his cell phone, he had a premonition something was up.

"Ricardo? Gonzalo here," the enthusiastic voice shouted over the phone. "I think we're right on his tail!"

"Hold on, Gonzalo." A jolt of adrenaline shot through Ricardo Lima's veins. He instinctively saved the Word text he was laboring on. He knew whom Gonzalo was shouting about. *Mora!* And the five days since Friday, when they first discussed the bandit, flashed by in a split second.

"Tell me, Gonzalo." Ricardo was nervous as hell.

"Firmín of Pilotos had the scum in his office minutes ago. It was the guy we talked about last week, Mora, for sure. Security carted the bandit off. He'd pulled a gun on Firmín. He'd threatened to kill Firmín because our friend wouldn't give him the Cessna ride he'd been promised."

"How did Firmín know it was him?"

"Well, he talked to me, still a bit shaken up, his words a little confusing, but he said it was exactly the guy in Dr. Decker's pictures. I'd shown Firmín the pictures Decker gave me. Firmín immediately thought of the guy as soon as the ugly bandit walked in. He described him to me over the phone. There wasn't any doubt this was Decker's man, he said: nose, voice, mean eyes, exactly the guy in the pictures. Firmín also heard the lisp. It's clear this was the bastard we're chasing. After I turned him down a few days ago, he tried his luck at Pilotos."

Ricardo was shaking his legs under his desk. He stopped this nervous movement, but he started again without realizing it. "So the bandit's locked up now. Does Decker know yet, Gonzalo?"

"Firmín wanted to call him right away, but I asked him not to—not yet. I used the words 'Venezuela' and 'murderer' and said that I had a friend who could put two and two together to get this creep in jail for life. He was happy enough to let me carry on. Who likes to openly frame a murderer? The creep may have friends who can get to anybody."

"Did you just ask me who'd want to frame the bastard? You're speaking to the man—me. I'm telling you it'll be my pleasure, Gonzalo. A real pleasure. I have my reasons. And I can see a couple more heads in the same frame you mentioned." Ricardo chuckled. "Not all of them that ugly, though."

"Good luck, buddy. Let me know."

Ricardo called Silvia, although he was sure she wouldn't answer. She didn't.

He sighed. *I'm stuck. For now. But it won't be long before the dam breaks. Then there will be a big flood of events. I see Barone crawling desperately, gasping for air, looking for a straw. And who else?* He got up from his chair, pushed his two arms in the air, fists clenched. Then he opened a box on his desk and lit a *Puro de Hostos* with deliberate slowness that allowed him to savor the moment.

CHAPTER 35

When Silvia met with Father Francesco, Carla, Tim, and Liese on Thursday at 5:00 p.m. to nail down the details of Carla's imminent departure, she felt bad as she saw the old man sad and embarrassed. He lamented that he had failed Carla, having been unable to fully guarantee her safety under his wings, that he had been a very imperfect host.

"But I'll go and check on you in Santa Elena often, Carla," he promised her, tears welling up in his eyes.

He never has had a son or daughter, and he has started projecting some of his caring instincts on her. He's losing a child, my dear, generous uncle.

"The operator of the small airline we work with in Santa Elena has assured me that a well-maintained plane will be waiting at the airport in Kavanayén from 1:45 on, for a punctual 2:00 a.m. departure. The two pilots will be sober and well-behaved ..." He shook his head and smiled lightly. "Of course."

That last promise shouldn't be necessary, my uncle thinks.

Father Francesco went on. "One of our Capuchin monks, I know him well, will be awaiting their new guest in Santa Elena from 2:00 a.m. on—early, to make sure. The monks in Santa Elena will pay the bill, and, Carla, you can repay at your convenience."

Silvia told the father and Carla that she, with Tim and Liese, had explored the routes. "From the guest building, around the mission, and to the door in the rear beneath the sacristy. And we've walked the route from that door to the airport, pretending to be out for a stroll."

"Don't count on any lights at the strip. The little shack at the strip itself won't be lighted," the father warned. "But hopefully the stars will be out to help Liese and Carla."

Carla listened calmly, her frown indicating she was paying attention to every detail. She didn't ask questions except for an estimate, again, of the time it would take from the door to the airport in the dark.

"Twenty minutes or less," Tim said.

"I told you that before, Carla," the father said, his face friendlier than his tone, "but I understand that you're getting nervous and a bit confused. And don't forget that under dark skies the walk can take a little longer."

"I must apologize for the inconvenience I'm causing with the horribly early departure time," Carla said.

"I'll be waiting for you, Carla," the father immediately responded, "in front of my confessional from 1:00 a.m. on. I'm sure you know where that is. You may have to give me a little tap on the shoulder when you get there."

"Again, I could come too, Uncle," Silvia suggested. "Keep you company."

"No, no. No need for that. I know you'll be dreaming sweet dreams by then, Silvita."

Liese smiled.

Tim nodded. He seemed to be in deep thought.

"Thank you so much, Father," Carla said. "And you, Silvia, Liese, and Tim, I don't know how to thank you. We'll be in touch, I know. From Santa Elena, I'll be able to call, I think."

"When we're getting close to Ciudad Guayana, on our way back in a couple of days, we'll have phone coverage," Silvia assured her. She gave Carla her new cell number.

Carla embraced her saviors and said good-bye to all except to Liese, who assured her she would be on time. She thanked Liese, turned brusquely, and walked away with quick, forceful steps.

Silvia rocked her head slowly. *What's the mystery she's leaving with?* She whispered to Tim, "I feel so sad."

CHAPTER

When on Thursday, April 9, Dr. Decker heard of the arrest of Mickey, José Mora, he immediately ordered the criminal records of the bandit. For his earlier visit to the hangars at the Las Américas airport, on Tuesday, he had had a sheet prepared that listed all of the man's misdeeds, but that document had been dressed up, enhanced by his subordinates for maximum effect. It had simply served as the crucial part of his sales pitch to the airline operators when he asked them to look out for the criminal. As a result, it contained several unsubstantiated charges that had been deleted from the official records later.

When he received the official documents on José Mora, he noted with dismay that they contained a disappointingly small number of convictions. Most of them were minor. *The bastard had, of course, the protection of our system. We are the ones who had almost everything against him dismissed or wiped off his record. Charles operates with the best lawyers and knows how to spread his bribes.*

When Charles had informed him about Mickey's pursuit of Carla, Decker had expressed his concern about the damage the bandit could do to their system. When he had heard about Mickey's arrest for a minor altercation, his first assumption, his gut reaction and hope, had been that the man's rap sheet would be enough to keep him in prison for a long time. But now, having read the official documents, Dr.

Decker feared rough Mickey would soon be back on the street and able to continue his dreadful pursuit of Carla.

I must keep him away from her. Decker decided it was time to talk sense into Mickey. He asked Charles to visit him in prison.

For a person like Charles, with connections and money, it wasn't a big deal to secure a discussion with Mickey, even without using the power of his ties to Decker. A letter from the powerful politician would of course have opened every prison gate for Charles, but it was better to keep the big name out of the picture if at all possible.

He soon found out that getting Mickey to act reasonably and to promise a halt to his pursuit of Carla was quite another undertaking. As he sat across a little metal table from Charles, complete in striped uniform, unshaven, and his nose uglier than ever with sunrays from a ceiling window shining right on it, Mickey looked cocky and self-assured. Defiant.

"Mickey, listen," Charles said after a long back and forth, leaning close to him over the table and trying to be friendly. "You pretend you have the goods on me and my partners. You're wrong. We know how to take care of things, wipe our slates clean. That's no secret for you." *But he* does *have stuff on us, in his head, on all of us in the system. It's going to be an uphill battle to convince him, unless we tighten the screws on him—and the sooner, the better.*

"You're the first one whose name I'll put in the paper," Mickey hissed.

Charles felt like hit by lightning. *My God, he's coming after me. But I'm just an instrument of the rich and the powerful, like Barone, who caused all this trouble.* He felt goose bumps on his arms but managed to state, "That would be unfair, Mickey. I just did what Barone wanted me to do. He was livid with Flores. That loudmouth had to be shut up, or we'd all be in trouble. Barone was right about that. And it was Barone."

Mickey sat back, a look of disdain on his face. Then he unloaded. "Bullshit!" He pounded the table. "You're a bunch of liars, all of you—Barone and you and the rest. I'll get the ones who got me in this trouble, all of you. You bastards! I'm paying for your greed! I had to help you fill your pockets. It's my ass for your yachts! I'm done with you."

Charles had to leave empty handed. He called Dr. Barone.

"Our system is in danger, Doctor. I don't see any solution but shutting Mickey up for good. He's livid. He'll either shoot Carla or start shooting his mouth off about us. In both cases, he'd destroy our system."

"But he's locked up now. Decker must have quite a record on him. He can threaten to keep him there till he rots away."

Charles felt dejected and responded, "Not so. Decker doesn't have much. We've protected Mickey too well in the past—too well for our own good. Got his slate wiped clean too often. He can play games with us. He can be out any day, he figures."

"Shit. Yes, we protected the bastard too well. Okay, tell me how we get out of this mess." Barone sounded as if Charles had applicable routine suggestions for the case lying around in his drawer.

Charles lowered his voice and said, "Doctor, Carla has disappeared already. Nobody knows exactly where she is, except probably her family and your Dr. Silvia. We could make that disappearance permanent, quietly. Few would notice if we do it properly. And Mickey would calm down overnight. End of story."

"Hmm. But we must find her. Isn't that what Mickey's trying to do? Find her and then …"

He's afraid to speak the word.

"What would Decker suggest?" Barone went on, his voice weakening.

"You're right. We need his support for this. I'll get him on the speakerphone. He'll understand, but he won't like the call. But we have to."

Charles made the connection.

"Are you guys nuts? Killing Carla? Another murder?" Decker

screamed before Charles even had had the time to speak two sentences explaining the logic for the proposal.

"We thought—"

"You didn't think enough, Charles," Decker shouted back. "She's gone anyway. She may never show up in this country again. She must be too scared for that. She'll hook up with a hunk of a Venezuelan or a Brazilian, and she'll be gone. All we have to do is to make sure Mickey doesn't harm her and create a mess. He has two choices: he can prefer to be taken out by us, or he can lay off her, leave her alone with her new guy on whatever continent."

"But her parents could raise hell if their daughter doesn't show up in a while," Charles tried to argue.

"No. They wouldn't. Mickey got them scared stiff when he went for their phones. They'll play smart, let their daughter live in peace. If they just know she's okay, they're okay. That's how parents are. I don't want to hear about another murder. I never should have let anyone talk me into the Flores case. A stupid mistake. Yours, Barone, in the first place. You hear me, Barone?"

Barone coughed and said, "Yes."

"So what do we do about Mickey? He may get out in no time," Charles lamented. "And I know he doesn't trust us. Even if he agrees to the deal you propose, laying off, he'll feel that sooner or later he'll get a knife in his back anyway. He says he wasn't born yesterday."

"Charles, whose job do you think it is to handle that? Not mine. Is that clear?" Decker yelled.

"Yes, sir. I'll get back to you."

Why is he so scared of liquidating a meddlesome girl in a faraway country? It's a neat solution. I'll never understand these "scholars."

CHAPTER 37

Friday morning at 1:00 a.m., Father Francesco sat in the church, waiting for Carla. He wouldn't need that tap on the shoulder he had mentioned to her; his sadness kept him from dozing off as he prayed for her in front of his confessional. He checked his watch every minute or so. Now and then he slowly turned his upper body and head to spare his arthritic neck as he looked behind him. *Carla will be walking in soon from the back.*

As the minutes kept ticking by, he became slightly irritated. *I'm punctual. She should be too. I'm helping her,* he fretted. *She should feel responsible. She's not that young. Miss Liese will be waiting in the dark, all alone. But with her gun.*

At 1:10, he decided to go to Carla's room. *If she shows up here in the church before I get back, she'll have to wait a minute. Not my fault.*

The father ran through the halls to Carla's cell, as fast as his weakened quadriceps and his garb allowed him, but slowly enough not to make unusual noise that would alert the guard. His heart was pounding. *The pilot may already have landed in Kavanayén.* The airline had told him the plane would be early.

As he arrived, panting and perspiring, he knocked on Carla's door. There was no response. He knocked again. She didn't open the door. He was going to knock again but decided against it. *I don't want to awaken any sister. I must have missed Carla.* He rushed back to the church. She wasn't there. He called Carla softly. "Carla? Carla?" All he heard was two weak echoes. He quickly checked the confessionals, hastily lifting the curtains that shield confessants. He opened some of the little confessor doors. *She may have fallen asleep hiding.* There was no Carla.

He rushed back to his cell and took the master key from the wall next to his desk, his hand shaking. He ran again to Carla's cell. He found it empty, except for some food rests. Her bed had been slept on. He saw no luggage or clothes hanging on the chair. A towel was wet. *My Lord. And I can't ask anybody for help.*

He locked the door of the cell and hurried back to the church. He had to calm down to remember the code for the sacristy. He stumbled down the steps to the heavy door, opened it in a panic, saw the sky, and found Liese. He was out of breath.

"Where's Carla, Father?" she asked, sounding nervous and looking concerned.

"Don't know," the father panted. "Didn't show up in church. Not in her room either."

Liese checked her watch. "It's 1:25. I heard dogs barking. I'm scared. Why do they bark so loud during the night?"

"They must smell your presence, Miss Liese."

"They sound pretty far away, Father. Where could Carla be? Did she change her mind? Or … I have too many questions. Quick. We must talk to Tim and Silvia."

They stormed to the guest building. As they got close, they saw three lights on in three rooms: Liese's, Tim's, and Silvia's.

They're already waiting for Liese's return from the strip.

Liese opened her door and offered the father a drink of juice. She said, "Let me fetch the youngsters. Half a minute. Just relax, Father. We'll solve the mystery. I'll knock on both doors. Please, lie down on my bed. You must be exhausted." *He'll rest with my perfume.*

❀ ❀ ❀

Silvia woke up. She heard Tim rushing to the door and veered up. She didn't have time to grab a towel to cover herself before he opened the door, a towel around his hips. She saw Liese gesturing and talking to him.

"Hurry—put some clothes on. The father is in my room. Carla didn't show up," she blurted.

"She overslept," Tim stated and shook his head.

"Not at all. She's not in her room," Liese snapped.

"Huh?"

"Get dressed, guys, and wipe the lipstick off, Tim. Father Francesco's in a panic. We must act. No time to waste. She may be in grave danger. Hurry."

In Liese's room, they deliberated frantically.

Silvia tried to put her emotions aside, face facts, and look cool-headedly at the possible scenarios with her friends.

"All her stuff is gone, Silvia. You saw it, Father," Tim said. "Doesn't look much like a hurried abduction."

"Maybe it wasn't a hurried one, Tim. It may have been well organized. They may have wanted to wipe away all traces and cleaned up the room after …" Silvia couldn't finish her sentence and started sobbing.

"She may have left voluntarily. Or somebody tricked her into … what? Romance?" Liese ventured.

"No," Father Francesco responded. "She didn't run away voluntarily with anybody. She didn't know anybody outside the mission to run away with."

"Except Omar from the restaurant," Tim interjected.

"Come on, Tim. Omar? No way," Liese argued, frowning and tilting her head.

Silvia couldn't help thinking, *Are Liese and I the only ones who noticed that belly protruding over Omar's belt?*

Liese turned to the father and said, "I shouldn't mention this,

Father, but I will. Could somebody within the mission have talked her into leaving? For whatever good reason, and with the best intentions, to save her?"

The father sounded indignant and breathed hard as he retorted, "Miss Liese, I know my flock. Any well-intentioned plan would have been discussed with me. I know that. And no other kind of plan could sprout within the sacred walls of the mission; the Lord wouldn't let it take hold in any of our minds or hearts." He looked around. His eyes dared his friends to disagree.

She went too far. But nobody says a word.

Liese continued, "Let's get practical, Father. I know it's early, even for you, but I think you should have every nook and cranny in the mission checked. And maybe we could go with you to talk to a number of villagers you feel we can awaken at this ghastly hour. Should we start with Omar? He's the only one who might, maybe, have talked about her, right? It's a big maybe. But you never know."

"It will be necessary to talk to many, and certainly to him. He knows much of the ins and outs of the village, as I do." Father Francesco sighed.

"Hold it for a second. Father, one more time before we start the search: I *did* hear dogs barking," Liese said. "That keeps bothering me. What did they want to tell me? They made me shiver as I waited for Carla at the door. Did they really bark because of me? Or were other people out there? Bandits?"

Father Francesco shrugged. "Who knows why they barked? I hear them almost every night. It could have been for a cat or a stray dog."

"If you say so." Liese didn't sound entirely satisfied. She sighed, "Okay then."

The father hurriedly dictated to Silvia a short list of some of his most trusted parishioners and explained where they lived. Then he told her he would rush back home to organize the search inside the mission. "Go now. Knock on doors. I will join you as soon as I can. Please hurry," he begged her as he stepped out, leaving the door open.

Silvia and Tim threw some more clothes on and, list in hand, went with Liese into the village. Twenty minutes later, the father joined them.

"I saw light. I knew immediately where you were," he said, panting, but looking happy he found them. Between 2:00 and 4:00 a.m., they saw a lot of Kavanayén sleepwear, faces with dentures missing, and long stubbles as small doors of little houses opened. Silvia discovered smells and facial expressions she was unfamiliar with. But she didn't hear of any trace of Carla or of any stranger heard or seen leaving the village during the night or even since early evening. And she was assured again and again that no villager would ever abduct or hurt a guest of Father Francesco.

At 4:00 a.m., Silvia, her friends, and the father were back in the mission, where a brother awaited Father Francesco. The young man seemed crushed by the disappearance of Carla.

"We looked everywhere, Father. I awoke even Sister Cornelia."

"She's ninety-five," the father explained.

"We checked the pond. We looked between the benches in the church; she might have gone there and fainted. We shouted her name everywhere. She never answered. We don't ..." His voice broke.

"You go in peace, Brother Marcus," Father Francesco said soothingly. "I know you have made your best effort. She's in the hands of the Lord till he lets us find her. Thank you."

The brother was in tears as he bowed and left.

The father sent another of his monks to the airport with a message telling the pilots to return to Santa Elena. Silvia then suggested the father join her and Tim and Liese in the SUV around 7:00 a.m. to start a search on the road to Luepá. It was all they could think of as something they could do. Villagers could search the immediate surroundings of Kavanayén and the village itself, being familiar with them.

By noon, they still had no trace of Carla.

CHAPTER

Aboard the Beechcraft Bonanza aircraft, Carla stretched her legs as best she could. It was getting close to 2:00 a.m. on Friday the tenth. The plane had been in the air for almost an hour, and the ride had become smooth. The pilot informed her that he had radioed his flight plan to the airline operator in Santo Domingo. She was exhausted. *This Coca-Cola Classic tastes heavenly.* She was accompanied by the pilot and by two guards sent from Santo Domingo for her protection by her good friend. He was the one who also had arranged her quick and trouble-free travel to Ciudad Guayana a little over two weeks ago, and the car to Kavanayén.

He didn't like it that I kept calling him Ana during my call from the confessional, she remembered with pleasure.

Although the pressurization in the plane was weak, she felt good, a little lightheaded, and also proud about the way she had made it to the plane.

She had waited for Marcus in the confessional from ten minutes before midnight. She had tucked her bag in the penitent's space, behind the curtain, and she had waited on the confessor's bench inside, where she had spent hours and hours with Marcus over the last two weeks.

When he showed up at midnight, she said right away, "I have a big surprise for you, my love. We're leaving right now."

He froze, eyes bulging, mouth open, and stuttered, "What? Right now? I have nothing with me. Not even a toothbrush or a Bible. No change of clothes." Then he stared at her jeans.

She saw the fear in his eyes. "Don't you worry, darling. It's all taken care of. Ana's great. She's planned it all very meticulously, and you and I are going to be just fine."

"Without papers?"

"Sure. Our friend will meet us when we arrive, and she'll help us sail through the formalities. She can get you new papers, no problem. I mean it. She has the connections."

"Carla, that sounds so easy …" Marcus slid a small distance away from her, looking apprehensive.

"Because it is, my man. It is when you have the right friends." Carla laughed to reassure him, and she put her finger on his cheek before she reached over and kissed him. "Don't you worry, *amor*. Just think what it will be like. We'll have beautiful children. We'll buy a house; I have the money."

"Did Ana send a car?"

"No car. An airplane. The landing strip is twenty minutes from here, I understand."

"An airplane? You never told me."

"I couldn't, darling. I was sworn to secrecy. It's our only chance to escape together."

"But they'll see us walk out. The guard may be awake …"

"I'm sure my smart *caballero* will know of some secret exit, no?" She pressed her body against his and felt it shaking.

"I can't show you that, Carla. I'm bound by secrecy," he stammered and kept shaking his head.

I'll bluff my way out of this. "Okay, then we'll have to take the front door."

"I can't go there." He sounded like he was begging for mercy.

"Yes, you can. And I need my rock with me," she pleaded, her hands searching his hips.

Marcus looked torn and still apprehensive when he said, "No, no.

Not the front door. I can lead you to an exit. Follow me and be very quiet."

"Oh, Marcus. Thanks so much. I knew you loved me. Can you take my bag? It's heavy."

"Yes, and the stairs are steep. Come with me." He stepped out of the confessional and picked up the bag from the confessant bench behind the curtain as she watched.

"Stairs, you said?"

"I'll show you. Be very quiet."

They went to the door of the sacristy. He put in the code. Carla acted surprised. They entered. Then he guided her to a narrow stairway that led down to a heavy door. He found a key and opened the door. He asked Carla to hold it open. He lifted her bag and put it on the grass outside. He put the key back in its spot, stepped out with Carla, turned briefly to look at the stairs inside, closed his eyes, and pulled the door shut. They were staring at the stars and a field of very high grass. Carla feigned complete amazement and kissed Marcus. She whispered, "You're unbelievable, Marcus. Won't the bag be too heavy to carry so far? I can help. But I know you have strong muscles. Of course I know," she whispered as she ran her hands over his arms and thighs as he stood ready to lift the bag again. "Shall we go?"

Marcus couldn't speak and didn't move.

He's scared to death, but he's also mortally in love with me.

He turned again and looked at the main mission building and up at the church and the sky. She saw sadness in his face. Then he grabbed Carla's bag and started walking toward the airport without saying a word. Carla's jeans and shoes protected her from the sharp grass, but she saw Marcus having trouble in his sandals and bare legs under the habit. She heard dogs barking. *Wishing their farewells.*

She threw one arm around Marcus's waist as he labored with the heavy bag, and she kept whispering her thanks and encouragement.

"Soon we can start our new life," she said, pushing her hair against his face while they walked.

When they arrived at the strip, there was no living soul in sight, but a small plane sat in a corner, lights off. As Carla and Marcus got close, two men emerged from the plane, moving slowly, with long, deliberate steps.

"Carla Fuentes?" one of the men asked and stared at Marcus.

"Yes," Carla responded. She showed him her passport.

"Ready? We've been waiting for forty minutes."

"Thank you. I have my friend here. My boyfriend. My fiancé. He's going with me. He'll get papers in Santo Domingo. It's been arranged. He and I will spend all the days of our lives together, my Marcus and I."

"Hmm. Great. Except tonight," one of the men said, his eyes on Marcus's garb.

"What? Why not?"

"Can't do it."

"Huh? Why? You have room in the plane. I know this kind of plane," Carla exclaimed.

"You're right; we have room. But we fueled up in Ciudad Guayana before landing here, and we're very heavy on fuel now. We have an unusually long stretch ahead. We're not allowed more than four persons. We expected you only. And you guys have quite a bag. Another ninety pounds?"

"Unbelievable!" Carla said. "We have a bad misunderstanding. I can't leave my love behind!"

"Your choice. You can go back to your bed. We've already been paid for the roundtrip," the man said to Carla and looked at Marcus as well.

Carla turned to Marcus and said, "Marcus, this is terrible. I have to go. My life is at stake. I must ask you to come and join me soon. I'll give you a phone number where you can call me, and I'll be waiting for you in my country with open arms. We'll be happy forever, together. You can make it back into the mission unseen, right?" *That won't be easy, but he'll crawl his way in.*

She saw Marcus's face telling a tale of two forces. One two-fisted force pushed him toward her, into her arms and to Santo Domingo, where he would never find her. Another force pulled him back to the peace and security of the mission. *He still doesn't see I'm lying.*

Trembling with disappointment, fear, and relief, Marcus said, "I'll do as you say, Carla. Your safety is more important than anything else to me. I'll join you soon." He stared at his feet.

She took a small sheet of paper, wrote a number down on it, handed it to Marcus, and told him, softly, "Here is the number where you can reach me, Marcus. You have access to the satellite phone. Call me anytime. Please call."

Carla looked at the men, who checked their watches.

Marcus looked dazed.

"I must go now, Marcus," Carla whispered. "Be careful on the way back. The dogs will wonder what happened. I love you." She looked him in the eyes as she spoke. *I bet he's relieved I'm out of his life. He'll wipe the slate clean and start all over again, with a new stylus. But he and the bench in his confessional will miss me and feel cold at midnight.* She kissed him on the cheek.

Marcus left, silent. He walked, head down, shoulders pulled up, and then started running in the direction of the mission. He disappeared in the night.

As she now sat back and stretched her legs, she felt proud and guilty.

"Well, we've got you some extra leg room, lady," one of the men said and then laughed. "A good act, I'd say. You got your luggage handled free of charge."

"You guys played the game well. Thanks again. For me it was a little hard, but I had to. I prepared this for two weeks. I had to build the foundation. It held."

The man nodded.

He nods but doesn't understand. She felt rascal-like inner pleasure as she thought back and conveniently rationalized, *Marcus had the time of his life in the confessional. I know that for a fact.* Then she mused, *My first trip ever down that lane with a monk. An inexperienced one, but a fast learner. One with a great body loaded with testosterone. He sure made the clock tick faster for me at the mission. And his heart too.*

CHAPTER

Friday afternoon, Silvia had to console her uncle. He kept finding reasons why he should feel guilty for Carla's disappearance. The man was in tears. Silvia had put her right hand on his left forearm as she listened to him with Tim and Liese.

"In a few hours, somebody will bring me the news that she's been found in a ravine. Maybe I'll have to look at a picture of her dead body," the old man lamented.

"Dear uncle, don't blame yourself. You did all you could. We all tried our best. I know she's not dead. She'll still need our support. Maybe we still can give it. Let's see what we can do for her."

"You don't understand, Silvita. Somebody abducted her. The grass at the door beneath the sacristy looks all trampled. It can't just have been from Liese, who waited there for Carla and me. I saw steps farther out, toward the airport path."

"Easy, Father," Tim answered. "We reconnoitered the area to prepare Liese. We trampled that grass."

"No, Tim. The trampling was fresh. Not from the day before," the father insisted.

Silvia looked at Liese, soliciting help with her eyes.

"Father, I waited there a long time around 1:00 a.m.," Liese said calmly. "You came down late, and I sauntered back and forth a lot in the grass. My feet must have done it. I was getting nervous."

Father Francesco looked at Liese's feet. He did not look convinced and kept shaking his head and sighing.

Silvia took her hand off her uncle's arm, stood up straight, tucked her white blouse neatly into her jeans, and said, "The best we can do is get to a place from where we can take action. If Carla's not here, there is nothing we can do for her from here; we'll be more useful in any place other than Kavanayén."

Father Francesco looked up. He sounded disappointed but also relieved as he said, "You're right, Silvita. Kavanayén has done all it could. You should move on." Now his tears flowed.

Silvia sat down again next to him. He grabbed her hand.

On Saturday, Silvia, Tim, and Liese started their trip back from Kavanayén to Ciudad Guayana around 7:00 a.m. Father Francesco had provided them with food and drinks that would last well beyond Kilómetro 88, the point from where normal facilities could be found.

Silvia noticed that Liese had become quite an expert, and a proud one, in navigating the maze of huge potholes, slippery slopes, little shaky bridges not worth the name, and low-hanging tree branches.

"It's child's play compared to what we in Switzerland have to go through sometimes to get to the ski slopes," Liese said, acting as if on the trip down to Kavanayén she hadn't been scared stiff and hadn't screamed a few times.

They made it to Luepá and the main road north without accident, mechanical failure, or flat tires. They had decided to stay in a hotel in Ciudad Guayana and proceed to Caracas and Santo Domingo the next day, Sunday.

When they were about twenty kilometers north of Luepá, they all switched on their cell phones and tried their luck. Liese was the first one to have coverage with her T-Mobile, but she didn't want to let go of "her" steering wheel, although she saw right away she had a ton of messages. "We'll have to take a break soon. I'll wait till then," she advised.

A few minutes later, Codetel came alive, and Silvia was again connected to civilization. Scrolling down, she immediately found a voicemail from Ricardo Lima. It had been sent just Friday morning. It said, "Ricardo here. Friday the tenth. I cannot connect with you on your new phone. Call me as soon as you can. Have been shaking up things here. Will get the bastards. Bye."

"I must make a call. We must. It'll be an important one, I think," Silvia exclaimed, excited. "Ricardo sounded really upbeat. I wonder what plan he hatched."

A minute later, Liese pulled off the road under a couple of trees offering a little shade. She said she was anxious to check her correspondence too.

Once out of the Montero, Silvia dialed Ricardo's number and switched her speakerphone on.

"Ricardo Lima. *Dime*," they heard.

"Ricardo, Silvia here, with Tim. You remember him. And my friend Liese's here too. We're standing under a couple of big trees, in the shade, and my friends are listening in," Silvia said.

"Oh! Good. I'm glad I found you. Or you found me. Finally. Where are you?"

"In Venezuela."

"Venezuela! Well, that figures."

"On our way back home from Kavanayén."

"I understand."

Maybe he thinks we gave up. "No, you don't, Ricardo. We didn't abandon Carla. We were together with her in the village, but about thirty-six hours ago, she disappeared from her hiding place. We have no clue, but we're 99 percent sure she's not in the village anymore."

"I did say I understand, right? I knew you would head back soon!" Ricardo boasted.

"What? You knew?"

"Yes. Listen well. Gonzalo, my partner in my little airline here in Santo Domingo, keeps an eye on suspicious passengers. I asked him. Our maintenance guy came in around 5:30 yesterday morning and saw a good-looking lady getting off a Beechcraft. From what he told me about the woman—'a ten,' he said—I conclude it could have been Carla. Two sturdy guys were with her, apparently armed. They stepped in a dark green Jaguar that sat waiting in an unauthorized zone, hidden under the trees. It sped away."

"And that was of course Carla," Tim commented, sounding more than skeptical, almost mocking.

"Cool it, Tim. Hear me out." Ricardo sounded irritated. He went on, "I happen to know somebody else with a dark green Jaguar. Somebody with clout, who can park his car unpunished in prohibited zones. An official, high up there. His name is Dr. Decker, of the Ministry of Justice."

"And then?"

"Well, Tim, I wasn't born yesterday, but I got intrigued and went to the guys handling that Beechcraft. The plane was from Servicios Generales. I know these guys, we're all friends, and I was told by a technician that the plane had come in from somewhere in Venezuela. The man didn't remember the name of the place, but I said, 'Kavanayén?' and he nodded. See why this old fart got excited and wanted to talk to you guys? We must put our heads together and connect some dots."

"Let's get together as soon as we get back, Ricardo," Silvia suggested, suddenly worried about higher-ups, Decker or others, listening in on Ricardo. "This is an open line. We must meet face-to-face. We should be back tomorrow night. How about first thing Monday morning in the Santo Domingo Hotel, in the garden? No listening devices there. Eight? Meet in the lobby first?"

"Great. Well, I just knew it." Ricardo sounded like a winner. "Quickly, one more thing. This Decker is chasing our bandit for some reason. That scum's real name is Mora, but he calls himself Delgado. Mora's the guy Decker is after. 'Delgado' sits in prison. I'll explain later. Too much."

"Quite a load, Ricardo. See you Monday. Careful," Silvia said, wanting to cut the conversation short. *I know how naked you feel when you've been hacked. And it can get worse than that.*

"Okay," Liese said when the call had ended, "let's call this a pit stop. The bushes are low but dense and reasonably dry here. Inviting! I'll be back in a minute."

Tim and Silvia laughed.

Then Tim said, "Those Swiss are efficient. I should be able to find a French facility somewhere here too." He disappeared before Silvia could object.

❀ ❀ ❀

It was still a long way from the shade under those trees to Ciudad Guayana.

Nature and the Gran Sabana offered the Montero passengers a spectacular visual treat, but Silvia kept discussing the situation with Tim, trying to put two and two together regarding Carla.

Tim opined, "Ricardo's right. He may be on to something. Strangely, this Decker apparently shows major interest in a creep like Delgado, or whatever his name is, Mora, who's chasing Carla. And Decker may well be the one who had Carla picked up. She must be the reason why he's tracking down Delgado. How many 'Carlas' can Delgado be chasing? This Decker may be a player in the Barone system."

"We don't know that, Tim. And I wouldn't call it 'the Barone system,' although he had, no doubt, some involvement in the death of Luis Flores," Silvia commented. "The network may be much bigger; we may just see the tip of the iceberg. There may be other Carlas out there. In Puerto Plata or Santiago, or who knows where. Crime breeds more crime, and always more to keep covering up. The system may be national or even wider."

She kept quiet for a while, allowing Tim to enjoy the scenery. But her mental gears kept spinning. *A Mafia offering a concierge service without a cancelation clause for a "little" fee that comes due every month till you die, and increases as reliably as the sun rises in the morning. Extortion. A Mafia enforcing its rules brutally. With support from high up.* It was gradually taking a clearer shape in her mind.

"Tim the tourist" now came back to the business at hand. "We'll have to get things confirmed and explained by Ricardo first, and I think then we must get in Decker's face. Confront the man to find out who he actually is. He'll certainly seem to have clean hands, because, I'm sure, he uses good gloves. But it's of course also possible that he keeps his hands clean without the help of gloves."

Liese jumped in to say, "Yes, Tim. Good tactics. We tell him we know he picked Carla up."

"Or we think we know he had her picked up."

"No, Tim, we must do real bluffing," Liese insisted. "None of that sissy 'we think' stuff."

"And then?" Silvia wanted to know.

"He may laugh, entirely relaxed, and say we're barking up the wrong tree. Or he may fall off his chair, floored. But he also could, guilty or not, be really smart, not tip his hand, and ask us for help to find Carla," Tim figured.

"And can we ask him *why* he's spending his energy so generously to help Carla?" Silvia wondered.

Tim started teasing, "I think I already know why. I have a hunch. A very simple one." Tim winked at Liese and Silvia and said, "Don't you, Silvia? You do. But I also know most of the fifteen other reasons he could recite."

Silvia was slightly annoyed and asked, "Is that your way of saying you don't have a clue, Tim? I'm not sure either, but what I do know is that he'll give us five smooth, pious, emotional, convincing reasons, and we'll still know nothing. He must be good at that kind of talk. I say, as you do, that before we bluff, we must talk face-to-face with Ricardo. He may be taking some of his wishes for reality. Let's keep our feet on the ground; Ricardo's anger may be a bad guide."

As they reached Kilómetro 88, Silvia suggested they take a break. "We can take gas and stock up on drinks there."

"I really wonder what superman Decker is like," Liese said as she

189

sat in the car with Silvia while Tim had the tank filled up. She fixed her sunglasses and took a look at herself in the mirror.

"His *looks* are great," Silvia said.

"The way you guys talk about him, he sounds like the real thing." Liese giggled.

Around 5:00 p.m., Silvia visited the computer room in the Hotel Figueroa in Ciudad Guayana, where she and her friends had checked in around 4:00 p.m., and went through her e-mail. She found a message from Carla. *Sent two hours ago.* She felt goose bumps as she read it.

> *Dear Silvia, thank you for all your help. I can't explain now, but I had to take steps to save my life. Please accept apologies for my rudeness. I'm safe now but can't tell you where I am. Don't worry about me any longer. Don't try to find me and help me; your efforts would endanger me. Do not respond to this message; I will cancel the Hotmail address I'm using as soon as I've sent this message. Please offer your uncle my sincere thanks and tell him I'm sorry. Un abrazo. Carla.*

She's alive, but … Silvia read the message again, happy but stunned, and trying to figure out who her friend Carla was. Soon she felt extremely disappointed. She tried to anticipate Tim's and Liese's reaction to this message. *They'll think I'm this credulous, naïve, bleeding-heart little ditz begging to be duped. I'll talk to Carla's parents as soon as I get back to Santo Domingo. They may resolve the mystery for me.*

Tim scratched his head as Silvia briefed him and Liese. "Can't we e-mail Ricardo? Maybe he can clear it all up. We'll be racking our brains for nothing till Monday morning. Can't we call Carla's parents now?"

"Tim," Silvia said soothingly, as if kindly reprimanding a little boy, "why do you want to keep putting your head under the guillotine? E-mail is an open book in the DR. You should know that by now. No?"

Tim frowned. "Hmm. But we should try the parents."

Silvia shook her head. "They won't say anything over the phone. They went through enough already, and they're not done, with Carla gone. If I visit them alone on Monday, or maybe tomorrow night, I may have a chance to hear something. A chance."

Tim rolled his eyes but then said, throwing his hands up, "*Merde,* I need a beer. I wonder whether Liese and I should set up a joint listening, hacking service in the DR. Good business."

He doesn't have the faintest idea where this leads. Neither do I. But my friend lives. At least that's what she, or somebody else who knows me and her, wrote me.

They all went down and soon were looking for inspiration on the bottoms of their beer glasses.

"A wild dream tonight will help," Liese declared with an encouraging but not very convincing smile. She then waved to the waiter, winked at him, and put three fingers up.

Tim didn't object.

Silvia didn't either. *Wild dream? Anyway, in a decent bed tonight. Decent?* She looked at Tim from the corner of her eye.

CHAPTER

At six o'clock on Monday morning, Charles drove his steel-reinforced Explorer to the gate of the Santa Ana prison, not far from the Santo Domingo airport. He had to visit Mickey again, who had been there for five days.

He knew he would have no problem getting access to the prison at this early hour because he regularly paid off the officer on duty. That officer clung to his early shift so he could continue his assistance to good citizens who happened to also be generous.

Charles asked the guard for his friend, the officer, who was expecting him and showed up within minutes. Together they walked across the drab and dirty outside yard within the small square prison complex. Garbage, plastic bottles, cigarette stubs, and matches littered the place, which had a basketball hoop without a net and smelled of urine. They quickly proceeded to a small room adjacent to the officer's.

Charles waited nervously, searching for the right position on one of the two rickety chairs in the room. His friend had brought him a cup of sugary coffee and had left to fetch Mickey. This was not an easy morning for Charles. He had a hard message for his friend Mickey, one that he had lost an entire weekend on rehearsing.

He put his hands on his knees to control his legs.

The officer knocked on the door and swung it open. He signaled that he would be in his office next door.

A sleepy Mickey walked in and grumbled, "Morning." He looked bored. "You're here again. Must like the place," he said, his eyes on the table instead of Charles. "What's up?"

"Well, Mickey, as it often happens in life—"

"Spare me the bullshit. What do you want? I'm still sleepy. What do you offer?"

"Listen, Mickey, I mean well with you—"

"I said no bullshit."

Charles saw his speech go out the window. He had lost control. He tried to be friendly and said, "Please sit down. We'll help you leave the country. All will be fine."

"And how do I make a living?" Mickey didn't sit down.

"We'll pay you."

"Till I'm a hundred? You think I believe you? Trust you? I know you wish I'd shoot myself."

"Come on. You can't mean that after all we've gone through together."

"I'm a threat to you and the system and to the big shots, much bigger than you." He pointed at Charles, his voice loud and angry. "You know damn well I'll be out of this dump in no time. I'll do what I want. And I have the goods on you and your buddies and masters." His eyes delivered the exclamation marks as he looked down on his visitor.

Charles let Mickey's rage run its course and gathered his thoughts. *I'll have to get nasty.* He stood up and whispered, his head inches away from Mickey's, "Look, you know what kind of place you're in. All kinds of scum around you. Half a million pesos will buy me a silent bullet in your head while you sleep. Or a fire in your locked cell. Or a spoon of rat poison in your bowl of soup. Or just a couple of strong arms to strangle you, if you prefer that. Get it?" He snapped his fingers to show how easy it was to get rid of Mickey, the sitting duck.

"Look Charles, Mister, I have friends too. Don't underestimate me. And I can send messages to the press within half an hour. *You* get it?" He snapped his fingers too, much more forcefully than Charles.

He pressed his lips together under his huge nose and stared intensely at him.

Charles tried once more. "Mickey, let's be reasonable. Let's say I went too far. Nobody means you harm."

"And I don't believe a frigging word that comes out of your mouth. I'm done with you. I won't say one more word." He sat down.

Charles knocked on the door. His friend, the officer, came in. Charles looked at him and shook his head, disgusted. The officer nodded. He told Mickey to get up and called for a guard to lead the prisoner back to his cell.

Charles had to leave empty handed again. He said to his friend the officer, "We must keep an eye on him. If he seems to prepare for an escape, act as if you're not noticing anything, and alert me. We let him go, follow him, and give him ten minutes before we chase him off a cliff or into a wall. Or a bullet, if necessary."

"Who are the 'we' in this game, Charles?" the officer asked. "What's the deal?"

"Well, we're all together in this, of course. I'll pay you well. You should manage the 'escape,' and I take care of things once he's out on the street. I've hired a promising backup chap for Mickey. He'll be glad to take on that matter as his baptism of fire. He'll pass with flying colors," Charles chuckled.

"And if Mickey doesn't make preparations to flee?"

"Plan B could be as simple as leaving his door unlocked or putting him to work close to the front door. If things go really wrong, if he still doesn't flee, we have other ways."

"Let me think about that, Charles."

"During the night, you can do all you want. I know. Nobody around. And night-work pays overtime, right?"

"Got you. How much?"

Charley was a little irritated. "We've known each other for a while, haven't we? We'll take good care of you. Trust me."

As he walked back to his cell, Mickey's legs were weak, and he admitted to himself he was scared. *They'll kill me. I don't have friends here. Whom can I trust? I shouldn't have threatened to go public.* He felt like vomiting and started looking for something he could make into a rope.

CHAPTER

"You're spilling coffee on my white pants!" Silvia yelled at Tim as she suddenly felt burning hot drops on her thigh and jumped up.

Ten minutes before, Tim had kindly stopped by the main restaurant of the Santo Domingo Hotel to ask for a tray with coffee and cups. The restaurant was about fifty meters away from the table in the snack bar next to the pool, where Silvia, Liese, and Ricardo had gathered for their Monday morning meeting. This little bar, situated in a spacious, lush tropical garden with an abundance of exquisitely colored flowers, had not opened yet at the early hour of eight. Tim was now pouring his brew for his friends and apologized to Silvia for his clumsiness with a kiss on her cheek. He looked at the spot on her thigh and made a mea culpa gesture. She gave him a short, pretend-angry stare.

Ricardo had brought the tray with papaya, pineapple, and toast Tim had also ordered in the restaurant, and distributed little forks and napkins.

A lonely swimmer quietly logged his smooth, noiseless twenty-five-meter laps and seemed oblivious to the intrusion by the foursome.

"Definitely a European, Tim. Look at the Speedo," Silvia said, pointing with her head and raising her eyebrows.

"Just keep looking. Enjoy his 'technique.' Liese's checking him out too." Tim laughed.

"Not fair, Tim. You can see very well that I'm all eyes for the pineapple," Liese quickly retorted with a piece of the fruit still in her mouth.

"I appreciate your invitation, Silvia," Ricardo said, "and the opportunity to meet you and your friends in person. Thank you for the introductions in the lobby."

"You call this an invitation? To me it sounded more like a summons by 'General' Silvia, Ricardo," Tim joked.

"Have some papaya," Silvia told Tim with a smile.

Ricardo checked his watch, made a serious frown, and dove right into the subject matter. "I gave this meeting absolute priority, my friends, and I think we should get to the meat right away. I'm in a hurry to get to my Monday morning schedule. That's always a hectic mess. I already told you most of what I know in that phone call on Saturday that Silvia said we had to cut short. I didn't have a chance to tell you how our bandit ended up in prison: he pulled a gun on one of my friends and got arrested by security at the airport."

"Do you think Decker knows that?" Silvia asked.

"I'm sure he does by now. He must be tickled pink; he really wanted that guy caught. I can explain in detail why and how this Delgado got nabbed, but it's a long story."

"Some other time, Ricardo," Silvia said. "Right now we would like to ask you how sure you are that we're talking about the right man, this Mora who, you said, calls himself Delgado. And we have the same question about Carla. Was she the person who was seen returning from Venezuela?"

Ricardo looked a bit annoyed and sighed.

The businessman at the top isn't used to being questioned, Silvia discovered.

"Look," Ricardo said after a second sigh, "to your question number two, I just say that you told me you believe Carla ran away from Kavanayén very early Friday morning, just after midnight. The person I mentioned to you arrived here by plane from Kavanayén Friday morning. And from what I heard from my maintenance man at the airport, she looked pretty much like Carla. I'll spare you his language.

He and his buddy must have had their eyes on her for a while. Believe me, it was Carla. Now, for number one, all descriptions I've heard or seen about the bandit fit the one of the guy who tormented Carla's parents. And strangely enough, they also fit with Decker's pictures. But, no, we don't have ironclad proof that Delgado, Mora, and the bandit the Fuenteses saw are one and the same person."

"Can you give me pictures? Copies? I'll go and see Carla's parents right after this meeting," Silvia said, convinced she would resolve the matter.

"I can, but not right now. Gonzalo has them."

"The parents may speak up—or not—Silvia," Tim worried aloud. "These people are probably still scared to death, and they may just say it was so dark and that they were so overwhelmed by fear and that, unlike in the pictures, he wore a huge hat and glasses, hard to tell, etc. They'll beg you not to insist with more questions. They'll say that if they help identify the wrong guy, some goon could come and ... They might not even complete that sentence."

"Right." Ricardo nodded, a grave expression on his face.

Tim sounded impatient when he said, "What intrigues me most, Ricardo, is why our bandit, now in prison or not, is or was so feverishly pursuing Carla—she never explained it—and why Dr. Decker, a man high up there, is so fiercely protecting a foot soldier like Carla. I'll forget my hunches about Decker and Carla for now. I know Silvia doesn't like them."

"We must talk to both, Tim—to the man in prison and to Dr. Decker. Confront them," Liese interjected. She quickly added, "But of course, I don't know how we get to them." She looked at each of her three breakfast companions.

All Silvia could do was keep quiet. *Ricardo's checking his built-in rolodex. Tim's and mine are near empty.*

Ricardo coughed, showing measured gravitas, and said, "I can get indirectly and discreetly to the prison warden. But it remains to be seen whether Mora will agree to speak with us. And Decker? He's pretty active in the Rotary Club, I heard. Not in my chapter, but I'll check out in which one. I'll have to get myself invited to one of his chapter's functions, with Liese."

"Just like that?" Silvia wondered. "What if Decker doesn't show up?"

"Then we try the next function. Don't worry too much; we'll find a way to make him show up," Ricardo said, and after a short pause, he continued, chuckling, "The best I can think of is to offer the head of his chapter and Mr. Decker a chance to meet a 'stunningly attractive, distinguished Swiss journalist who is an authority on Caribbean social issues.' Liese will be a reputed scholar henceforth."

"Oh, thanks, Ricardo. Dressed how?" Liese laughed. "And wearing heavy-rimmed zero-prescription glasses? I can always take them off, later in the evening."

Nobody reacted.

"But who meets whom?" Silvia wondered.

"I think I just said Liese should see Decker at the Rotary, with me of course. Decker doesn't know Liese, but he may feel pretty safe talking to her, a foreigner, about his policies and challenges. And he may appreciate an opportunity to voice his opinions in the international press."

"He would feel safe, you said? You meant flattered, right?" Tim teased. "Or intrigued?"

"Never mind, Tim. Any of those will do," Liese said and winked at Ricardo.

Ricardo showed a knowing smile while he checked his watch.

"So that means Silvia and I go to prison, visiting," Tim went on. "Ricardo, how soon can this be set up, assuming the bandit is prepared to talk to us? Our chances are darn slim, I'd think."

"Wait and see, Tim. I'll contact my friend, a buddy of the warden. Flies on my airline sometimes. Regarding Mora and those slim chances, there may be more to his little story than we think, and new reasons may pop up for the bandit to talk. With an enemy like Decker, the poor guy could soon be looking for love in all possible places. A lot will depend on how we approach him. Maybe Silvia can 'unzip' him. Let me first see when I can get you and Silvia in. One step at a time."

They finished the coffee, pushed back their metal chairs—the screeching noise of the shuffle causing the tireless swimmer to look up—stretched their legs, the men anyway, and prepared to leave for the real world, as Ricardo said. Then Silvia turned back to the table and started arranging the cups and the can, the plates and fruit leftovers on the tray.

"Come on, Silvia, this isn't McDonald's. The waiters will get the stuff," Tim commented, already walking in the direction of the lobby. He stopped, looked back at the table, and joked, "The birds must have breakfast too. Some breadcrumbs with their worms. A balanced diet. I see them waiting up there on the gutter edges."

"Right. How generous and thoughtful you are. The bird lover. But everybody knows me here. I don't want to score bad points." She continued the clean up without looking up.

Tim came back to pick up and then carry the tray all the way back to the main restaurant, Silvia in tow.

"Frenchmen are gentlemen," Silvia commented with a smile to the grateful waiter who accepted the tray. *But I'm still waiting to be served breakfast in bed.*

CHAPTER

Around midmorning, Silvia had started her drive back from the Fuentes residence in Valencia to her apartment, located on Avenida República de Colombia and overlooking the botanical gardens in Santo Domingo, when she decided to take the plunge and call the receptionist at Barone's office. She hadn't shown her face there for more than ten days. She could imagine what Barone was thinking. *I'm persona non grata at his place. But I must find out what he's been doing, how much he let slip to some of his staff, mouthing off in anger, as he did once with me. He must know that that bandit Mora is in prison.*

When the phones connected, she said, "Angela, this is Silvia."

"Huh? What? Dr. Herrera? Where are you? How are you?"

Silvia didn't want to create waves in the office and attract unwanted listeners. She said calmly, "Quiet, Angela. All is fine. I hope you're well too. Please speak softly. I'm looking for Teresa. Is she in?"

Teresa was the nurse who worked closely with Silvia and would take occasional weekend trips with her.

"She's in with a patient. Do you want to speak with Dr. Barone?"

"I'm in a hurry now. I'll get to him later. Don't alarm him. Could you tell Teresa? I'm holding and in a hurry. I'm fine and will be back soon from my long break." *How much of my blabber does she believe? She must know something's up. What the hell.* She shrugged.

"Yes, of course, Doctor. I look forward to your return. I'm sure Dr. Barone does too. I'll connect you now with Teresa. Take care."

Silvia thanked Angela and waited.

After about fifteen seconds, she heard Teresa, who was breathing fast and sounded very happy. "Dr. Herrera, welcome back. We missed you. Where are you? It's so good to hear from you! I bet you ran away with your boyfriend! Pregnant yet?" she joked. "You've known this guy for a while. What French name did you decide on for the baby?"

Teresa's humor is a little special. She's been looking for Mr. Right for the last twenty years. "Shh. Quiet. I'm right here, alone, two kilometers from the office. Can I see you?"

"Oh. I'm with a patient, but come on over … make sure Barone doesn't kick you out." Teresa chuckled.

"Oh. Would he? Quiet. Listen. Within three minutes, I'll be in the parking lot of the gas station next door. Can I talk to you there?"

"Hmm. Well, I can say my tank is in the red. Okay. In your Jetta, right?"

"Yes. *Hasta pronto.*"

Silvia sat in her car, parked in the shade near the gas station, air-conditioning running, waiting, when she saw Teresa sneak to her Jetta, looking left and right.

She's afraid.

Teresa slipped in and embraced Silvia. A long embrace. *An eternity.* Silvia felt her perspiration.

When Teresa finally let go, a torrent of words flowed in Silvia's direction. "I was so worried about you, baby. Both you and Carla gone, the doctor bent out of shape for the slightest, miniscule reason, ranting and raving about ungrateful employees. Looking at us as if we know what he means. And where's Carla? You know?"

She's nervous as hell. "I'm sorry to hear all of that, *amiga.* And I have no idea where Carla is."

"Dr. Barone thinks you do."

"He's wrong. Has he said anything further about the death of Luis Flores?" *Careful now. Wait for her words, even when she leaves space between them.*

"Not to me. Why would he? But we all know he has discussed the matter repeatedly and loudly, sometimes with big shots. One day, Dr. Decker from Justice stormed into the office, looking furious. We all could hear there was a heated screaming match between the two. It got really bad. At some point, we thought Dr. Decker had a heart attack. He didn't. We took care of him." Teresa kept looking around. "But what have *you* been doing?"

Silvia sat up straight and made big eyes. *Decker?* She was surprised and didn't answer Teresa's question. She said, controlled and in a neutral tone, "It's of course possible that Dr. Decker is concerned about recent incidents, such as the death of Mr. Flores. It's his area of responsibility in the government, as we all know. It's one more load on his shoulders."

"Yeah. Of course," Teresa said and shifted to whispering, her face so close that Silvia smelled her coffee breath. "Keep this to yourself, what I'm going to say. We all know Decker is a ladies' man. He has them swarming around him all the time—all shapes and shades and reputations. The successful politician … Of course Barone must know that too. When Decker fainted, Barone came to the lab and put half of the vial we had for the enzyme test in his pocket. José, the technician, saw him do that. He knew what Barone was up to; José wasn't born yesterday. So he saved a little of the blood from the other half and ran his own test on Decker. The man has HIV. José told me."

Silvia was dumbstruck. She decided to look for a mint in her purse and offer Teresa one. Then, holding her mint in her left cheek, she said matter-of-factly, "How sad. A man with such a future. HIV." *And Dr. Barone knows.* She went on, "I feel sorry for Dr. Decker. He may not even know himself about his status."

"That's possible. You and I know most people who carry the virus don't realize it. You feel sorry for him just as you always do, for every HIV-positive patient, Silvia. That's the way you are. Now, when do we go to Juan Dolio and talk about all the *good* stuff? Of course, I understand, you have that baby to take care of with your hunk." She laughed and pointed at Silvia's stomach.

"We can all go. Without the baby, Teresa."

"I must go back to the office, you understand. Stay in touch now."

They kissed good-bye. Teresa walked to her car, and Silvia saw her stopping at the gas pump. *Her alibi.*

Silvia drove away and called Tim, who was at her apartment.

"Preparing lunch," he said.

Silvia laughed. "Oh my!" *This may be the day I kick-start my diet.* She told Tim she had good and bad news.

The bad news was that the Fuenteses had kept mum every second she was at their house after the breakfast meeting with Ricardo. They repeated, "We don't know anything about Carla," the way politicians recite their prepackaged answers on TV. Silvia had concluded the poor parents were either paralyzed by fear, still, even after she told them the bandit was in prison. Or maybe they knew where Carla was but were bound by secrecy.

"And are you going to spill the good news too?" Tim inquired.

"When I said good news, I meant to say that I've succeeded in discovering worthwhile information. Very delicate stuff. Too delicate for the phone. I'll tell you when I get there. You won't believe where I got it."

"You know I believe anything you say, *amor.*"

"Watch the oven, Tim." *His French cuisine. I hope I survive it. I'll* have *to like it.*

When she made it home, she briefed Tim immediately, her voice muffled, on Decker and Barone.

Tim didn't act that surprised by her big story.

They had a drink and lunch on the little balcony, oblivious to the noise and fumes of cars racing by under them. Then Silvia and her chef went inside. They more or less closed the curtains, but not the balcony door, and found time for a little lovemaking, Tim's French dessert, on the rug near the curtain, a soft, sultry breeze inspiring romance.

Shortly thereafter, rearranging her clothes and hair as if she were on a video call, she shared, from near the curtain, her stunning news in phone calls with Ricardo and Liese. She paraphrased carefully and avoided names. Liese said twice that she was writing at the pool at the Sofitel Hotel, and Ricardo sounded busy at his office.

Tim slid into a nap on the rug while Silvia talked at length with her mother, who still sounded worried despite Silvia's assurances that her daughter was now safely back.

CHAPTER 43

"How did you get this set up so smoothly? And so soon?" Liese marveled as Ricardo drove her to the meeting at the Rotary Club of San Cristóbal, not far south of Santo Domingo, on Wednesday around 6:00 p.m.

"I found out that Dr. Decker's a loyal member and driving force of the Rotary chapter of the city of San Cristóbal. I'm a board member of the Valencia chapter and used your credentials to get myself invited to tonight's regular meeting of his chapter with you. Really short notice. I mentioned to Dr. Orozco, the head of the chapter, your intense interest in the DR's social issues and your skill and authority to produce powerful messages. I explained that you're visiting various locations in the country for an article you've been working on and researching for months."

"And you didn't exaggerate at all, right?" Liese laughed.

"Of course not!" he played along. "You can put San Cristóbal on the international map with your sharp pen if you get the right inputs."

"It's a good thing that I don't blush easily, Ricardo."

"Just wait. I'm not done yet," he said.

While he talked, she took mental notes of the list Ricardo had rattled off to Orozco. *I'd better remember my "credentials."*

Liese felt right at home in the luxurious Lexus Ricardo was driving. She was dressed in a classy, dark gray skirt of Indian silk and a thin, vivid yellow blouse, the cut of which left little to the imagination. She kept admiring Ricardo's pleasant voice and demeanor and his skill in negotiations, analysis, and traffic navigation. She wondered ... *No, he's married.* She felt sorry for this spectacularly handsome man who was HIV positive.

When Liese and Ricardo arrived, about thirty members had shown up at the fancy Restaurante París. After formal introductions had been made, Dr. Decker still hadn't arrived. When he finally showed up, Dr. Orozco ushered him to the table where Ricardo and Liese were seated side by side. He asked them to move their chairs a little so an additional one could be placed between them for Dr. Decker.

I took care of that, Ricardo gestured, his right hand on his chest, his index finger almost invisibly pointing to himself, and his left eye winking.

Liese thanked Ricardo with her glance. *Great, Decker is at my good side, and my best ear. He didn't bring a girlfriend. And my English must be better than his. I'm in control.*

The discussions centered first on the donation drive for a new library in the city. Later when they turned more informal, Ricardo volunteered his opinion regarding electronic readers and formats in libraries. Liese nodded at some occasions, when she happened to understand slivers of the discussion. She said in English, "I'm here to absorb and rephrase for German audiences whatever I can pick up in the country, including tonight, about social and gender issues."

"We do address those quite often," the head of the chapter explained, producing his best English for Liese, smiling at her, "but right now we are in fundraising season. My honest apologies." He looked around the table.

Should I compliment him on his English?

Ricardo promised financial support for literacy promotion.

Decker nodded approvingly.

Liese said she understood. "Any moment is a good one for meaningful discussions, but now and then we have to set aside time for raking in hard cash."

"We could sit together in the bar, after the session, Miss Kung, Miss

Liese. I think I can provide some useful insights to you, and in turn you could further our cause by describing our challenges and efforts in your writings. Foreign support is greatly appreciated by our city and, frankly, needed for many of our projects," Dr. Orozco said, his eyes trained on hers, then her lips, and down to the edges of her blouse.

Decker smiled lightly and said to Liese, looking also at Orozco for a second, "I'm sure Dr. Orozco can enlighten you, beautiful. If you'd allow me to join you, I would appreciate your kindness."

Wow. Already. Well, a minute ago, my leg happened to touch his. "I know your knowledge and experience will be invaluable for both Dr. Orozco and me, Dr. Decker," Liese responded.

✻ ✻ ✻

In a cozy corner of the bar, the light soft and of warm color, the trio sat down for a drink. Ricardo had wished them good night and left after Orozco and Decker had assured him one of them would drive Liese to the Sofitel, no problem. Ricardo had explained he had a busy day ahead tomorrow.

Liese had noticed how Decker had made sure that he sat next to Orozco, facing her. *He doesn't want Orozco to read his eyes.*

She listened intently to Orozco's wisdom, and more so to Decker's, leaning forward close to him as he would jump in to expand or clarify some of Orozco's statements. The wine flowed. Decker barely sipped; Orozco gulped. *Demonstrating his manhood.* Liese ran her fingers over the rim of her glass now and then. She unobtrusively turned down refills.

When the clock said eleven, Liese took Decker's hand, looked at him, and whispered to him, for a moment pointing her head at Orozco. "Are you my ride today?"

The drinks had taken their toll on Orozco, who didn't even listen but kept staring in his glass, dazed, looking ugly now—drunk. Decker

208

checked his watch, stood up, bowed at Liese, and offered her his hand. He nodded and smiled.

He looks so confident. "Oh, Doctor, you're so charming. Thank you." Liese sighed. "Thank you so much. Your days must be very full."

"You made this one so much brighter, beautiful. It will be my pleasure to drive you safely wherever you want to go."

Liese got up, threw her hair back while looking at Decker, and did not say a word more.

He asked a waiter to make sure Orozco got a ride to his residence. The poor chapter president had now dozed off, his head resting on the table.

Liese walked out with Decker, and she felt his leg briefly graze her hip from behind as they got in line to wait for his car at the front door of the restaurant. Liese handed the guard on duty her cell phone and asked him to take her picture, Decker's arm firmly around her waist, her hair in good order.

The valet pulled up with Decker's car and bowed when he accepted the tip.

Decker took the wheel.

"Is this the road to Santo Domingo, Doctor?" Liese asked as she noticed that he skipped the sign for the city and kept driving east instead of north.

Decker smiled at her. His warm hand rested on her left leg as he said, "For you, I'm Mauricio. Everything's very close by here. I'll show you the real country. At this hour, we'll reach my boat in Boca Chica in no time. I can show you the real Santo Domingo from there. I'll surprise you."

Liese reflected for a second. *Boca Chica? Out of the city. Am I safe? The man has his reputation to protect.* She told herself she was on a mission and had to succeed. She whispered, "You already did surprise me … Mauritz. Call me Liese. I can't wait to take in the views." *I think he likes "Mauritz." And the feel of silk.*

"The views will be great, especially for me, with you in them …"

"Thank you, Mauritz. Also for taking the time. I know about your antidiscrimination work and can't even imagine how demanding it must be."

"We've a long way to go, but we persevere, Liese."

"I heard from Ricardo about the case of Mr. Flores. Did I get the name right? I understand they caught the shooter."

"Yes, that's what I've been told," he responded, his eyes trained on the road. Taking a right turn, he said, "Well, here we are. Half a kilometer to go to my dock, darling. Boca Chica awaits you."

I have to time my points better.

They arrived at his dock. Decker stepped out and looked for keys. Then he guided Liese over the small ramp leading down to the twenty-footer.

She gingerly made it into the boat down a few steps on the unsteady ladder and immediately turned her sights west, where the majestic skyline and the bright lights of Santo Domingo rose up before her eyes. She smelled the sultry air—fish, oil burning on grills not far away. *My kind of place. Hot in every sense.*

Decker opened a cabinet in the little bar. "Whiskey? Rum, Liese?"

"A little rum, Mauritz. I want to feel Dominican."

"Okay, Barceló for my Dominicana," Decker agreed enthusiastically. "I'll join you with the rum. I'll drink to my new partner in the fight against discrimination, to the woman with the almighty pen, her irresistible weapon."

"Irresistible?"

"Just like you. Your face and smile struck me as soon as I walked in for dinner."

Anything else? Well put, anyway, and straight to the point. Self-assured, experienced, a hell of a body, well preserved, and he knows it. She answered by taking a step away from him. *The rum can wait.* She looked him in the eyes, brushed her hair back with two hands, held them behind her head, and flaunted her body. She kept looking at him and liked what she saw. Then she put her hands on his shoulder and eased him down on a bench. She quickly sat down next to him, turned, and put her head on his thighs, her left leg stretched out over the length of the bench, and her right one slightly bent over her left knee. She felt his leg muscles contracting and relaxing. *They're massaging my neck. I must let this last a bit.* She said, her voice fluttery, "Oh, I'm so relaxed. I felt tired, but no more, Mauritz. And I bet I have the best view in Santo Domingo." She looked up and admired his features from below. *And almost no nose hair.*

"No, *I* have the best view, Liese. I'd like to call you Lisa," Decker said. "Lisa *mía*."

"Hmm. Okay, anything to please my Mauritz." *I have work to do.* With her left hand, she squeezed the arm he had lying on her chest. She moved her head slightly, looking for a new position, and said, staring at her smooth right knee, her right hand slowly, furtively pulling her skirt up an inch, "To get back to this Flores matter, if you don't mind, I read that a woman accomplice may be on the run. Carla, right?" Her nape felt Decker's quads suddenly contract forcefully. *I gave him a thousand-volt jolt.* Then she felt him getting things under control again.

"I've read it too, Lisa. It's for the police to resolve. It's probably not exactly what you heard. But hell, we have other matters to worry about. Like children not being let into their school because they have the HIV virus. I can't fight hard enough for them. Would you like the Barceló now? Do you like the breeze?" He held her head and softly moved her upper body with his other arm so she was sitting upright, next to him. He looked ready to stand up.

Patience. "How many smashing young ladies have shared this bench with you, Mauritz?" she teased as she fixed her hair. *He must have heard that question a hundred times.*

He now had stood up and gestured he would lead her somewhere else. "I have a comfortable bed downstairs …"

"I assumed that, *caballero*. An outrageously wild guess, of course." She laughed and remained seated. "But you didn't answer my question. You don't have to. Let's just enjoy the moment. Anyway, I heard this Carla worked with a Dr. Barone."

"Yes. I guess that's right. He's a good man. Handles many patients successfully." He caressed her hair and her neck, massaging it lightly. "Do you feel good?" he asked, sounding almost mechanic.

He's exploring how far he can go. His hands.

211

"You have great hands, Mauritz. I'm enjoying the tranquility here on the water." She stood up and said, straightening out her skirt, "I heard this Carla showed up again somewhere recently."

"Could be. They'll get her if she's guilty. Shall we move downstairs? I'll bring the rum."

"You want that? Downstairs?" Liese asked. She realized she hadn't finished her task. *Downstairs will offer me opportunity.* She knew she was rationalizing. *I love the game,* she had to admit to herself.

Decker guided her down the steps. He quickly went back upstairs for the rum and then cautiously down again the little steps, a glass in each hand, the little bottle sticking out of his pants pocket. He proposed they drink to serendipity.

Liese felt the rum invading her body, her legs, and then her mind. *Careful.*

Decker kissed her on the cheek.

Liese looked at him, put her glass down on the little bedside table, and slowly lay down on the bed. She curled up on her left side, her left hand under her head, her eyes on Decker, who started undressing. *Another one who hates to waste time.*

"You don't have to worry about a thing with me, precious. And I always use condoms," he volunteered, smiling encouragingly as he flung his socks on the floor.

"I hate condoms. I like the real thing," she whispered, her voice slightly sulky. She tried to sound as innocent and pure as she could and curled up more.

"Oh, we can handle that," Decker assured her. He towered over her as he stood next to the bed in his boxers.

"You think so? Can we, darling?"

"Of course."

Push a little harder. "Sure?"

Liese suddenly detected some unease in his voice. And his macho pose was gone. *I deflated his balloon.*

He looked away, at his clothes thrown on the floor.

I'll have to let him save face. Her voice kind and soft as she grabbed his hand and tried not to look at his shrinking bulge, she said, "I feel so good here, Mauritz, but I lie here thinking that we're both very tired. I would like our first time to be really great, spectacular. I want you. But I think it's better to wait till tomorrow or the day after. Maybe a nice long weekend together in Casa de Campo, when we can be rested and thoroughly enjoy, if you want."

Decker's response came fast. "I do want you, Lisa. You're driving me crazy. I'm not tired, but I respect your condition; you are tired but still looking splendid." He already had started to put his pants on. He said, one leg in and one leg out, "Give me your number. I'll call you."

"Don't you have a card? I'll call you."

He didn't answer but kept concentrating on getting dressed.

She had seen him handing a card to another guest at the Rotary Club. She now saw a bunch of cards sitting in the pocket of his shirt as he put it on. When he finished, she stood up and kissed him. She put two fingers in the pocket and asked, "Do you mind?" as she slipped a card out and checked the name. She quickly asked, her eyes trained on his, "Around what time can we meet tomorrow?"

Decker looked slightly annoyed and then reflective. He said, "You can't call me early enough, Lisa, my treasure. I won't sleep tonight. You can even call me to your hotel, anytime. I'll cancel meetings for you."

"Good. My first activity tomorrow will be a discussion with the staff of the Alliance, somewhere on Calle Robles. Do you know them?"

"Yeah. The French. You won't pick up much for your articles there. I think they're useless."

"Oh. But I have set up the appointment. Maybe I should quickly catch a flu bug ..."

"Do that."

"I have one more question, Mauritz. It's a delicate one." *I don't really have to ask this one, but I want to see him squirm.*

He frowned, looking a little apprehensive.

Liese went ahead before he could wave her off. "You don't mind being seen with me, your newest conquest? Your umpteenth, I bet. A Dominican politician with a *gringa*? Heads will turn." *I know his answer.*

He smiled and said, "No doubt. You and I will see lots of jealous heads. And I'll love it, darling." He squeezed her tight.

I was right again. And he's got a smart tongue.

She knew from Silvia that politicians here always looked good parading beautiful women. In his case, there was more. Swarms of women were obviously a shield, a veil he used to hide his HIV status. Tim had added to Silvia's point, using the analogy that gay US politicians often made the most virulent gay-bashing speeches, wanting to look straight in the eyes of their voters. But then such self-righteous, hypocritical bastards got caught in an affair themselves with a man or in a massage parlor.

"Good then, my *caballero*. I like to see you proud. Now I need rest. Can gentleman Decker drive his 'treasure' to the Sofitel?" she asked. "And kiss me once more on the cheek when I go my way and you yours at the front door?"

"Anything else, Lisa?"

When they had kissed good-bye at the hotel in the old city, Liese walked to the elevator with spring in her step. *I still have it; my sit-ups, crunches, and yoga pay off. I have a valuable report for Tim and Silvia and Ricardo. Zürich will like my article.*

CHAPTER

Silvia and Tim arrived at the Libertad prison, near the Las Américas Airport, at 9:00 a.m. on Thursday, April 16. On Wednesday afternoon, they had received the good news from Ricardo that he had managed to arrange a special visit for them at the prison for a discussion with José Mora. Ricardo had also briefed them on his discussions with the warden, a friend of a friend.

Ricardo had assured the warden that the visitors would religiously follow instructions to keep the visit confidential. It would take place in his office, which had a back entry door. Ricardo had told him that José Mora might well refuse to talk to Silvia and Tim. The prisoner had probably come to distrust the entire world. The warden had then told Ricardo that Mora had started acting erratically, with increasing anger, sounding desperate when he had his rages. Mora had no family visiting him, but some friends had shown up. Those visits had, however, not improved his mood.

The warden welcomed Silvia and Tim and explained to staff they were contractors, here to discuss a food supply contract. All three went to his office. The warden summoned inmate Mora to his office. Silvia assumed that the bandit would be smart enough not to resist the summons.

When José Mora slumped into the office through the back door,

Silvia and Tim saw a man who appeared smaller and frailer than they had pictured him from the descriptions they had heard and seen. He wore regular clothes. *He's not your average prisoner; he has money,* Silvia thought to herself. He sat down without greeting and stared at the floor. *He fears a trick.* The warden left.

"I'm Dr. Herrera from Dr. Barone's group," Silvia said, "and this is my friend Tim. Carla Fuentes has left Kavanayén. We're looking for her, and we think you are too. Can you help us?" *Voilà, I said it.* She looked for impact. Tim gave her a small thumbs-up, hiding it beside his hip.

Mora didn't acknowledge her or Tim's presence and kept looking at the floor.

He's shaking. He looks scared. "How do you feel?" Silvia asked, suppressing her anger, speaking in a neutral tone.

Mora looked up. He stared at Silvia.

He's looking for friends.

Mora sat up and said, almost inaudibly, "*Señora,* I shouldn't trust you, but I'm a marked man. I have nothing to lose. My days, my hours are counted. People I know have made life hell for me here, instead of helping me, as they should. The first three days here, I still had money and could afford a key to my cell. The *llavero,* the guy who controls the keys, took mine away this morning. The guards will move me out, because I have no money left, to a common area where I'll have to sleep on the floor with the rats and the mice. I'll have to defecate in public, in a hole in the ground. I have no family or friends bringing me food. If I don't kill myself here, somebody will drag me out of this place, shoot or strangle me, and throw me in a garbage dump. Please believe me; I know what I'm saying. I need help, and I'll tell you all I know about Carla. I'm scared."

Silvia knew all about prison conditions, but she couldn't believe her ears when she heard about the threats against Mora. *They want to silence him.*

"We'll talk to the warden to make sure you're safe," she assured him. *It's the warden's job.*

"I know it'll take more than that, *Señora*. You'll have to get to the big shots to save me."

"Tell us what happened. We may be able to help," Silvia said, half-fearing she might be overpromising.

"Carla Fuentes saw me shoot Flores. Higher-ups told me Barone ordered Flores shot. Barone worked behind the scenes. I told him Carla Fuentes saw me do it. Now he wants me to take care of her too. Shut her up for good. Save his butt. And others' asses. Believe me now?"

Silvia listened open-mouthed but managed to respond, looking at Tim first. "We'll talk to Dr. Barone." *I don't believe a word of what Mora says. It's all one gigantic lie. He knows I know Barone. He thinks that I can get to Barone but not to the higher-ups, so he accuses Barone.* "Anything else we should know? The more you tell us, the better we can help you."

"No," Mora said. He looked down again.

✤ ✤ ✤

On their way back to her apartment, Silvia told Tim that Barone couldn't have ordered the murder on Luis Flores. "He's not that kind of person. And he would never want Carla harmed. He was rather close to her, if you know what I mean."

"Hmm. We must see Barone soonest, Silvia."

"Right. We don't know how many hours Mora has left. He's a murderer, but others are clearly guilty too. Once Mora starts speaking the truth, he can help us unravel this thing. We need him alive. But today he was lying about Barone."

Silvia called the office and asked for Barone. *He'll fall off his chair when he hears my voice. Or he may dive under his desk.* The receptionist said that the doctor was out for the day. Silvia called his cell phone. It was off. Silvia was disappointed and getting more nervous by the minute.

"It may be a good thing that we don't get hold of Barone today; we'd better talk to Liese first," Tim opined.

Silvia didn't answer. *He's just trying to make me feel a little better.*

They stopped at a small snack bar on the Malecón for *tostones*. From there, Silvia called Liese and Ricardo and asked them to come to her apartment by eleven if at all possible. "We have very urgent work to do."

Ricardo said he couldn't make it.

❈ ❈ ❈

At 10:40 a.m., Silvia heard Liese's enthusiastic voice over the intercom. "I'm twenty minutes early, I know. Sorry! Swiss punctuality slightly overdone."

"Come in, Liese," Silvia said and pushed the button.

A minute later, a radiant Liese stepped out of the elevator at Silvia's floor. "Silvia's and Tim's hideaway," she said as she met her hosts and entered the apartment. She refused the cup of coffee Tim started to pour for her. "I'm already going full blast," she explained. She walked over to the sliding glass door opening onto the balcony and took in the view over the Jardín Botánico. Then she sat down with her hosts.

"Who goes first?" Tim asked.

"I will, if you don't mind," Liese squealed impatiently. "You know, I had a blast last night, and now I have a hot date waiting for me. I also have ... Ready? ... All we need to know about Decker stored up here!" She pointed at her forehead and waited.

Silvia frowned and said, "Well, Liese, tell us what you've hidden up there." *I could have said "behind the Botox."*

"Of course he wanted my body, the horny liar. He still does." She giggled. "I have his phone number, his picture for my article, the smell of his breath, his measurements, the color and cut of his underwear, the size of ..."

"His shoes." Tim laughed.

218

"His shoes. Exactly, Tim. My Mauricio has a good, good body, I can say. I have all we need to know." She looked triumphant.

Silvia was thoroughly put off. She had been looking at a family picture on the wall while listening.

"How about the lies? His. You said he lied," Tim said.

"He lies about everything. He insinuates he has no HIV, that he has no clear idea of who Carla is—except that she worked for Barone and has disappeared—and that he works his butt off to help HIV victims. But he's not bashful about his hundred girlfriends. I'm now number 101, he thinks. I've left him his illusion for now."

"Okay. Thank you. Well, our mission was less enjoyable," Tim reported. "Mora feels his life is threatened. He has the looks of a marked man. He says Carla saw him kill Luis Flores, on orders from Barone. And that Barone wants him to kill Carla too."

"Aha. I'm not too surprised, but I guess Silvia is. So that solves the mystery, right?" Liese figured. "Our Barone's at the core of the matter. Carla feared being eliminated by Mora because she witnessed a murder committed by Mora for Barone. Decker has HIV but no blood on his hands. We're done. So … all my hard work of last night was for nothing?" She smiled.

"There's more, Liese," Silvia said, unwilling and unable to share Liese's exuberance. "It's not that simple. Carla's still missing as far as I'm concerned. Mora lies; Barone wouldn't order murder. Never. I know him. But we'll have to confront him to get to the truth. He may know what we need to know. And I don't think he's entirely innocent either. Far from. But things may have gotten out of hand. Out of his hands."

"And the half-only saint will be happy to tell us what we need to know," Liese stated, looking at Silvia askance.

Mocking me. "We'll have to unsettle him, Liese. Spring a surprise on him, hit him over the head with a two-by-four from behind, shock him," Silvia said. Her words about Barone grew harsher as doubts and anger started to ferment in her mind about the doctor and about Carla, who hadn't been honest with her. *Carla may be lying to me right now, while I am trying to help her. And Barone may have lied his entire life.* The thought made her feel bitter, betrayed, used.

"Wow. Let's go then," Liese said.

"He's not in today. We can't find him now, but I have a plan. Tim and I must be at his office at 7:30 tomorrow morning. We surprise Barone; scare him. I can ascertain he's there before we enter. Then he'll discover what kind of wood his lowly staffer Dr. Herrera is carved out of," Silvia said resolutely and angrily.

"And once he's discovered that, can I ask him what kind of wood it is, Silvia?" Tim joked.

Silvia almost blew her top but held back and just said stiffly, "This is a serious matter."

His face told her he knew he was out of order.

He means well.

At that moment, Liese's phone rang.

"It's Ricardo," Liese said and kept listening to him. After a few seconds, she told Tim and Silvia, "He's very busy but anxious to know how things went last night with Decker. He had expected a call from me." She put her hand over the phone and said, "Who tells him about Barone?"

"Go ahead, but paraphrase the doctor's name," Silvia answered as she walked over to Tim. She bent down and whispered in his ear, "I'm sorry, *caballero*. You don't have to ask Barone about the wood. I'm bamboo for you. I'll show you after lunch."

CHAPTER

On Friday morning, Silvia and Tim waited in her Jetta just around the corner from Dr. Barone's office, in a spot from where they could observe his parking spot. They had been there since seven. Silvia knew Barone's routine, which included quiet, personal phone calls to family and sometimes laboratories from around 7:30 till 8:00.

At 7:15, Silvia saw Barone's BMW appear and find its spot in the parking lot. The doctor walked in, already chatting on the phone.

"Ready," Silvia said. "I do the talking."

"Good. What's new?"

"Don't hold my language against me. I may go overboard. But I can swim."

"Straight ahead, *amor*. I'm your buoy."

Two minutes after Barone had entered, they pushed the front door of the building open. Nobody was there to greet them. They headed for Barone's office. Its door was closed. Silvia opened it brusquely without knocking, barged in, Tim in tow, and shouted, "You'd better put that frigging phone down, Doctor!"

Barone looked up, seemed to see a ghost, and screamed, "Where the hell have you been?"

"Did you order the murder of Luis Flores?" Silvia thundered, her eyes ice-cold, her voice firm.

"Huh. Huh. What?" Barone shot back, holding the phone. "You know me. I'd never do that."

"How clean are your trembling hands, Doctor? Aren't you part of the damn organization? Mora says you ordered the frigging murder of Luis Flores. And that you now want the bloody bastard to kill Carla too."

"What? Nonsense! Why are you talking to me like that? Vulgar. Mora's lying. He's afraid to accuse the real killers. They may be threatening him!" Barone yelled. "The higher-ups are behind this," he blurted. He stopped talking. He looked surprised by his own statement.

"So you know that? How come you know? Did you ask them to murder?"

Barone looked at Tim before he started explaining, his voice low, "Silvia, you know I'm just a bit player in the circus I have to work in. You're in it too. Don't you forget that. I'm clean. You know that, don't you?"

"I don't believe a frigging thing anymore from you, damn liar. So the creep named Decker did it, right?" she provoked him.

Barone didn't take the bait. He had recovered. He kept his composure, and he measured his words as he said, "Dr. Herrera, may I ask you in decent language to leave the premises. Your presence here is no longer appreciated. Never again. Please go. Don't make me call my guards. I'm an innocent man."

Silvia decided her best comment was stony silence.

Tim and Silvia left. As soon as they were out of earshot, she said, "He's no murderer, but he's guilty. He'll be on the phone to Decker by now. And I'd better look for a bullet-proof vest."

"Good. And, *à propos*, congratulations on the tremendous expansion of your 'frigging' vocabulary."

Bad imitation, Tim.

Barone was seething. *That shameless bitch. She knows damn well I don't murder or order it. What got into her? Where did she pick up that filthy language? Now she'll run to Decker and tell him I accused him. No, she can't get to him. Wait. She can!* He picked up the phone to call Decker on the secure line.

"Mauricio, are you by yourself there?" he asked. He tried to keep his voice steady.

"Yep. Good morning, Doctor. You're early." Decker sounded busy.

"Not a minute to waste. I just got accused of having had Flores murdered and planning the killing of Carla Fuentes. Somebody told my accuser that Carla saw the Flores shooting."

"Another rumor? What accuser?" By now Decker had changed his tone.

"One of my staff, Dr. Herrera. She screamed it into my face a minute ago. She's worried about Carla; she said she knows I want Carla dead."

"I hear you're out of breath. Calm down. Nobody should worry about Carla. She's gone and out of reach. Even we can't find her. Forget she exists. And we all know who killed Flores. The bandit sits in Libertad, a good, uncomfortable little prison."

"And he has a big mouth. He's the source of this nonsense. You know very well I never ordered anybody killed," Barone lamented.

"Hmm. That's one way to put it. You're part of the system. You know Charles is handling this. Don't ask me how. I don't ask him questions about his work."

"Mauricio. Let's talk turkey. Your Mickey must be the one who's talking, and Charles has to silence him one way or another. Shut him up. Tell your damn Charles," Barone boomed, suddenly having found his voice.

"Sure," Decker mocked. "This is an order for murder from …?"

Barone measured his words, conscious of the power he had over Decker. He said slowly, his voice low but threatening, "From a guy who can put your HIV status out in the public within minutes. Clear? Understand?" He waited for an answer. *I got him by the short hairs.*

"You can't possibly be serious about this," Decker hissed almost inaudibly. Then he added, loudly sounding his own threat, "I don't know how you found out, but you're bound by confidentiality rules. I can sue your ass off if you talk about it."

"By then it would be too late for you, Mauricio."

"Calm down, I said. And tell your little doctor she'd better keep her mouth shut."

"You know what you have to do." Barone hung up.

CHAPTER

Around 9:00 a.m., on her way home with Tim from Barone's place, Silvia got a call from her mother.

"Silvita! Canal 25 Breaking News shows pictures of a bullet-riddled car!" The woman gasped and shouted, "Mora in it! Killed. Blood all over. The reporter said prison guards pursued the escapee and shot him. His name is Mora! The one you told me about. I'm scared for you. Are you at home?"

"My God! Mora? Unbelievable," Silvia said and looked at Tim. *He's heard Mom's screams.* She forced herself to calm down and said, "Don't worry, Mama. I'm in my car with Tim. I'll be at my place in a few minutes."

"Why don't you come here? Hide here?"

"I'm fine, and with a strong man. And close to home. Are you sure about the name?"

"Yes. The officials showed the man's prison badge on TV. And a picture, exactly as you told me."

"Anyway, don't worry about me; I don't shoot people. I'll be in touch soon. *Hasta pronto.* Relax."

After the call, Silvia had another worry. "Tim, I hope her heart survives this. In her mind, I'm fighting a gang, and she's not too far off."

"You don't shoot people, but you do bother some pretty badly," Tim commented. "Let's play it safe and wait things out for a couple of hours. See what transpires. I wonder … That killing must have been a setup."

"No doubt."

"Somebody on the inside must have tricked him into escaping, helped him get out, provided a car, and then done a super-marvelous job of pursuing him, killing him, and producing instantaneous identification on the spot. Nice work. Too nice."

"But well-paid," Silvia agreed. "Mora could have seen through this kind of setup. I'm sure it was one, but he must have been so desperate he'd grasp at any straw. Even if he had only a 1 percent chance. The poor man."

"You can't mean that … 'poor man.'"

"He's not the worst, Tim."

"And who fixed this shooting, you think?"

He knows the answer. "Liese should go and see him, the real fixer. Confront Decker the way we did Barone. She's got the introduction, it seems. She thinks so anyway, the bragger."

"Right. But we can't ask her to just go there, just like that, by herself," Tim cautioned.

"You mean she needs a gun again?"

"No, she can't carry a gun into a government office. She needs us. She may end up in trouble if she pushes too hard. It's hardball now."

CHAPTER  47

Silvia told Liese over the phone about the death of Mora and her and Tim's visit to Barone. It was now 9:45 in the morning.

Liese sounded shocked. "All day long yesterday and during the night, I couldn't get my mind off my encounter with Mauricio Decker the day before yesterday. I was tempted to call him yesterday, just to see how he would react, but I concluded that any further contact between him and me had to wait for the outcome of your confrontation with Barone this morning," she explained.

Silvia said, "You were right. And now we need expert help, Liese, from somebody who has the nerve to confront Decker."

"No problem. I'm ready to look Decker in the eye and ask him what's going on. Wherever. Whenever."

"Tim wants you to go and see Decker as soon as possible."

"Okay. I will. My hair's still a mess. And Decker hasn't seen me in harsh daylight yet. But I will. His office is on Avenida Leopoldo Navarro, not far from the American Embassy, I found. I'll surprise him."

"Call him first, Liese, to set up an encounter with him somewhere else for later today. Those officials have time on their hands on hot, lazy afternoons. They can do what pleases them, go wherever they want," Silvia said. "He wouldn't take too well to being surprised at his office.

Better meet him at some hot … Well, I think I made myself clear already. You know how to handle him."

"Yes. Very clear. I'll call him now."

Silvia was concerned and said, "Wait. If you get something set up, we'll go with you, to be in the area, just in case."

"Okay, Silvia. Okay. Talk to you soon." She hung up.

Silvia wrinkled her brow and looked at Tim. "She sounds a bit upset that we want to go too. She must feel that amateurs shouldn't think they can protect pros."

Ten minutes after they had hung up, Silvia received a call back from Liese.

"I called him three times. Each time, I was asked to leave a voicemail. He must be very busy." Liese sighed, sounding exasperated.

"We have no time to waste. Let's drive together to the area where his office is on Leopoldo Navarro, and we'll wait around there. You can call from there," Silvia said. "We'll pick you up in fifteen minutes."

CHAPTER

Sitting in her parked Jetta, fifty meters away from Decker's office entrance with Liese and Tim, Silvia suggested Liese call Decker again. It was around 11:00 a.m. About forty minutes had gone by since Liese's last attempt. She had her phone on conference.

He picked up. "Oh, Lisa. Good morning. Good to hear from you, darling. How's your day?"

He sounds very quiet. His voice is entirely flat. Silvia looked at Tim, a little surprised.

"I'm fine. And how's my hunk? You forgot about me, I bet."

"Lisa, come on. Never. But I'm terribly busy right now. Could you call me back later? Tomorrow maybe."

Silvia showed Tim a frown. *The last two words sounded like an afterthought. They weren't even a question. Just a statement.*

"I see. Are you sure you want to see me again?"

"Lisa, you're asking me *that*? Of course, darling. Talk to you later."

Silvia nodded. *He's fobbing her off.*

"Hold it, Mauricio. Did you hear about the Mora murder this morning?"

"Mora?"

"Didn't you hear? Or see? You don't know him?"

"I don't have time to watch all murder reports. We've got so many in Santo Domingo."

"Mora doesn't ring a bell?"

"Not really."

"It does for Dr. Barone, I know."

"You do? How do you know?"

"Who do you think is behind this, Mauricio? A terrible shooting, I heard." Liese looked at Tim. He made a fist.

"I asked you how you know!" he shouted.

"You don't have to shout, Mauricio. You know very well that I can understand you even when you whisper. Is Dr. Barone behind this?"

"How would I know?"

"Doesn't he take orders from you? He and others in the system?"

"What? Stupid question!" His voice boomed through the Jetta.

"Are you lying to me, Mauricio?"

"Hell! What is this? An inquisition?" he thundered.

"You lied to me the day before yesterday. About your HIV status. And I think you lied about Carla."

"What?"

"Do I have to make a sketch over the phone? I can read between the lines. You're a liar, and I have many reasons to think you're responsible for the murder of Mora."

"What? You're accusing me? Go to hell. Who cares about what you think? Who are you anyway? I'll get you kicked out of the country for slander. Or do you prefer prison?" The sound grew deafening.

"Make my day, my friend," Liese said, her voice calm and mocking now.

Decker didn't answer but didn't hang up either. Deafening silence on the line.

Liese waited, silent, questioning Silvia and Tim with her eyes as the seconds went by.

Then they heard a groan over the phone, a weak sound, Decker begging, "Maria … can you help me? … Ooh … nauseous … lie down …"

There was a click, and the conversation ended.

He fainted. Silvia stared at her friends.

"Let's think. We already know that Decker was involved in the killing," Tim said. "What's the next step? The police? Can one simple citizen and two simple foreigners take on a high government official? Should we …"

Suddenly Silvia saw a green Jaguar leave the office parking lot. It moved slowly.

"The green Jaguar!" Liese exclaimed. "Decker with a driver. An employee? Let's follow them."

Silvia started the Jetta and soon caught up with Decker's vehicle. They took just a few turns and within a couple of minutes saw the Jaguar come to a halt in Calle Santiago. Decker stumbled out of the car and to the front door of a residence.

Must be his home. Big. Fancy.

The Jaguar then disappeared behind the residence, and a couple of minutes later the driver reappeared and started walking in the direction of Decker's office.

"He's walking back. It's a few hundred meters," Silvia said.

"Decker got a good kick in the stomach from you, Liese, and probably one in the crotch from Barone this morning. The guy's collapsing," Tim concluded. "His girlfriend had better take good care of him or call a doctor."

CHAPTER

"Let's watch things from here for a while," Silvia proposed as she sat in the Jetta with Tim and Liese. They were now parked about twenty meters away from the Decker residence. "It's all in a state of flux. Crazy things could happen. Barone might show up. Or an ambulance."

"Or Carla." Liese laughed.

Silvia frowned.

Close to noon, the green Jaguar bolted onto the street from behind the Decker residence, dust flying and tires screeching.

"Where's Decker speeding? Quick, Silvia. Follow him, right on his tail!" Tim shouted.

"He's racing in the direction of the airport. My God, he'll see us. He may have a gun," Silvia said, scared.

"He doesn't know your car. No worries. And he needs all his attention on the road at this crazy speed. Go!" Tim shouted. He sounded as if he wanted to push the Jetta with his hands.

The Jaguar kept racing east on Avenida Independencia.

"He *is* going to the airport. Taking the freeway. Fleeing the country. He must have recovered pretty quickly. Probably had a suitcase and his documents ready. Felt the noose tighten," Tim figured.

The chase continued. They reached the airport exit ramp.

"He's going farther east, Silvia," Tim said. "Staying on Route 3. Where's he headed?"

"Boca Chica," Liese ventured. Then she laughed.

"Your playground, Liese!" Tim said.

"Liese's right," Silvia said. "I mean he's headed there."

She saw the Jaguar come to a halt at the docking space of Decker's small yacht.

"Wow. I feel at home," Liese commented.

They waited in the Jetta, about fifty meters away from the Jaguar.

A person stepped out of the Jaguar and opened the trunk, in a big hurry.

"It's a woman!" Tim exclaimed.

"Carla!" Silvia shouted, surprised. "I know it! Carla! Look. She can barely lift her suitcases. What is she doing?"

Silvia stepped out and ran to Carla. Tim and Liese followed.

"Carla! You're alive. I can't believe it." Silvia was ecstatic.

Carla looked nervous. She showed a quick smile and said, "I told you I was. But I needed privacy, then and now. Go away or my life will be in danger. Go away." Her tone was harsh. She started walking hurriedly to the yacht, groaning under the weight of her two suitcases.

Silvia looked around. The area was entirely quiet and peaceful.

At that moment, another car arrived, a small Ford Focus. Two people exited the car, one strongly built, young guy helping the other, who looked weak.

"My God, Decker, he can barely stand on his legs," Liese gasped, her hand over her mouth.

Carla was getting close to the boat, perspiring and panting.

She didn't look back at Decker when he howled, "Stop! You thief!" She moved faster.

She's in a big hurry. And Decker doesn't even seem to notice we're here too. "Can you call the police, Tim?"

"What's the number?" Tim asked in hushed tones.

"999. We need them here."

"Yeah. I bet Decker's guy's got a gun." Tim turned his face away from the scene to make the call.

Silvia noticed that Liese was furtively recording the action from a few meters away.

Carla struggled on the narrow ramp. She looked back, not even halfway.

Decker reached the boat ramp, leaning on his sturdy companion, who helped him block her.

"Let me go! I want to get out of this country!" she yelled. She dropped the suitcases as she fought off Decker's helper. The youngster grabbed them.

"Not with my money," Decker thundered.

"It's mine too! I earned it more than you, wimp," Carla taunted him.

"I used to love you, bitch. I gave you all you have. All I could. Jewelry, bank accounts, houses, travel, protection. You ungrateful piece of—"

"You? You're a nothing. *I* gave you the idea for your system, you moron. It's my brainchild. My money. You didn't know an iota about making money out of power," Carla responded, her voice full of loathing.

"My God," Silvia whispered.

Tim tilted his head, his eyes asking, "Are you surprised?"

Liese gasped. She stopped filming.

"Shut up, you serpent!" Decker yelled as he tried to pull Carla back off the ramp.

"Watch your language, loser. You're finished. You with your hordes of women, the veil of flesh hiding your virus!"

Another veil. Just like his speeches against discrimination.

"You're the one who gave me HIV," he hissed.

"Liar! You know better, you murderer! First Luis. Now Mickey. Who else? And who's next? Get out of my way. It's my boat more than yours." She tried to force her way forward, her eyes drilling into Decker's.

Decker's companion put the bags down and pulled a gun. He shouted at Tim, "You, *flaco*, scrag, take the bags and put them in the Jaguar. Hurry."

Silvia looked at Tim.

Tim lifted the first bag and looked at Silvia.

234

Tim's eyes are telling me I call him flaco *too when I'm angry.*

Within a second, Decker pulled a gun himself and threatened, his voice weak and trembling, "Anybody who speaks a word about this will end up in a garbage dump. I have frigging power. Hear me? I can have you thrown in the water ten miles out, with concrete blocks as companions." His eyes raced from one person to the next. Nobody reacted. Then he pointed at Carla and said, his voice full of scorn, "This bitch, she ran away with my hard-earned money. She's a frigging liar."

He's gone crazy. Silvia stood silent, looking at Carla.

Liese quietly put her camera away.

"Give me that toy, you spy. The game's over!" Decker, visibly exhausted, half-shouted at Liese as Tim picked up the other suitcase to carry both to the Jaguar. "You, in the car," Decker barked at Carla. "You're toast. Move!"

His legs unsteady, his eyes wild, he looked ready for revenge.

Silvia looked up.

"Hands up! Police! Drop the guns!" It came as a lightning strike from a blue sky. Silvia heard a deep, calm voice. Four policemen descended, guns drawn. They were still about twenty meters away. Their two cars were parked about seventy meters farther out, partly hidden in the shade.

Decker's guard looked up and cocked his gun.

"Ernesto. Put it down," Decker said and dropped his.

So did his guard.

Mauricio Decker had to be supported to proceed to the police car. He glanced at Liese on his way there.

Liese checked her hair and smiled at the police officer escorting Decker. She asked the officer for her camera.

He said, "Later."

As she was led away handcuffed and walked by Silvia, Carla said, her voice expressionless, "I'm sorry."

Silvia nodded.

CHAPTER

Six weeks after Luis Flores was found shot to death, Silvia and Tim heard on FM 101 that Dominican authorities had indicted Mauricio Decker and Charles Montenegro for instigation and complicity in the murders of Luis Flores and José Mora.

The authorities hinted that they pinned their hopes for finding the murderer of Mora on their continued efforts to make Montenegro turn witness against Decker.

Dr. Barone and Carla Fuentes faced charges, along with Decker and Montenegro, of bribery, extortion, and violating the country's antidiscrimination laws.

Although he was not formally charged with murder, well-informed citizens and certain press outlets kept pointing to Dr. Barone as an instigator and culprit in both murder cases. They hoped that the legal procedures would unearth the real driving forces behind the murders and the extortion schemes.

All accused pleaded innocent to all charges. The legal process could drag on for years while they walked free on bail they had no problem making.

Silvia was convinced all would be convicted and given lengthy prison terms, as much as twenty years. But she fretted that one didn't have to be an oracle, prophet, or seer to confidently predict that they would serve just fractions of their jail terms. "Buying your way out is even easier and safer than escaping," she commented to Tim, dejected. The accused in this case would not be subject to the prison hardships that the *ranas*, the "frogs"—poor prisoners—had to suffer daily. *Acido del diablo,* the dreaded acid used to maim enemies in prison, would not be a concern for them, protected as they would be by their money and power. Food, hygienic care, visits, and passes would be no problem since they all would be generous, enthusiastic contributors to the "favorite charity of the warden," the euphemism for the vehicle of choice for bribes in many prisons.

The announcement on FM 101 revived waves of talk in Santo Domingo and the entire country about toothless and unenforced antidiscrimination laws on the country's books—about circumventing them, about officials and their bribers boycotting them and turning them into cruel tools for illicit, hidden, and untaxed profits. These rumors seeped into any meaningful discussion of the Decker case and were gratefully accepted as a topic for sanctimonious editorials in the press and over the airwaves. Calls for a cleanup of the stables were legion for a while.

The Minister of Justice had removed Mauricio Decker from his responsibilities as the country's antidiscrimination enforcer. His replacement had immediately pledged strict adherence to the letter and the spirit of the law. The press had applauded him. Mauricio Decker had made the same statement a few years ago and had also harvested applause.

Liese Kung had returned to her business in Zürich, but not before she had taken two more Rapid tests, from Silvia this time, which showed no HIV virus. Her first project, once she arrived back in Zürich, was an article about an attractive, mature woman out for a good time in Nueve Ríos, in the tropical country of Idílica, and the pitfalls of socializing too closely with young, local Adonises. She made it abundantly clear that, with her stories about a distant friend, she didn't want to badmouth Idílican tourism; to the contrary.

Ricardo Lima was proud that so many misdeeds had been exposed with his valiant support. Since he had dual US-Dominican citizenship, he moved to Coral Gables, near Miami, with Marcelo and Rosita and enrolled Marcelo in a local school where soccer was the number-one sport. Marcelo was scoring goals, and Rosita was happy. Ricardo ran his businesses from Florida. He wondered how long it would take for Decker's successor to discover smart, illicit ways to earn his fortune, ways that would have to be smarter than Decker's, ways that, Ricardo feared, could be found.

CHAPTER  51

As they saw Tim's sabbatical drawing to an end, Silvia and Tim had long conversations about "the system," and longer ones, often late at night, about themselves. Silvia found the latter most enjoyable, but now the couple felt they could no longer postpone critical decisions and choices.

They drew up idealistic, sometimes grandiose plans and then discarded them, joking about their own naiveté. A few times, they were on the verge of going to the priest to get married, but then one or both got cold feet when they "approached the altar." They drank beer with friends who offered well-meant advice. They were inclined to accept it and then rejected it when they were by themselves again.

One evening as they stood on the balcony of Silvia's apartment, Tim said he had decided to be just himself, the procrastinator, and to simply ask for a three-month extension of his sabbatical.

Silvia wasn't pleased. Tears welled up in her eyes. "I'm thirty-eight, Tim, and I need a baby," she said softly.

Reality set in. Tim looked her in the eyes, tenderly, and said, "You're right, *amor*, we have no time to waste." As he saw darkness set in over the Jardín Botánico, he caressed her face, held her tight, and whispered, "I think it would be a shame to waste *any* time before ordering that baby, particularly the next hour."

Silvia cried.

They went in and closed the glass door. Suddenly the traffic noise was gone, and so was the rest of the world.

That night, after their lovemaking, Tim told Silvia that he had decided to become a freelance contributor to *En Avant* and other publications.

Silvia said she would accept Jorge Riquelme's oft-repeated invitation to join the Alliance NGO, where she would make half of her old Barone salary and work double hours in a building with poor air-conditioning, if any, but she would work with people aiming for the good.

"What's the date today, Silvia? The eighteenth?" Tim asked later that night as they lay in bed.

"The seventeenth, Tim."

"Thanks. Good that you corrected me. I'm going to figure out the exact day our first baby will come into the world."